To Jac

#Trust No-one!

Underneath

Andie M. Long

Andie M Long
x

Copyright

This book is a work of fiction. Names, characters, places and incidents are either the product of the author's imagination or are used fictitiously, and any resemblance to actual persons, living or dead, events or locales is entirely coincidental.

No part of this book may be reproduced or transmitted in any form or by any means, electronic or mechanical, including photocopying, recording or by any information storage and retrieval system without the written permission of the author, except for the use of brief quotations in a book review.

ISBN-13: 978-1495422782
ISBN-10: 149542278X

Dedication

To Adam.
The best son any mum could wish
to be blessed with, and my
No 1 fan.

ANDIE M. LONG

ACKNOWLEDGEMENTS

Firstly to my son whose words 'You are an author, mum,' made me feel I could actually achieve this.

For Den. Yes I admit I was lax with the housework whilst writing. Get used to it.

To my sister who read the book in a day and loved it. Thank goodness, because sister or not, she'd have told me if she didn't. I love you bliss.

For my parents who have cheered me on throughout. Thank you for the love.

For all who read the early drafts, Janet Hanson, Katie Hanson, Annmarie Bradley, Ruth Loizides and Tracey Sutton. Thank you for your words of encouragement, or in Ruth's case, "Get on with it, I need more".

Major thanks to my friend Michelle Dunbar for editing the book. You've been a fantastic support to me.

To Sharon Therese Nuttall for all your expert advice and support.

To the girls on my street team Andie's Army. I salute you!

My fellow Indies at the Indie Erogenous Zone. I would not be sane without you people, you keep me upright.

Extra special thanks to Annmarie again for taking my chosen picture and making it into a beautiful book cover.

A shout out to all the bloggers, readers and fellow Indies who listen to my craziness and promote and advise me like you do. I heart you all big time.

Lastly, Sandrine Oodian, thanks for the loan of your apartment for Monique. I redecorated ;)

After twenty years of thinking about it, I finally wrote a book.
It's been released second, but this was my first.

CHAPTER ONE

I've spent so much time lying on my bed I'm surprised I don't have bedsores on my backside.

People tell me I have a perfect life, so how come I find myself staring at walls in a state of catatonia? Being a mother can bore you rigid, no matter how much you love your child. Where's the fun in telling your son fourteen times to get out of bed? Trying to get Joe ready for school whilst he ignores my every instruction means my throat will be hoarse by around half eight. He's like his father in that respect. Niall has avoidance as his most-perfected trait.

I spend my days doing chores, whilst running my little vintage empire and my line in refurbished Barbie dolls via eBay. I do coffee with my bestie when she's not working. People are always telling me how lucky I am that I have such freedom, but sometimes I get so bored I put my pyjamas on and go back to sleep. It makes the clock tick faster.

If Niall's home for dinner he expects a home cooked meal on the table as I 'don't work.' My eBaying is seen as a hobby. I've learnt to ensure I'm mid-chore when he gets home, or he'll comment that it must be nice to have time to sit or read. That's another reason I sometimes take myself to bed. Might as well do what I'm accused of anyway.

Attempts at adult conversation with Niall are for the most part rejected. I can count one minute tops before he's huffing and puffing that he's missing the news, that he's been at work all day and wants a few minutes peace to catch up. With Joe in the other room watching the Simpsons or playing on his DS, I retreat to Facebook, but there's limited solace found in what people I've never met have eaten that evening.

More often than not that's it for the evening. Niall starts snoring on the sofa from about half past ten. I'll lie in bed and read until my eyes start closing. When I can't recall the sentence I've just read I put my book down and go to sleep. I'm embarrassed to admit it, but I skip past any rude bits. They make me depressed and unhappy. How bad is that? I think I've got a more than alright figure for a thirty-one year old mother of one, but Niall doesn't appear to have any interest in seeing it at the moment. I wonder if he's addicted to computer porn or, being as he's ten years older than I am, just too knackered after work.

Niall feels life is mapped out – wife and kid, steady job, house and cars – I'm totally lost.

Anyway, tonight is going to be different. It's time to bring sexy back.

I run my hands down the black satin chemise I've bought. The stretchy, glossy material pushes my breasts up like Moll Flanders and does a good job of holding in my post-childbirth stomach. On goes a pair of hold ups with a lacy trim and some black stilettos with a pink sole, 'Car to Bar' shoes that I've never actually worn because I can hardly balance in them. I bought them because they were pretty and on sale. Looking at them makes me happy. Don't tell anyone, but I've been known to stroke my shoes.

Checking myself out in the full length mirror at the top of the stairs, I'm surprised to see I look quite fit. Enthused, and just a little turned on, I return to our room. I lie back on the bed and wait for Niall to come in to set his alarm clock. This is his evening ritual, post settling Joe down, and prior to switching the TV back on.

The door opens and Niall enters the room. His blonde, wavy hair is all floppy, as if he's just run his hands through it. He still has a hint of a tan from our holidays. His newly appearing lines add to his handsomeness in a craggy, but sexy kind of way. He barely glimpses at me as he tiptoes past and reaches for his clock. I flex one of my shag-me shoes in his direction.

He nods towards the shoes. 'Not very hygienic is it? I'm nagged to death if I sit on the bed with my work clothes on, but it's alright for you to have your shoes on?'

I grit my teeth, kick off the shoes and raise myself. My breasts spill out over the top of the outfit, and I curl my legs up under myself. I let a lock of my own blonde hair fall across my face. In my mind I am a total sex kitten. He sets his alarm and after placing it on the bedside table turns towards me. I attempt what I hope is an alluring look, raising my eyebrows and giving him a hint of a smile.

'Love…' He looks at me like he's found me wandering the streets confused. 'You don't have to get dressed up for me. It's just going to come off anyway.' He sits on the bed at the side of me, then points and smirks. 'How much of my overtime have you spent on that thing? It's like a taped up bin bag. I could've made you one just like it for about seventeen pence and still had enough left to line the bins.'

My mouth drops open as he undoes his trousers.

'Fuck off.' I throw myself under the duvet. The tears in my eyes sting against the non-waterproof mascara I've left on. He mutters that he can't do anything right, re-zips and walks back around the bed. The door clicks and his footsteps tread down the stairs. Within a minute, the low hum of the television travels through the floor.

I cry, wondering if I'm just not attractive anymore. I replay the scene over and over in my head, trying to work out how it went from the hot, mind blowing sex I'd been imagining to this. Rage takes over again. I sit up, breathing rapidly and wondering whether to go downstairs and kick the television set in with my heel; at least then they would have proved a useful purchase. My eyes dart around the room, searching. My jaw is firm with tension. I grab hold of Niall's pillow and pretend it's his face. I punch it until I'm out of breath.

Spotting his alarm clock, an idea forms. Pressing buttons, I change it to go off at seven pm. He'll oversleep and think he set it wrong. It's a small thing, but it makes me smile. My head throbs with tension, and as I lay my head on my pillow, I imagine it will take me ages to get to sleep. However my brain must wish to block out the evening's trauma and I am out within minutes.

The next morning, I slip out of bed, wake Joe and head downstairs. Part of me feels guilty about the alarm clock and I pause on the stairs. Sucking at my lip, I consider going back up and waking Niall, but I just can't bring myself to do it. Instead, I decide to make Joe his favourite pancakes with strawberry sauce for breakfast. I creep back up to Joe's room to tell him. Whereas it usually takes forever for him to get out of bed, I get a 'Yay' and a thump as his feet hit the floor. He's out of bed, and in two minutes he's dressed and racing down the stairs for pancakes I won't be able to cook up fast enough for him. At nine, Joe is all skinniness and angles. His face has elongated over the last couple of months, looking more adult, and his shoulders have broadened. In contrast, his legs and feet resemble golf clubs, but his brain activity seems to be decreasing as his body grows. Yesterday I discovered him trying to saw Lego in half with my best knife when he'd supposedly gone in the kitchen for a biscuit. My heart melts when I see him enter the dining room. His short blonde hair is mussed up from sleeping and he's only half-awake. He looks at me with one eye scrunched up, as he does when he's trying to get used to the light.

'Can I have three pancakes today please, Mum?'

I laugh, telling him to try to eat one first and see how he goes and head to the kitchen to start cooking. He does indeed manage to eat three, thanks to a soft mother who makes them small enough so he can manage it. He's so pleased with himself that he gets ready for school easily this morning, which is a godsend.

Just before we put on our coats to head out of the door, I pop upstairs to the bedroom and feign alarm, whilst inside rejoicing with an inner monologue of 'Take that you bastard.'

'Niall,' I say. 'Niall?'

There's a grunt from under the covers, of which I can't make out a word.

'Niall, its eight thirty. Shouldn't you be up?'

Niall shoots up so fast that in trying to pick up the clock, his muscular hairy arm sends it flying across the floor. 'Shit,' he says. 'Why didn't you wake me?'

I note the fact that he immediately blames me for his predicament, even if this time he is correct.

'I saw you set your alarm last night, so I never gave it a thought until now.'

'Damn,' says Niall, the clock now in his hand. He rubs his eye with the other hand. 'I set it for pm instead.'

I hitch the strap of my bag further up my shoulder. 'Well, I have to go or Joe will be late for school,' I say. 'I hope you don't get into much trouble with work.'

He waves his arm at me. 'Naw,' he states. 'I'll just phone and tell them I had to go to the doctors.' With that, he lays his head back down on the pillow.

I feel my chest tighten and try to swallow the acid rising up from my gut. Does nothing ever rattle this man? I'm beginning to think I have a Stepford husband.

'Well, see you later,' I say. My smile fixed and teeth gritted, I close the door, head back downstairs, grab my bag and keys and take Joe to school.

Joe dropped off, I get back into my lovely metallic blue Nissan Micra and pull the lever until the seat is further back and I have more leg room. I lean back into the comfy padded upholstery, a creamy-beige colour that Joe does his best to turn grey, and reach into my bag for my mobile phone. I love my bag. It's a black leather Betty Barclay, with lots of pockets for keys and a mobile. I was forever unable to find things and kept being told off by Niall for not hearing the phone. I pull out my Nokia and fire off a quick text to my friend Monique.

Fed up. U free for cofi n chat?

Within seconds I have a reply.

God yes. Get here asap.

Texting that I'm on my way, I throw my phone in my bag, completely ignoring its designated pocket. I pull my seat forward and set off, calling at the supermarket bakery en-route for two pain au chocolats.

My friend's apartment is part of a large Victorian building that from a distance looks like a stately home. An elegant stone staircase leads to the front entrance. The grounds have large swathes of green grass and established shrubbery and trees. A Consultant at the local hospital, where Monique works part-time as a Research Assistant, told her he thought she owned it all after giving her a lift home. Monique would make you think that though. She is immaculate. Tall with short brown hair in a pixie crop, she is the colour of the finest milk chocolate and has a row of freckles across her cheeks that add to her exoticness. She has exacting standards and will not leave the house without full make up and painted nails. If it's summer, this self-rule extends to her toe-nails. Her clothing looks like it cost hundreds of pounds, and yet I know that the majority of it comes from the charity shops located in her local area. She lives in Ecclesall, a district full of yummy mummies who want the latest of everything and dispose of their attire the moment the next season is on the runway.

I first met Monique at yoga class five years ago, when I was desperately trying to shake off my frumpy mummy self image. We hit it off and she took me under her wing, seeing me as both a friend and a little project. Now I feel I can hold my own with clothes and make-up, though I have to confess to making more of an effort on the days I'm seeing her. Today I'm dressed in Levi's, a royal blue Reiss blouse, which was a car boot find, and some black Office sandals. My toes are painted orange to match the belt around my jeans. I walk up to her apartment entrance and hit the buzzer.

She opens her door and I'm greeted with a wide smile that makes her look even more gorgeous.

'Hi, Lo.'

She never gets bored of this.

I roll my eyes. 'You letting me in or what? I have breakfast.' I hold up the bag and crinkle it before her eyes.

She scrunches her nose up. 'Ugh. An Asda carrier bag? Where on earth is that swish shopper bag I got you with Paris on it?'

'That's not as much fun as seeing your face when you have to touch a carrier bag.' I giggle, and hand it to her as I step through to the foyer. 'I was going to bring a Poundland one, but couldn't find it.'

She mock shivers and leads the way to her apartment, all the while holding the bag like it's a used nappy.

Monique's apartment is on the ground floor. She takes the bag through to the kitchen while I go straight through the hallway, removing my sandals to carry in my hand. I move past the sitting room and through the patio doors to outside. I claim one of the two wrought iron chairs and slip my footwear back on. There are strict rules in her apartment block about garden furniture; no plastic rubbish will do. The patio is part of a large, enclosed communal garden, shared by around four residents. Two large ceramic pots frame Monique's doorway, overflowing with multi-coloured floral displays. I could sit on her patio all day, and can't help but compare it to my reasonable sized lawn, which has Joe's cycle marks all over it and not a hint of a flower in sight. There's not much point when footballs are forever being kicked around it. I learnt that lesson the hard way, enjoying some home sown black tulips for a whole hour before he knocked all but one of their heads off with his football. He did pick me the last one though, bringing it to me as a gift because it was 'pretty... like mummy.' That was a few years ago now and I haven't grown a flower since.

Within a few minutes, Monique comes outside bearing a cream vintage tray covered in tiny pink roses – a present from me. Upon it are two steaming cups of coffee in pink tipped cream tea cups, nestled on pink tipped cream saucers with space for the Amaretti biscuit which lies beside it. Our pain au chocolats sit on matching side plates. No mismatching crockery for Monique.

She raises an eyebrow. 'What's up with you then misery guts?'

I fill her in on my night of seduction. Monique is no fan of Niall and the way he fails to ever give me compliments. She shakes her head as I get to the part where I told him to get out. She stays silent for a moment and I wait to hear her verdict, and then she looks at me and falls about laughing. I can't help it. Her laughter's infectious and I start giggling. Huge fat tears roll down my face as I think how funny it was, and then I think about how utterly humiliating it was.

'Lo, he's Niall. He doesn't do seduction. He never notices your normal clothes, never mind your night attire,' she says. 'You've spent the last God knows how many years just getting into bed and getting on with it, and then you go and dress like a porn star. It probably blew a gasket in his brain. If he didn't want you he wouldn't have tried to get into bed. It's obvious he sees the attire as an unnecessary barrier.'

I sigh. 'I know you're right.' I take a bite of biscuit. 'I tried it once before when we'd been going out a couple of years,' I confess, before pausing to swallow. 'While he was at footie practice I dressed in a lace Basque. When he walked in he asked why I was dressed in a doily.' I sniff up and search my pocket for a tissue I don't have. Monique, whilst desperately trying to keep a straight face, pops back into the house and returns with a leopard print tissue. I look at her before I blow my nose. 'Seriously, they make these? You co-ordinated your snot rags with your handbag?'

'It takes no extra time to choose between a stylish tissue and a boring old white one,' she replies. 'Now back to Niall. You do remember who he is, right? Mr Unromantic. Mr Moody. You expected him to turn all Christian Grey on your ass? Seriously?'

'Okay, okay, I admit in hindsight I was a tad deluded. I just thought he'd think whoa and—'

'Take them off? As I keep saying, Niall just thinks you're wasting VBT.'

'VBT?'

'Valuable bonking time. Now stop talking and eat your pastry. I need to tell you about my Friday night hottie, and I don't mean a wheat bag.'

I partake of my delicious, pain au chocolat, chasing the sauce escaping from the corner of my mouth with my tongue. Monique tells me about the twenty-six year old Medical Student she pulled Friday night. She hasn't had a serious relationship since Toby left her ten years ago after her refusal to have children. I didn't know her then. She was thirty-two and Toby was thirty-eight. He felt it was time. He left, and within six months had a pregnant girlfriend. Monique moved to Sheffield to start over. She's ten and a bit years older than me, although you wouldn't know it to look at her. She says she's inherited her mother's skin; there's barely a line on her face and sometimes I feel very jealous. My crow's feet and frown lines have deepened over the last few years. I think having children must be an ageing factor. All that stress is enough to give anyone a few extra lines. Monique is blunt about why she doesn't want children and I love her for it.

'They make a mess and I can't deal with it. Plus they want constant attention and I want all my attention.'

That said, she still makes the effort to see Joe a few times a year, and she really makes a big effort when she does. I selfishly and secretly like the fact that she's my child-free friend. She's the one I can talk to about books, fashion and the latest reality TV programme. I don't have to chat about school, SATs and the things about having a child that bore me rigid to be honest. I don't do well with routine and having to get up at the same time to go to the same place twice a day nearly sends me demented.

'So how's Joe?' she says, like she's reading my mind.

'Oh. Well he totally loves school, and must be the only child not looking forward to the summer break. He says he wishes school was carrying on. I think he's scared he's going to be stuck with me. I'm becoming less cool the older he gets.'

'Yeah right,' replies Monique. 'Joe totally adores you and you know it. You are Cool Mum personified. When are the holidays anyway? And more importantly, are you going to be able to ditch him for some girl time?'

'There's seven weeks left of the term, and yes, I've lined up some holiday clubs so we can skive off. You'll have to let me know when you're free so I can put it in my diary.' Monique looks satisfied at this and I know it was the correct response, though Joe hates holiday clubs and I feel torn between them both. 'Joe was extra excited today because a new boy was starting in class. I told him to be nice to him.'

'Strange time to start school?'

'I know. I can only think that his mum's doing it to get him introduced to the kids before the break. I hope he's a good kid, cos that class has its fair share of troublemakers as it is.'

Monique starts looking around the room, my signal that she's getting bored.

'Anyway, enough about men and children,' I say. 'Show me the new clothes you've bought this week, you know you're dying to.' She claps her hands on her knees, smiles and goes off to get them whilst I move inside to the sofa and make myself comfortable. This is what I love, fashion. I smile to myself as I wait to see her latest collection.

She doesn't disappoint. A black knee length Wallis jacket sits amongst the items she piles at the side of me. I feel my mouth get wet as I look at it. She grins. 'See you don't need sex when you have fashion porn. Try it on. I picked it for you.'

I pull it around myself. The waist nips in and the bottom of the jacket flares out ever so slightly. I shimmy so it swings. Monique looks at me like a mother at her child's first school uniform fitting. I hug her. 'Thank you, it's beautiful.'

'You're very welcome. Now, how about another coffee and Real Housewives of NYC?'

'Mon, my life is complete,' I giggle, sitting back on the sofa and keeping my new jacket on so I can keep touching it.

Back at home I catch up with the 'Chore of the Day' (my latest project to alleviate boredom, courtesy of Pinterest). Today's exciting chore is vacuuming the house, and then I check my eBay account. I've not got much for sale at the moment, but I hope the weekend's nice for trawling car boots in search of bedraggled Barbie dolls and pretty vintage pieces. My business started off as a hobby when Joe was younger. A lot of my friends had daughters at a similar time and I was secretly jealous that they got to play with dolls. I don't think I've ever totally grown up. I'd got into eBaying while Niall had been nurse training. We were broke, so I'd sold anything I thought I might make some money to help pay the bills. I noticed that Barbie clothes went for a lot of money and started looking around for them at summer fairs and car boots. Then I took to buying dolls that looked like they had seen better days; washing them, brushing their hair, mending their clothes and then selling them online in the run up to Christmas. I made a few hundred pounds and earned a good reputation for selling them, so I started my little eBay shop, 'Lauren's pre-loved'. My obsession with all things vintage followed; pretty tea-cups, jewellery, the odd piece of clothing. It's grown into a little part-time job that fits in perfectly around Joe, and apart from Monique, I think it's the only thing that keeps me sane. I make a mental note to list the nine or so items in the box at the side of the desk later on tonight, and then head off to school to collect Joe.

I always park up on one of the back streets near the school. It means a few minutes' walk, but the main drag is full of crazy mummy maniacs who despite repeated warnings from the school and the local police, still persevere with parking on zigzags and corners of junctions. You fear for your life walking down to school as they whirl around the corners in their haste to get the nearest parking slot available at the last possible moment. I meet Tanya, one of the other school mums, at the bottom of the drive. Tall and slender, with her red hair tied in a ponytail with a huge scarf, she's easily identifiable from some distance away. I get on well with most of the school mums and we have the odd coffee, but I keep a distance as I have Monique and that's enough for me.

The walk up the drive only takes a few minutes. It leads past the main school building into a playground complete with two small benches, a wooden climbing frame and a large grassed area. In the corner of the playground are two Portakabins, one of which is Joe's classroom. We all gather nearby and await the release of our little angels. For once it's not raining.

'Did you know there's a new boy in school? Our Billy told me.' Tanya says.

'Yep, Joe said. I think he started today.'

'I've heard his mum's a footballer's wife,' she adds.

'What?' I laugh. 'A WAG, in Handsworth? You've got to be kidding; surely she wouldn't come to live here? Not being funny, because I love living here myself, but it's hardly chock full of McMansions is it?'

Tanya shrugs. 'Just saying what I heard. We'll find out in a minute anyway, cos she's over there.'

We head over to the tiny woman standing sideways to us. It has to be her as she is a stereotypical WAG. Her hair is almost yellow blonde and reaches the bottom of her back in spiralled tendrils. She flicks it with her pink glitter ended nails and turns to us showing an over-tanned face. It's either sunbed or real tan, because her skin resembles the part of my leather sofa where Niall's bottom has worn the seat out. Her mouth opens to reveal white teeth that might be alright in London, but in Sheffield, and against the tanned skin, look ridiculous, like snow on a beach.

She turns towards me. Her eyes open wide. 'Lauren,' she shouts and throws her arms around me. My forehead creases and I tense as I'm locked in her embrace, because I don't know who the hell she is. She releases me and I step back to look at her. Her eyes look familiar and I'm just trying to place her when she adds, 'You muppet, it's me. Liz Parker, from Brook.'

I stare at her, and then try and plant a smile on my face as I realise an old echo from my life is back – one I didn't wish to hear again.

CHAPTER TWO

'Gosh Liz, er, I haven't seen you for years,' I state, my hand held to my chest.

'Yeah, well Danny went to play for Leeds United, so we were there for a while.'

There's a silence whilst I process the fact she's in front of me. The Liz I knew was a spotty, mousy haired loner. I made the mistake of standing up for her when a rumour spread around school that she'd been caught masturbating in the toilets with her lunch box banana. She thanked me by reporting the culprits to the teachers and misguidedly told them I was being picked on too. I can only think she said it in some pathetic attempt to be my friend, but I was furious and joined in the rumour-mongering instead. I remember how she looked at me as she walked out of the Head teacher's office while I sat outside awaiting my fate. I was threatened with suspension and had my Prefect badge taken away. Liz's parents took her out of school shortly after that and I didn't see her again. I'd heard a rumour later that her parents had discovered she was pregnant to Danny Southwell, one of the school hard cases who played football any time he could, and just like that, the WAG thing clicked. 'So you and Danny stuck together? Wow.'

'You hadn't heard how successful Danny was?'

'I'm not into sports.'

She stares at me like she doesn't quite believe me and sighs. 'So you didn't hear about me being made to marry Danny cos I was pregnant? You must have been the only person in South Yorkshire who didn't.'

I grit my teeth and shake my head.

'I lost the baby, but we stayed together and had Tyler. Danny did well at Leeds, but we're divorced now. I've moved back to Sheffield to be nearer my mum. She isn't getting any younger and she dotes on Tyler.'

Good God, an over-sharer. I've only been standing here five minutes and I have her whole life history.

'Fancy you being here anyway. So you've children too?'

'Just the one, Joe. Well, I hope you get sorted soon.' I look towards the classroom door as the kids start coming out of class. Thank goodness I can get out of here. 'I'm sure Joe will keep an eye on Tyler to make sure he settles.'

'Oh, that's so kind,' she says as a child comes sloping towards her with a face so sneering it looks like the kid's had a stroke.

'Well, see you later Liz,' I state.

'Oh,' she makes a small tinkly laugh. 'It's Bettina now. Bettina Southwell. I gave myself a fresh start when we moved to Leeds.

I dread to think what my face looks like in response to this; Niall says I am incapable of masking my emotions.

'Hey,' she adds, 'before you go let's swap numbers. I'm out of touch with people around here. We must do coffee sometime.'

I hesitate as I've no wish to get involved with a girl I barely knew at school. 'I've not got my phone on me at the mo, but I'll bring it some other time.'

'Sure,' she says and smiles. 'Catch you tomorrow.'

When we get to the car, I ask Joe what his new school friend is like.

'He's ace mum, dead cool,' he says. 'He's got over five-hundred Pokemon cards and loads of spares he says I can have.' Pokemon is Joe's new obsession, so Tyler will be a God now in his eyes.

'He seemed moody when he came out of school,' I mention. 'Was he like that in class?'

'Nope, he said his mum gets on his nerves. She's always making him do things he doesn't want to do, like moving.'

'Well, he'll be missing his friends from Leeds.'

'Suppose so,' Joe sucks on his bottom lip. 'But he's got me now.'

I walk into the house and for once I don't chastise my child as he leaves his coat and bag on the stairs and his shoes strewn in the hallway. Instead, I put the kettle on, make myself a coffee and reach into one of the high up kitchen cupboards. I take out a bottle of whisky, my tipple of choice on the few occasions I drink. I throw a good measure in, before finally plonking myself in a dining room chair.

'Can I play with my Lego?' Joe asks, seeing a chance to take advantage over the mother who usually gets him to practice his reading first.

'Whatever you want.' Joe looks at me strangely, but runs off to his room before the alien leaves and his mother returns.

I sink back in the chair, coffee in my hands and close my eyes. I can feel a tension headache starting. I've loved being part of that school since Joe started, but now I feel a sense of dread. I was never friends with this woman, so how do I put her off without seeming mean? I can only hope she befriends some of the other mothers. Or maybe, I chastise myself, after all these years she's turned out okay and I should get to know her. I take a large swig of my coffee; the whisky warms my mouth as much as the hot drink and I decide I'm ditching tonight's planned tea and will walk to the chippy. Then I'll have a top up.

Niall comes home from work and I realise that Monique's chat and the latest school events have overtaken my frustration with him. As I ask him my usual 'Have you had an okay day?' I can see the relief in his face, and then he looks at me with a furrowed brow. 'Have you been drinking?'

This behaviour is completely out of character for me on a school day. My anxieties about needing to be able to drive in case of an emergency with Joe mean I only usually drink on special occasions, or if I have a cold to help me sleep. I fill him in on the events of the afternoon, but I'm not sure how much of it he's taken in as he turns the news on at the same time, and then sits in the chair I vacated to let him in the house. 'Niall what'll I do?'

'You're worrying over nothing Lauren. Just smile at the woman, say hello and leave it at that,' he advises in his *men provide solutions not empathy* voice. 'That Danny Southwell's a proper headcase though. He was always getting red-carded, so we best keep a close eye on Joe's new friend.' Then he turns back to the news.

I pick up my bag ready to head to the chippy. I can see that my problem is already solved in Niall's eyes, and that's the only advice I'll get.

Later in the evening I go to the secret Facebook Group I set up with Monique and leave her a message about the new kid and his mother. Of course she knows nothing about my history with the now called Bettina. I leave Facebook open whilst adding my eBay listings, and flip back when I see someone has posted. Sure enough it's Monique.

'Jeez, if you're gonna change your name change it to something nice, but normal.'

'She looks like Donatella Versace,' I add with venom. Secret Facebook just makes me bitchier; I can't resist it when there's no-one else reading.

'Lol. So what's the WAG thing all about?'

'It's in her head; Danny played for Leeds. I googled him. He did okay, but he's hardly Beckham.'

'PMSL'

'Dreading tomorrow '

'Ask her to come for coffee with us next Monday. I need to meet her. It'll be a right laugh.'

'Noooooooo.'

'Yessssssss, pretty please.'

'Oh Mon, I dunno. I doubt she'll do our caff anyway. It's not Harvey Nicks.'

'She might turn up with a Chihuahua in her handbag. I bet she wears a Juicy Couture tracky with Uggs.'

'ROFLMAO. No I think she likes leopard print ;)'

'Piss off.'

'Nite Cougar.'

'Nite and INVITE her.'

Niall comes to bed about ten which is ridiculously early for him. I keep my face firmly on my book, but he undresses and snuggles up beside me, placing a hand on my boob. I'm feeling quite squiffy from all the whisky I've consumed. I do feel quite in the mood, but choose to ignore him. 'I'm sorry about last night,' he says. 'I didn't mean to upset you. I just wanted you to know you don't have to dress up for me.'

'S'okay.' I turn the page of my book.

'Anyway to make amends…'

He jumps out of bed to reveal a pair of crocodile pants. He runs around the bed with them on and I watch them snap, snap, snap. I collapse with giggles.

He lands next to me. 'So, d'ya think I'm sexy?'

'Quit while you're ahead mate,' I state and turn towards him, pushing him back on the bed.

The next morning I drop Joe off at the bottom of the school driveway. I know it's pathetic and in doing so I had to pull up on the very zigzags I berate the other parents for parking on, but I just can't face seeing Bettina this morning. I decide that the scheduled housework can stuff for the day as well. The weather is beautiful and I drive up to Ecclesall Road, which is chock full of second hand shops, gorgeous chocolatiers and coffee shops. I browse for vintage items and wander from shop to shop, just enjoying the day. I pick up some pieces of jewellery: a gorgeous bronze coloured sequined clutch bag and a handmade crocheted cream shrug. I have my latest book in my bag; a chick lit about someone travelling to Paris. At lunchtime I walk the few minutes to the local park, sit myself under a tree and eat a prawn baguette. The sun warms my skin and my head floats to the Champs Elysees. When it's time to drive back to school, I lean back against the tree, ignoring the bark digging in my back and sigh. I really don't want to go there. I take my phone out of my bag and ring Tanya instead.

'I'm stuck in traffic and going to be late. Will you take Joe to yours and I'll pick him up from there?'

'Yes of course, don't worry. Take your time. We'll see you whenever.'

I try to get back into my book, but my mind is distracted by thoughts of the past. I can't avoid Bettina forever, but after all these years I still feel like I want to shout at her for what she did to me. I still remember my mother's reaction. She was furious when she discovered I'd lost my prefect status and accused me of taking after my father, calling me a bully. I take a breath and tell myself I'm being completely irrational, that it was all such a long time ago. I resolve to see her tomorrow, ask her for coffee and stop being so ridiculous. I might even ask Tyler for tea if Joe continues to get on well with him. I pick up my baguette wrapper and my spoils of the day and head back to the car to drive to Tanya's.

Later, I feel so much better for having a Me-day. I help Joe with his spellings and let all my Lego figures lose to his in battle. Then I spend the evening with Niall, even though he's watching a run of TV shows about pimping up cars. Before I get in bed, I have another little peek at my treasures from the shops. I cradle a delicate necklace in my hand and admire the white teacup pendant. Pink roses adorn the cup and saucer and gold leaf swirls around the rim and edges of the saucer. I decide to keep it for myself, to remind me of how lucky I am that I can spend my days this way.

The following morning Bettina spots me at the bottom of the drive. I decide to make an effort and wait for her to drop Tyler off as she's still taking him up to the classroom door.

'Has Tyler enjoyed his first few days?'

'He loves it. I'm so surprised. I thought he'd really miss his friends in Leeds. Joe is helping a lot. He's introduced him to the other lads.'

'It must be hard being the new kid.'

'Yeah,' Bettina says, breaking eye contact with me for a moment.

I remember she had to start again after she left our school. 'Are you doing anything now, or do you want to grab a coffee?' I say quickly, to get her mind back from wherever it is before I chicken out and abandon her.

'I'd love one,' she replies. 'Where shall we go?'

'I'll think of something. Leave your car here and we'll pick it up later.'

'Oh. I don't drive.'

'Okay, well I can drop you back at yours after. I'm parked this way.' I point up the hill. We head up the road to the car and once inside, I set off trying to think of a decent coffee shop. She asks me about my mum and dad and other things from the past. I move the conversation on to current times and ask where she's living. It's a house a few streets away from school in a popular catchment area, so she must have done okay by Danny in the divorce.

Handsworth only has the local supermarket cafe, so I drive further afield, to a garden centre cafe in Wentworth that I enjoy visiting. The cafe is surrounded by a row of small shops including a butcher's, a leather shop and a small craft shop. A little further on is a pet shop and a small petting zoo. I sometimes bring Joe to spend the day here. Bettina and I dodge branches from shrubs and take care not to knock into garden ornaments on our way into the cafe. I take us to the waitress service section where we order two coffees and two teacakes.

'Have you seen the sign for help with the summer fair at school?' Bettina asks.

'I have, but I don't usually get involved to be honest.'

'I thought it might be a good way for me to get to know some of the teachers, but I'd feel a bit stupid going on my own. Would you come to the meeting with me? You don't have to sign up for anything. Just come for moral support.'

I chew my lip as I try to think of a way to get out of it, and then remember I'm meant to be making an effort. 'Go on then, when is it?'

'Tonight at six.'

Inwardly cursing, I decide we can have a quick pizza tea and that the curry I took out of the freezer will keep for tomorrow. I don't want to arrive at the meeting smelling of garlic. I don't realise I'm daydreaming, mentally planning the evening meals, until Bettina touches my arm.

'Is that okay? It's not too short notice, is it?'

'No that's fine. I'll text Niall and let him know to get straight home after work. I'll meet you outside the school at five to.'

'Thank you so much. I'm so pleased I know you. You and Joe are being so kind to us.' She reaches across the table and gives my hand a squeeze.

'Honestly, don't worry about it.' I feign a cough so I can take my hand away and have a sip of my coffee.

'But you really are being so helpful.'

'I believe in treating everyone as I'd like to be treated myself.'

'Oh, I agree with that,' she replies, looking towards the window for a moment. She turns back. 'Any ideas as to what we'll get roped into at the fair?'

'Hey, no *we*. I'm the moral support, remember? But I'll put your hand up if there's any custard pie throwing.'

'Don't you dare,' Bettina flicks a stray currant at me. We start laughing and I relax a little. Maybe she's not so bad after all.

The meeting starts at six pm prompt. In the school hall there's Mrs Sullivan, the Head Teacher, and an assortment of other teachers, assistants and parents. Amongst them is Mr Kingsley, who'll be Joe's form teacher next year. The Year Five classroom is on the opposite side of the school in the main building. He started halfway through the year to cover maternity leave, so I've only seen him once or twice. He's a bit of a nerdy looking thing, with his gelled back tufty brown hair and glasses. The green pullover and grey slacks don't help either. I guess he's over six feet tall because he looks similar in height to Niall. I find myself thinking that he must be around his mid-thirties because he doesn't have the beginning of Niall's middle-aged spread. It'll be a nice change for Joe to have a male teacher though, another male mentor. Mr Kingsley pulls up a chair up next to mine and gives a small nod in greeting. Bettina looks at me.

'Who's the geek?' she whispers.

'Sssshhh, you'll miss the pie casting.'

She sticks her tongue out at me and laughs. 'I'm so putting you up for something now.'

Mrs Sullivan explains how she's hoping that this year we'll raise even more funds for the school as the library is in need of a makeover. I adore books and reading and decide to volunteer to run the book stall. I whisper the idea to Bettina and she gives me a thumbs up. Mrs Sullivan says she has a number of roles to fill and will then discuss any further issues. She's a formidable looking woman, I guess in her late fifties, with bobbed light brown hair. She frowns a lot which has left two vivid crease marks over her brow. She gives us the date of the fair – just under three weeks away, on Saturday the twenty-second of June. I quickly check my diary, but we have nothing down for that day so I know I'm clear to volunteer.

'Right I'll go through the roles we have to fill. Please raise your hand if you're interested. Okay, firstly there's the cake stall ...'

She goes through a few of the more usual stalls including tombola and 'guess the amount of marbles in the jar'. Bettina's yet to volunteer and I'm waiting for the book stall to be called out.

'Now we need a very willing volunteer for the sponge stocks ...'

Quick as a flash Bettina lifts my hand up. 'Lauren'll do that. She said she wanted to do something along those lines.'

'Brilliant Mrs Lawler, that's so kind. It's usually difficult to get a volunteer for that one, so thank you.'

I look at Bettina, a half smile on my face, wondering what she's playing at.

'And now the book stall,' says Mrs Sullivan.

Bettina looks at me, biting her lip. 'Err, could Lauren help me with that instead of doing the sponge stocks?'

'I hardly think a small book stall requires two people,' Mrs Sullivan berates in her scary head-teacher voice.

Bettina visibly shrinks and then turns to me mouthing. 'I'm so sorry.'

'Don't worry about it,' I say. 'You can always swap with me.'

'I would, but I'm scared of water,' she replies, her eyes filling with tears.

'I'll help Mrs Lawler with the sponge stocks,' says the male voice to my right. Mr Kingsley has finally spoken up. 'The kids would much rather pelt a teacher, and Mrs Lawler can collect the money and pass me towels to help me dry off.'

'A good point,' says Mrs Sullivan. 'Well, that's the roles all decided then. I suggest you take some time to consider what you need for your stalls, and we'll reconvene at the same time next week. If there's nothing else, I'll see you then.' Her tone suggests that the 'discussion' part of the meeting isn't something she's required for and we're all dismissed.

I turn to find Mr Kingsley hovering beside me. 'Can you spare me ten minutes to go through what we need to do?'

'Sure,' I say turning round to Bettina. 'I'll catch you tomorrow missus, and you'd better watch out on fair day for stray flying sponges.'

'I'll do you proud with the book stall,' she says in a quiet voice.

'You'd better,' I say to her retreating back.

'Right, well, school's closing. Any chance you can nip round the corner to the Queen's Head?' Mr Kingsley shifts from foot to foot.

'Why not?' I reply. I feel riled with Bettina and consider I need a drink after being roped in to being hit with wet sponges all day. At this rate I'll be in The Priory by the end of the term.

The Queen's Head is about a five minute walk from school. It's an old fashioned pub that's been there for years and is badly in need of redecoration. The burgundy leather seating is worn, but comfy, and I deposit myself on it. Mr Kingsley takes the seat opposite me on a purple and gold chair in need of some TLC.

'What would you like to drink?'

I go to get my purse from my bag.

'Oh, no, this is on me.'

'Oh, okay, thanks. A whisky with ice then please, Mr Kingsley.'

He bursts out laughing, which suits him. His teeth would be flawless except for one at the front that twists just slightly.

'Seb, please,' he says, 'or I just won't answer you.'

'Okay, Seb please,' I josh back. 'I still want a whisky.'

He smiles and heads to the bar.

Drink placed in front of me I watch as Seb looks around and removes his glasses. 'Phew, that's better.'

'Do you wear contacts?' I ask, taking a drink.

'I'll let you into a secret Mrs Lawler,' he leans over the table towards me and whispers near my ear. 'I don't need glasses, they're just for show.'

The mouthful of whisky I've taken splatters ungainly from my mouth. 'It's Lauren, sorry. I don't get it.'

'Well, Lauren sorry I don't get it,' he deadpans back at me. 'I'm just dressing for the job.'

'What?' My forehead creases. I lean back into the seat and cross my legs. Seb gets up from his seat.

'Give me a couple of minutes,' he says.

The brown haired man who returns to the bar from the gents' loo bears little resemblance to the man I sat next to at the school fair meeting. His hair is tousled in very sexy waves. At a guess I'd say it's been wet and dried in the bathroom. Without the glasses, I see that he has the most beautiful dark brown eyes. He's removed the pullover and undone the collar of his shirt. I suddenly get the thought that Niall would not be happy to find me sitting here with this version of Mr Kingsley.

I rise from my seat and take a last swig of my drink. 'I need to go.'

'But I've not explained yet,' he says.

I hesitate. 'Okay, five more minutes then,' I reply as I am a little intrigued. I sit back down.

'I've not been very reliable in the past, so I decided to try a new tack.' He shrugs. 'I dressed up in my best impression of a stereotypical teacher, gelled my unruly hair down, put on a pair of fake reading glasses and went for an interview. I gave it everything I had. The head said she'd keep me on if I knuckled down and earned the respect of the other teachers. I've had to dress like it ever since. It works though; the other teachers love me, but it's killing me dressing like Clark Kent.'

'It serves you right for being fake.' I take out my ponytail and re-fix it.

'Hey, we're all fakes in some way,' he replies, his brown eyes on mine. 'People can be completely different with others. Look at you, acting like you were interested in being part of the fair tonight.'

I shuffle in my seat.

His mouth turns up at the corner and his eyes sparkle with mischief. 'I'd like to know what's underneath the surface of you, Lauren Lawler.'

I look down my nose at him. 'What you see is what you get. Anyway, now that I have your life story, what do we need to do about the fair?'

He stretches his hands behind his head. 'Well, we turn up on the day. Get the stocks, sponges and the bucket out of the store room and we're ready. Can you bring some towels?'

My voice turns sharp. 'You could have said that in the school hall.'

'But then I wouldn't have had the pleasure of your lovely company.'

'I'm married, Mr Kingsley.' I place emphasis on his name.

He puts his hands up in front of me. 'Have I stated any improper attentions towards you? No. It's very presumptuous of you, Mrs Lawler, to imply I was angling for a shag or something.'

I feel the heat rise in my cheeks, although I'm not someone who usually blushes.

He carries on, 'I just thought the pub would be nicer. I fancied a pint and don't like drinking alone.'

'Well, I need to head home now,' I state, and get up to leave.

'Of course, if you do fancy a ....'

'Goodnight Mr Kingsley.' I almost run towards the door. I turn back just before I leave to make sure he's not following me and he winks. I'm too shell-shocked to respond and head home where the whisky bottle comes out of the cupboard for the second time that week.

CHAPTER THREE

Niall is red in the face with mirth. 'Hey Joe, did you hear? We can pay to hit your mother in the face with wet sponges. Don't need any practice, do you, Love? We could always go out in the garden and hit you with the bath and kitchen ones?'

'Ha, bloody ha. I'm not being pelted. I'm the money collector.'

'It's a good job with your 36Ds. The husbands' would all be skint, the wives'd swap the sponges for rotten fruit, and the kids'd be scarred for life.'

'Aren't you jealous about me towelling down Seb Kingsley?'

'What am I supposed to be jealous of? Joe says he's lame. You're hardly planning on putting his arms in the stocks to have your wicked way with him are you?'

I huff and waltz into the kitchen to do the packing up. Niall follows me in.

'Don't suppose you can borrow those stocks?' He grins.

'Only thing on you I want to lock up is your mouth,' I fire back.

'Kinky,' he replies, smacks me on the rear and returns to his favourite chair.

That evening I sit on the sofa near Niall as he watches some sports programme. He doesn't utter a word. I'm wondering if he's no longer interested in my conversation, or if we've just run out of things to talk about. I know if I was to start talking now he'd get annoyed because I'd be interrupting his listening. I decide I'm going to talk anyway.

'Why do we always sit here in silence?'

'We don't sit in silence, Love, cos you can bet the minute I'm trying to listen to a crucial point, you yack on about something and interrupt me, like right now.'

'My conversation should be more important than anything on the television.'

'I've been at work all day -'

'Yeah, yeah, yeah, that's all I ever hear,' my voice rises as my temper does. 'Don't interrupt the news. Don't interrupt Gordon Fucking Ramsey. Don't interrupt me being a boring fart.'

'You're being ridiculous.' Niall mutes the television and turns to me. 'I'm sorry, what is it that's so important?'

Reasonable, never ruffled Niall. He drives me mad. I want him to argue back, to fight and show me some passion.

'It doesn't matter now, it'll seem stupid,' I say. 'I'm going to bed.'

I don't pick my book up straight away but lie back against the pillow, pull up the duvet and wonder how long it will actually be before we make love again. It's become about once a month, so after the other day that's June done with. It doesn't help that Joe's always getting out of bed and is settling down later and later, so by the time he finally falls asleep, it's my own bed time. I'm exhausted by then and just want to sleep, not go and see if Niall's up for it. I worry about us not having it enough, but if I ever raise the issue Niall just dismisses it and says he's happy and we don't need to be at it like rabbits. It makes me feel insecure though. I know I'm not bad looking for my age, and my figure is still trim and firm, but I worry I'm getting to the point where the wolf-whistles stop and no-one will find me attractive. I think about the evening in the pub. I was totally shocked. Who'd have thought that nerdy Mr Kingsley had all that going on under his clothes? As much as I felt irritated with how he spoke to me, I keep replaying the conversation in my head and I like the fact he flirted with me. I need to be flirted with. Maybe Niall would be a bit more interested in me if it were possible to dress up as a 1956 Ford Zephyr. I wonder how Seb would have reacted to my boudoir outfit? I realise I'm smiling and berate myself for thinking like this. I love my husband.

Monday comes around fast, and I meet Bettina at the school gates so we can travel in my car together to meet Monique. Bettina is quiet at first, twirling a piece of her hair around and staring out of the front window. After a few minutes of awkward silence she asks, 'You're not mad at me about the sponge stocks, are you?'

'How long have you been worrying about that?' I reply. 'And no, I'm over it. I'm not going in the stocks and it should be a laugh watching the kids pelt Seb.'

'Seb,' she says, considering the name. 'I wouldn't have thought him a Seb, more a Gordon or a Steve.'

'How stereotypical of you,' I mock. 'Whatever have the Gordons' and Steves' of the world done to you?'

'You know what I mean. He's dead straight looking. Sebastian's quite a cool name.'

'Yeah, well he's not quite as straight-laced as you might think,' I state, raising an eyebrow at her.

Her eyes fire up. 'Tell me more.'

I turn to her and wink. 'You'll have to wait til we get to the coffee shop. I want to fill Monique in so I'll tell you both together.'

'Ooh, I hope she's on time.'

We pull up just down the road from the coffee shop that is mine and Monique's favourite haunt on Ecclesall Road. Tucked in between all the charity and other shops is a modern red brick building with almost floor to ceiling glass windows. Today is sunny, but not all that warm, so I walk past the outside tables and head inside towards my favourite corner. I'm happy to see it's free, and sink down into the warm, comfy, tan leather sofa that I wish I could transport home. It makes me feel snug and protected. I quite often remove my shoes and sit sideways with my feet up on it when I'm chatting to Monique. Bettina has seated herself at the side of me where Monique usually sits.

'God they need new sofa's, I don't think I'll get back up from here.'

'It's lovely and comfy though.'

'You and your love of old things. Shall we wait for Monique before we get drinks?'

Monique charges through the door at that point. Dressed in a pale yellow dress with an A-line skirt and cream wedge sandals on her feet, she is once again immaculately turned out.

I watch Bettina's eyes widen and she sits up straight, rising partway to shake Monique's hand.

'Hi, I'm Bettina, lovely to meet you.'

'Likewise. I've been looking forward to meeting someone who knew Lo at fifteen, you can give me some new material for piss-taking.'

Bettina looks at me, her brow furrowing.

'I'm joking,' says Monique, mock thumping Bettina's arm lightly. 'Right, what are we having to drink?'

One thing about Monique is that she never shuts up talking, so within minutes of being seated, Bettina has relaxed and is joining in with the conversation, which has so far consisted of a critique of my outfit; a long black skirt with black sandals and a stringy-strapped lilac t-shirt that I thought looked okay.

'Good God woman, its summer. What're you doing in a long black skirt? As soon as you're home get it packed away. In fact, throw it out, those legs of yours should be seen. That top does nothing for your skin tone either. Where's the Jade green one you bought last time we were round here? And *why* are your toenails not painted?'

'I didn't have time,' I plead.

'Did you go on Facebook this morning?'

'Erm ...'

'Thought so, and if you were on there any longer than ten minutes you most certainly had time.'

I turn to Bettina. 'See what I have to put up with?'

'You two are hilarious,' she grins. 'It's like watching some kind of reality TV show. In fact, I think you should make a demo.'

'Hey, we could be the new Ant and Dec. We could call it The Lomon Show. If you say it in a Jamaican accent it sounds like Lemon,' I say.

'Right, you're in trouble,' states Monique turning to Bettina. 'You've started her on the lame joke telling. You don't know what you've done.'

'We could call it Bit r Lomon.'

'Shut up, *please*,' pleads Monique.

'Or learn sumo-wresting, and call it Lomon squash.'

'Stop,' they yell out in unison.

I pretend to look hurt and take a sip of my coffee and then smirk at them both. 'Bettina, say beer can.'

'Beer can.'

'See you can talk Jamaican too. Say I want a beer can sandwich.'

Monique lifts her shoulders and drops them with a sigh. 'I give up.'

There's a break in conversation for a short time. 'I wonder if I could do with a makeover?' says Bettina quietly.

Monique re-energises. 'Well to be honest, if you're intent on sticking around Sheffield you could do with going down a hair shade or two, and dropping the tan about three shades.' Monique's like my own personal Gok Wan and is always direct with her answers. I envy her confidence.

'I was wondering if I was a bit full-on, I've already sent the sunbed back. Thanks for being so honest,' Bettina replies. 'I'll get booked in. Do you know a good salon?'

'Bella's on the top of Handsworth is excellent,' I say. Monique nods in agreement.

'They are good, they've won awards. I'd definitely book in there.'

'Cool, I'll do that this week,' she says. 'Anyone fancy another coffee? Then you,' she points at me, 'need to fill us in on the gossip about Seb.' She gets up to order the drinks.

Monique appraises me. 'Who's Seb?'

'Aha, I've saved that gossip especially for today.' I bat my eyelashes at Monique.

'Get those coffees dead fast or else,' she shouts across at Bettina.

'Right, spill,' says Monique once Bettina returns with fresh drinks.

'Just before I do, where was it you got those great yoga pants from again?'

'Yeah right, get on with it woman.'

I recount the pub events to them both and they listen without interruption, which for Monique is new territory, although she does sit twiddling her friendship bracelet round and round her arm.

'Oh my God, I just can't believe that of Mr Kingsley,' says Bettina. 'He looks so…boring.'

'Yes, well, I did find it boring.'

'Would you shag him if you were single?'

'Mon!'

'Well, would you? Does he live up to his hype?'

'Well there's definitely no faulting the TV', I state, 'but the picture's a bit dubious.'

'Oh jeez. Can't you just talk normally?'

'Stop picking on me,' I pout. 'You're causing interference.'

Bettina rolls her eyes and laughs. 'Reality show,' she repeats.

'So what're you going to do about Sexy Seb's seduction?' Monique pronounces each 's' like an Adult Chat-Line operator.

'You'll have to tell Mrs Sullivan. It's inappropriate to attempt to seduce a pupil's mother,' adds Bettina.

'Nah. It was amusing, and he's not going to get anywhere, so let him do his worst,' I say. 'I'm quite looking forward to his next attempt actually.'

'What did Niall say?' says Monique.

'Nothing really. He doesn't feel threatened by a,' – I make air quotes – 'lame teacher. Not that I told him what he said to me. I'd just have been wasting my time. I'm thinking of entering Hell's Kitchen, or being arrested by the police for speeding to get him to pay me some attention.'

'If you wanted a romantic, you picked the wrong bloke,' says Monique.

'What's your husband like?' asks Bettina.

'He's a dickhead.' Monique is as delicate as ever.

'That's my husband you're talking about, Mon.'

'Okay. He's a nice guy who acts like a dickhead. He doesn't appreciate what he's got in Lauren. She's beautiful, a fab mother, and she runs a small business as well as keeping the household running. He continually ignores her. I think a compliment would kill him.'

'Oh don't listen to Monique,' I protest. 'I do all my whinging to her so he comes across worse than he actually is.'

'You let him get away with ignoring you and I can tell it makes you feel crap. It upsets me seeing you down and unconfident. That's why I think he's a dick.'

'Okay,' I sigh. We've had this conversation before and it's not worth getting in a row about. She doesn't really know him. They've only met a handful of times so I let it go and enjoy another taste of my decaf.

'Anyway, what about you Bettina?' asks Monique. 'I gather yours was a dick too if you divorced him?'

'Nosey much?' I berate. 'Did toy boy not give it up then? Is this why there's a sudden obsession with the male anatomy today?'

We look at Bettina. She's gone quiet. 'Hell, sorry,' says Monique. 'I didn't mean to pry. I can be brash sometimes, take no notice. Sit back, drink your coffee and watch the show.'

'No, it's okay', says Bettina. 'I don't mind talking about it. I've nothing to hide.' She twiddles a lock of her hair again, a sign I now realise indicates her nervousness. 'It's quite simple really. He kept cheating, and I put up with it because of Tyler. He hit me...a couple of times...I didn't want Tyler at risk living there, so I left. He offered to pay me to leave Tyler behind.' She looks us in the eye in turn. 'As if I'd sell my son, and when that didn't work he started setting me up, saying I was a psycho. He doused himself in scalding hot coffee and told the police I attacked him. I was at the police station for hours.'

'Were you charged?' I ask.

'They let me off with a caution at that point.'

'So then what?' asks Monique.

'Oh that's the best bit,' she answers, with a sniff. 'When I went back home to fetch Tyler, I told him he couldn't do a damn thing about it, so he got a kitchen knife and stabbed himself through the hand. It wasn't a serious wound, I mean, he wouldn't have wanted to do anything that would threaten his glorious career.'

My mouth is wide open. 'Oh my God!'

Bettina's eyes are teary but she carries on. 'He got his friend who lived next door to come round and say he'd been a witness to it all. The police dropped the case as a domestic in the end, I mean, they knew he wasn't a saint from what they heard about him from the press, but he still managed to get me committed to a mental health unit.'

Her voice cracks on the last word. I lean over and squeeze her hand.

She smiles weakly at me. 'It was only for a couple of days, thank goodness.' She closes her eyes and takes a breath. 'I went to court to retain custody of Tyler. It was a hard fight, no thanks to him, but I got it, although he has to spend every other weekend with his dad. I moved back near my mother as she'd told the courts she'd be close by.'

I'm at a loss for words. What must it be like to be married to such an awful man? Poor Tyler too, what sort of effect has this had on him? I reflect on what I have. It might be boring at times, but at least I'm not in an abusive relationship.

'This girl needs a good time,' says Monique. 'Let's hit a few charity shops, then Etta's wine bar.'

'No wonder you love it around here,' Bettina is in awe. 'Designer gear for like five pounds an item?'

'Yep, and all cos it's not in season.' I'm in my element having got myself a little Karen Millen khaki cardigan for three ninety-nine, which Monique pointed out for me, and another two bags full of vintage style stuff, including a tea service, more jewellery and a few crocheted style handbags.

We are positioned in a window seat at Etta's. Our spoils rest on the window behind us as we sit on high bar stools with a glass of rosé wine each. I don't usually drink and drive but it seems apt to have one given what Bettina revealed this morning.

We've ordered an Etta special for lunch: an open baguette with roast beef, rocket, horseradish and caramelised onions, served with a side salad and beer battered chunky chips. My mouth is salivating just thinking about it.

'What exactly do you do on eBay?' asks Bettina.

'I have a little shop,' I explain. 'The overheads have gone up a lot recently, so I have to make sure I sell quite a few things a month to cover my costs and make a profit, but I do okay. I sell vintage looking items, as you've seen.' I point to the bags.

'She also plays with dolls,' smirks Monique. 'Buys them from car boots all bedraggled and unloved from little girls who've moved onto Monster High.' She coughs and I elbow her in the side. 'Ahem, I mean she *refreshes* them, washes them, brushes out their hair and gets them looking absolutely gorgeous again. She's like Extreme Makeover for Mattel. But it works, she's got a good eBay rep and you do okay don't you?'

'Well, I'm not about to give Branson a run for his money, but it's a bit extra that comes in handy for treats and holidays. I doubt we'd have got to Tenerife in May without my additions to the bank account.'

'That sounds really cool,' says Bettina. 'I loved Barbie when I was little.'

'They're really popular,' I smile. 'Before you know it I'll be on the run up to Christmas and it'll really take off, like the Princess of Monaco on her wedding day.'

Monique groans.

'So how much do you sell each month?'

'About fifty items a month I guess, until the end of September. Then I can sell two-hundred a month in the run up to Christmas as it gets so busy. I've only got about twenty things listed at the moment, but I've got another couple of bags full to list now, so that's my evening sorted. I hate listing though, it takes forever.'

Monique tilts to the side. 'Nope, it doesn't, look just took me a sec.'

'You're so funnneeeee,' I state, 'and you tell me off for my jokes?' I shake my head from side to side.

Our food arrives at this point and we're silent whilst we consume the deliciousness that is the Etta special.

We're ready to leave and Monique asks me if I fancy going to the pictures on Friday evening to see the latest Romcom.

'I can't. Niall has a works leaving do,' I state in a sad voice.

'If it's alright with you, I'd love to go,' says Bettina, looking at me for permission. I turn to Monique who shrugs. 'It's okay with me.'

'That's great then,' I say. 'I can avoid the latest Romcom where it leads me to believe there are men in this world who *do* treat women like the most desirable objects on earth, only to go home and see the reality.'

'Excuse me. Aren't you the one with a solid fella and another sexy bloke who wants to get in your pants?' says Monique. 'Quit your moaning.'

'I haven't had a night out for ages. I'm really looking forward to it,' adds Bettina, whose face then falls. 'Oh no, I can't. I've no-one to look after Tyler that night.'

'I'm stuck in. Why doesn't he come round to mine for the night? You can pick him up after the cinema, as long as you're not going to be mega late.'

'I was thinking a seven-ish showing,' says Monique. 'Then, if the Romcom gets me in the mood I can booty call Dr Love.'

'Ewww,' I say, trying to keep a laugh down, whilst making it look like I may vomit.

'Thanks so much,' says Bettina.

'No problem. I'll take him from school and give him some tea, so you have plenty of time to get ready.'

'You're such a pal. I'm so glad you're back in my life, you've no idea how pleased I am.'

I smile at her and touch her arm. We say our goodbyes to Monique and head home.

Later that evening I'm back on Facebook to see what Monique made of our new friend.

'She seems okay. Obviously got over the school victim thing to become another victim, which is a shame. You'll have to introduce her to some school gate mums though. As nice as she seems, I don't want her with us all the time. Three's a crowd and all that.'

'Well maybe you should have made an excuse for Friday instead of taking her to the cinema.'

'Awww, you jel hun? I felt sorry for her, so just this once I've made an exception. Plus I really want to see the film and admit it, you didn't want to go.'

'I didn't want to go.'

'When you seeing Sexy Seb next?'

'It's the meeting tomorrow night, but I'll be quite safe cos the other parents and helpers will be there.'

'I'm going to call you Lo-is, as only you know his real identity.'

'And Bettina.'

'Yes, but only you have been charmed by Super Seb. Wonder if he has a muscly, manly chest under that nerdy teacher outfit?'

'I am not going there with this conversation.'

'I bet when they appointed him they went "this looks like a job for Super Seb"'

'*groan*, again, thought I did the lame jokes?'

'I've obviously been hanging around you for too long. I can hear a noise ... Is it a bird, is it a plane? ...'

'I'm going now.'

'ROFLMAO. Love ya, Lo-is. I want any gossip tomorrow night. Hot off the press for the Daily Planet.'

'Goodnight.'

'Is that kryptonite in your pocket or are you just pleased to see me?'

'GOODBYE.'

CHAPTER FOUR

Wednesday night. Six pm rolls around and I find myself once again entering the school hall for the summer fair update. I've dressed down in jeans and a t-shirt, my hair loose and I'm make-up free apart from foundation and blush. I spot Seb sitting in a chair with the Clark Kent look, alive and well, and see tonight's nerd look is helped along by a maroon tank top. He gives me a nod and a small smile and looks away. I sit at the side of Bettina who has saved me a chair. Her hair has been cut to shoulder length and is now honey blonde. She looks really different. As I sit I notice her nails are French polished, rather than the pink I've become accustomed to. She's dressed in jeans and a t-shirt, though I recognise her jeans are DVB.

'You look amazing.' She really does look fresher.

'Thanks. I'm pleased with it.'

'Did you go to Bella's?'

'Yes, who'd have thought you had such a treasure on your doorstep?'

'Yep, well ssh, we need to keep her local.'

Bettina appraises my hair. 'I've just realised it looks very similar to yours. We could be twins.'

I touch my hair. 'Er, yes, well it's similar, but mine's lighter, and wavy. I like that honey colour she's used though, it suits your skin tone.'

'I'm going lighter once I've let the tan fade.'

I feel uncomfortable and at a loss at what to add. I've never understood people who copy others. I look around, inadvertently catching Seb's eye. He gives me a wink.

Mrs Sullivan arrives dressed in a brown woollen suit that would bake anyone else half to death, and have them fainting, but she is as composed as always. Her hair remains in its immovable position as she turns to us like she's about to give a presidential address. 'Okay, so can everyone give me a progress update?'

Volunteers fill her in about where they've got to over the past week. Bettina has placed notices on the boards in the main building and in the classroom windows, asking for unwanted books and says that quite a few have been donated already. Of course the stocks are easy to set up and need no further discussion.

'This week's task is to create some posters,' states Mrs Sullivan. 'So if everyone can start by doing a poster for their own stall, and ensure it shows the price of the activity. Whilst you're doing that, I'll be having a think about any additional posters we might need, such as arrows for the toilets, refreshment signs et cetera.'

'Right I'll catch up with you later,' I tell Bettina as I get up to make my way over to Seb. The paper for the posters is being placed on the tables. I'm pleased I wore my dodgier clothes as I know from previous experience with Joe that the paint is notoriously difficult to wash out, even though the school professes that it's washable.

'Ooohh, Sexy Seb,' she giggles.

'Don't you start,' I playfully hit her on the shoulder. 'Just remember this is your entire fault for landing me in the water. You didn't realise it was hot water, did you?'

A groan indicates Bettina's response to my humour. 'Monique is right, *lame*.'

I laugh and go over to Seb's table.

He looks me up and down. I squirm under his gaze.

'Well if it isn't the lovely Lauren Lawler. Oh the alliteration. I could make a beautiful poem out of your name.'

'Leave it out.' I sit down at the table with my side to him so I don't have to look directly at him. 'Pass me the pencil to sketch out the poster before we paint it. The quicker we get this done, the quicker I get home to my family.'

'So we're not going to the pub then?'

I purse my lips. 'We are so *not* going to the pub.'

Seb watches me outline the sign for the fair. I sketch out the words 'get revenge on a teacher, sponge stocks, one pound for five goes'.

'Twenty pence a throw? Dear God, I'll be drenched,' Seb says. 'Then you'll have to go in the stocks. Lauren Lawler all wet. I like the sound of that.'

I glare at him. 'One more pathetic, lewd comment and I'm out of here. I don't know if this ladies man charm works with other mothers or women, but to be honest, it's as attractive to me as you in that get up.'

'Ouch, that hurts.' He makes a stabbing through his chest motion with his hands.

I push the poster towards him. 'I've sketched it, you can paint it. It's done.' I get up to walk away.

He puts his hand on my arm. 'I'm sorry. I can't seem to help myself. In my defence it does usually work very well on the fairer sex.'

'How many times do I have to point out I'm married?'

'Yes, but are you happily married, Lauren?

I wince at his words.

'You see if there's one thing I've picked up on since I've been *charming* the ladies as you so nicely call it, it's which ones are happy, and my guess, is that although you don't want to like me, you can't help it. You're getting attention from me and I'm guessing you're not getting it at home.'

I clap three times, slowly. 'Bravo. That deserves a standing ovation. What a crock of shit.'

He rubs his jaw. His usual patter not having worked, his shoulders slump. He fixes me with his chocolate eyed gaze. It hits me again just how attractive he is. It's a shame his mouth doesn't match up to his features.

'Well, gosh, I don't think I've ever been turned down before, married or not,' he says. 'I'm sorry Lauren. Can we just get on with the painting and forget about the total ass I've made of myself?'

'That would be nice,' I state.

We spend the rest of the painting time chatting about Joe, Seb's job at the school and my eBay work. It's companionable and pleasant, and I see a different side to Seb. He is so much nicer when the act's turned off. Mrs Sullivan announces that we have five more minutes left.

Seb pauses from painting and looks up at me. 'So you have a happy marriage then? I'm pleased for you.'

'Some of the time he's a complete arse.' I state, placing my bag on my shoulder ready to leave. 'And the last time I got a compliment was about 1995. But he doesn't play games. No-one likes a player.' He nods, his forehead wrinkling, as I walk away.

The following night I find myself at home alone. Bettina insisted on having Joe round at hers for tea, to take her turn before I had the kids Friday, and somehow Tyler and Joe have managed to negotiate a sleepover. Niall's shift had been changed to afternoons, so I text Monique to see if she wants to meet up for tea, but she's busy, which I translate as shagging Dr Love.

I sit on my settee, a coffee coloured, corner placement like the one in the café. It has lovely sink

into it seats. I look around the house. We live in a
three bed semi. The walls are painted a neutral
beige at Niall's insistence, so I've jazzed it up with
abstract red canvasses and assorted cushions in
different textures. I had to fight Niall's obstinacy to
get a rug in the lounge, a lovely thick brown one
with stripes graduating into shades of red. He thinks
they make rooms look too fussy. I like it because it
makes the room cosier. I can lie across the rug, rise
onto my wrists and read or watch TV. Once upon a
time Niall and I would have christened such a rug
within days of it being put on the floor, but I've had
it over seven months now and its only other use has
been as a racetrack for Joe's cars. I realise I'm back
getting maudlin and decide if no-one's available to
go out with me, I'll just go on my own. There's a
pizza place in Meadowhall I go to frequently with
Joe, and I reckon I can sit at a dark table at the back.
I grab my book to read in lieu of a partner and head
off.

After about six minutes walking around the
shopping centre, window shopping on my way to
the pizza place, I pass a shop that sells intimate
items. Usually I pay this shop no attention and walk
past. Today I stop. I haven't had a vibrator for
years. I think about how times change. I threw out
anything dubious looking when Joe was around four
and started going through all the drawers asking
what everything was. I suck on my bottom lip.
Maybe if I'm not getting much at home from Niall,
it wouldn't hurt to have a bit extra myself. I smile,

thinking next time I'm home alone I might not feel the need to rush off shopping.

I go in, and I'm immediately approached by a Shop Assistant. 'I'm just looking thanks.'

She moves away and leaves me to browse. The vibrators are situated at the back of the store, obscured by a corner so you can't be seen by outside shoppers. There are rows upon rows of them in assorted shapes and colours. I don't know where to start. I look at the Assistant and she must be used to reading faces like mine because she heads straight back over.

'Bit overwhelming isn't it?'

I nod. 'I've had one before but ...'

'Not a first timer then, that's useful to know.' She looks through the racks and hands me a few to look at, describing what they do. I decide on a simple pocket rocket after finding that some of them quite frankly scare me. I feel empowered when I've bought one and leave the shop proudly clutching my carrier bag. My stomach growls, so I walk quickly towards the restaurant.

'Lauren?'

I turn around slowly and look at Seb. He looks at my carrier bag. My face reddens to a deeper shade than ketchup.

'Normally, I would have to say something lewd and witty, but seeing as it's you, my mouth is closed.' He makes a zipping motion with his fingers across his lips.

'Well of all the people I could have met at this exact moment, of course it would have to be you,' I huff.

'Could've been Mrs Sullivan...'

The thought of Mrs Sullivan near a sexy store reduces me to laughter and the awkwardness evaporates.

'Right, well I must get going before I faint with hunger.'

He raises an eyebrow. 'You haven't eaten yet?'

'Niall and Joe are out, now don't think I'm being rude, but I need to get going.'

'Well that'll definitely get you going,' he nods towards the bag. 'Sorry, sorry, couldn't resist it. I saw an opening and had to take it. Oh my God, I actually didn't mean to say that one,' he says with a hand across his mouth, doing his best to hold down a smirk.

'There's obviously an underlying sexual repression or something with you,' I state. 'Go home, have a wank, and get it over with.'

'Mrs *Lawler*. I am shocked that you said that to me, a teacher at your son's school.'

I close my eyes for a few seconds and wish myself somewhere else. 'You're right, that was inappropriate, I'm sorry.'

'I promise not to tell Mrs Sullivan, but only if you eat with me.'

'What? Don't be ridiculous, you're not going to tell Mrs Sullivan.'

'I'll just follow you then, and sit opposite you anyway.'

I sigh. 'Oh my God, you are so annoying. Whatever, come on then, before I come to my senses and change my mind.'

I no longer need a corner table for one as I don't want it to look like an illicit encounter, so I ask for a seat in the middle of the restaurant, near several noisy children and infants in high chairs. The smell of garlic and tomato permeates the air. It makes my stomach rumble and my mouth water. I so need to eat. 'Are you going to behave normally?'

He holds up three fingers. 'Scout's promise. I'll even talk about the summer fair.'

The waitress comes to take our order. I ask for a plain Margarita and a coke. Seb orders the same.

'So I gather there's no significant other in your life, with your persistent need to annoy me?'

'Nope.' He sits back in his seat, legs wide open. 'I can't be doing with serious relationships. It gets to six months and then the pressure starts.'

I raise an eyebrow at him.

'I'm being serious. One kept inviting me to her friends' weddings and always managed to catch the bouquet. Another tried to make my mother her best friend. It does my head in; I'm just not that kind of guy. It's why I started having affairs with married women. I like non-committal sex, but sometimes even they get carried away.'

'Have you listened to yourself?'

'I'm just being honest.' He opens his hands apart in gesture.

The waitress brings our drinks and I have a long sip of mine.

'Are you enjoying being at Woodley?' I think a change of subject is a good move.

His face opens up into a large smile. 'I love it. The kids are mainly awesome.'

'It's nice to enjoy a job as well as just earn money from it,' I say.

'Absolutely. Total bonus. I love looking at a kid and seeing how there's all this information about the world they don't know yet, and I can teach them some of it. Some of those kids might make decisions in the future based on what I've taught them. It's just amazing. Sometimes I can't get up fast enough in a morning.'

I smirk and he realises what he's said. 'Oh, so now you're starting with the innuendo, steady on Mrs Lawler.'

I pick up my drink quickly and lose my grip on the glass. As it starts to drop his hand hits mine as he reaches over to catch it. We place the glass back down whilst somehow still having our hands touching. I move my hand away. I can't look at him as my traitorous mind thinks I actually wouldn't mind touching him again. He hesitates and then leans over the table. I look up at him and I don't know what to say.

'You careless sod,' he chucks me under the chin and the mood is broken, which is just as well as our pizzas arrive.

Seb insists on paying the bill and walking me to my car. The shopping centre closes at eight pm, except for the restaurant area, so there aren't many cars left around.

He breaks the silence. 'That poster you drew is really good. You have a talent for art.'

'Thanks, I love doing anything like that.'

At this point I realise I'm swinging the carrier bag containing my vibrator around.

Seb nods towards it. 'Is that vintage patterned as well then?'

I roll my eyes at him. 'Thanks for walking me to the car,' I say, and open the driver's side door.

'My pleasure,' he says, looks again at the bag and I feel my breathing get heavier.

'Well, night.'

'Good night Lauren.' He walks across the car park his hands in his pockets. I try not to notice that this causes the material of his trousers to pull tight, displaying a mighty fine bottom.

I get home feeling wired. Niall has not yet returned home from work. I go upstairs, remove the packaging from my new toy, clean it and put batteries in. It has noise reduction and whirrs quietly. I feel stupid as I lie back against the pillows and shut my eyes. Thoughts of Seb come into my mind and I drop a hand to my breast and imagine he's touching me with those soft fingers. I stop; feeling guilty. I'm thinking of a man who's not my husband. It's not even a movie star, which I'd give myself a pass for, but my son's next teacher. I turn the vibrator off, jump out of bed, and throw it at the back of the wardrobe. I'm tired, and feeling foolish. I decide there's no Facebooking tonight. I'll go straight to sleep. I didn't manage to get on Facebook last night either, so I know Monique will be waiting for an update on things. I go to turn my phone off and see I have a message from her asking to know what happened at the fair meeting. There's another text message from a number I don't recognise. I open it and read;

Remember your phone can vibrate too, so I might have to keep texting. Keep it in your pants ;)

I switch it off and get into bed for what turns out to be a most restless night's sleep.

CHAPTER FIVE

I spend Friday wasting time on the computer and watching daytime television, which is the one thing I have never succumbed to before at home. At three-fifteen I arrive at school and take Joe and Tyler home. They had an amazing time the previous evening and can't wait for round two. I'm just dropping the schoolbags into the house when my mobile rings.

'Lauren?' The voice is so loud I wince. 'Oh my God, Lauren, Tyler's missing. The teacher didn't see who took him. I've called the police. I think Danny's got him.' Bettina is sobbing hysterically down the phone and I have to shout to be heard.

'Bettina, I have them. It's Friday, remember? You're going to the cinema with Monique.' There's a pause.

'Oh my God', she bursts into tears down the phone. 'I totally forgot. Oh my God. I've rung the police. I reported him. I—'

'Take a breath, ring them back and then ring me and let me know you're okay.'

'I… I'll, yes, I'll do that now.'

She puts the phone down and I get the children a drink and a snack. When she phones again she is much calmer.

'I'll come through and see him, if that's okay. It's really,' her breath catches, 'got to me. I thought he had him.'

'Well of course you can. I was sure Mrs Baxter had seen me, you know.'

'As long as he's safe I don't care.'

'But doesn't Danny see him every other weekend anyway? Why would he pinch him?' I know I should be apologising. How would I feel if it was Joe? But how can she have forgotten? Surely Tyler and Joe would have been talking about it this morning?

'He threatened to do it before. He told me he might just take him and go abroad. It's not like he couldn't afford it.'

'I'm sorry Bettina, I didn't know. Okay, get yourself round here and I'll get the kettle on.' I end the call and sit on the bottom step for a few moments.

When she arrives at the house she's shaking and teary. I keep her in the hallway for a minute, apologise again and get her to compose herself. Tyler will only worry if he sees her upset.

'I don't think I can go out now. I'll stay here with the kids. You go.'

'Not a chance. Everything here is okay; it was just a mix up, that's all.

'I just want to be with Tyler.'

'He's fine, and he's with Joe. Look, I think you need this night out, get a break from things. Plus there is no way on this earth I am seeing that damn film, and Monique will kill you if you don't go. So cup of tea coming up, and you can have something to eat here if you like. Its casserole, so there's plenty, and you'll be able to meet Niall as he'll be home from work soon.' I shut up as I realise I'm rambling on and she's only half listening.

She rubs her eyes with the back of her hand and draws in a deep breath. 'Thank you. I just... I panicked. I keep thinking Danny's going to pull some kind of stunt to get Tyler.'

'Right, come through to the living room.' I say, 'but mind where you're walking, cos there is Lego everywhere and it flipping hurts when you step on it.' I wait for her acknowledgement. Mothers have a universal hatred of Lego on the floor, but there's nothing. She rushes straight for Tyler, who endures a hug from his mum, which is obviously so not cool in front of his mate. I see him look over her head and roll his eyes at Joe. I head into the kitchen to warm through the casserole, and decide to give the kids their meal first as they're complaining they're *starving*. We can wait for Niall to arrive home from work.

Kids seated and eating, I'm about to sit down when the phone rings. I curse under my breath but pick up anyway. 'Hello?'

'Hello Mrs Lawler, are you okay to have a quick word?' It's Mrs Sullivan.

'Yes of course.'

'It's about the incident at school tonight. We are obviously going to have to look into it because it could have potentially been very serious.'

My brow furrows. 'I understand, and I'm so sorry. I was sure Mrs Baxter had seen me.'

Bettina comes and hovers nearby.

'You may have actually done us a favour. At least this time it was a mum from school and everything was alright. I just need you to tell me exactly what happened.'

'Of course. Well it's very simple really, Joe came out of class with Tyler and I took them both home. I'd made arrangements with his mother for Tyler to stay for tea.'

'Hmm, well obviously security has got a little lax. We'll be reviewing our procedure, and will be making sure Mrs Baxter or her assistant are standing at the doorway at home time to ensure each child is collected by a person they know, which is what should happen anyway.'

'I should have made a point of telling Mrs Baxter I had them.'

'Not at all. The teacher should have been paying more attention. The situation won't arise again, but I do need you to pop in tomorrow to fill in an incident report.'

'Of course. Is there anything else?'

'Not at the moment Mrs Lawler. I'll see you tomorrow.'

I put the phone down and exhale sharply.

'I gather that was the school?' Bettina says.

'Yes, they've got to do some kind of report about the incident.'

'Oh, well good. They can't be letting kids go off with just anybody.'

'Bettina,' I say. 'It was a mix up, and anyway it sounds like its Mrs Baxter who's in trouble.'

'Why?'

'For not paying attention to who's collecting the kids. Anyway,' I say as a thought occurs to me. 'Why weren't you at the school gates if you'd forgotten I was getting Tyler?'

'I was running late. I'd had to get the bus from town and it took forever. By the time I'd got there, hardly any parents were around.'

I'm starting to wish I'd just gone to the cinema myself. There was probably less drama in the movie. I turn as I hear keys jangling in the door.

'Niall's here,' I smile. Bettina sits up straight and flicks her hair, putting a smile on her own face.

'Oh, hi,' Niall looks questioningly at Bettina as he walks into the room and then he sees Tyler. 'I'm guessing you're Bettina. Aren't you supposed to be at the cinema?'

'Hi, I am,' she stands up and holds out her hand for Niall to shake, which he does. 'Not for about another hour though.'

I stand also. 'I'll serve the meal. Do you want to go and sit at the dining table?'

As they do, I hear Joe saying, 'This is my mate, Tyler.'

'Well how do you do Tyler?' replies Niall. 'Are you two responsible for all this Lego mess?'

'I'll get them to clear it,' says Bettina quickly, and heads towards a seat.

'He's only teasing,' I say. 'We can't get Joe to pick anything up without nagging.'

'Apart from swear words at school,' Niall quips. 'Those he picks up just fine.'

Bettina giggles, a silly high girlish giggle that I've never heard her make before.

We send the kids off to play. Niall sits next to me, as usual, and Bettina sits opposite. I feel like I do when I'm waiting in the doctors, wanting it to all be over quickly.

'So, you're a nurse?' Bettina asks in her new girly tone.

'A Charge Nurse, yes. Dead important I am,' Niall winks, then turns and smiles at me. 'I have to work hard so Lauren can go out and buy pretty bags and jewellery.'

'Ha ha,' I say, a bit miffed by his insensitivity about my business.

Bettina lifts up her hand daintily. 'I'm sorry for mentioning work things, but my wrists been hurting and ...'

'I need to stop you there,' I say. 'Niall's a Charge Nurse at a Psychiatric Unit for the Elderly. He only did a few weeks placement in General Nursing, so he's hopeless unless you've gone bonkers.'

Bettina flinches and I realise what I've said. Oh God, she was a psychiatric patient. Foot in mouth again, well done, Lauren. She can tell I'm about to say something but gives me a warning with her eyes, she doesn't want Niall to know. I've told him anyway, but maybe he wasn't listening at the time. Right now he certainly seems to have no idea what's going on as he reaches to turn on the TV.

'Excuse me, ladies. I don't mean to be rude switching on the TV at mealtime, but I'm going out soon and haven't managed to catch up with the news yet.'

I raise an eyebrow. He puts it on every bloody night and never says its rude then. Hypocrite.

'Where are you off to Niall?' asks Bettina.

'A leaving do at the Chantry,' I state, speaking louder so it reaches Niall's ears. 'Which he needs to be at in about thirty minutes.'

He turns around to me. 'I can answer for myself you know. Actually I have to pass the cinema to get there,' he says looking at Bettina. 'Do you want a lift?'

'That'd be awesome,' she says.

Awesome?

When they've gone I catch up on eBay. The kids are great, and with the provision of some junk food, they keep themselves occupied with the toys in Joe's bedroom. The evening passes quickly. Bettina picks Tyler up at nine-thirty and takes him home in a taxi, saying she had a nice time. Niall arrives home not much later at ten. He's not one for staying at a do. He likes his own company and barely drinks, so he does the pleasantries and as soon as the booze starts flowing and tongues start loosening he leaves them to it. He says he doesn't mind hearing the gossip about what his colleagues have been up to, but would hate to witness any of it. I begin to tell him about the drama of the afternoon, but he stops me. 'Bettina told me in the car. Messed up there didn't you? Nearly gave the poor woman a heart attack.'

'She's the one who forgot,' my voice gets higher.

Niall walks into the kitchen and sticks the kettle on. He grabs a mug out of the shiny red kitchen cabinet and plonks a tea bag in it.

'For someone who didn't want much to do with her, you are certainly very involved.'

'You were the one who told me I was being stupid, so I decided to make an effort. She seems okay, bit paranoid about her husband though.'

'She seemed fine to me. Her husband sounds like a complete knob.'

'Yes,' I sigh, 'it would appear so. Tyler and Joe are getting on like a house on fire.'

'Owww, speaking of houses...' Niall picks up a Lego window that he's stood on in bare feet.

'What do you tell Joe all the time?' I mock. 'Should've had your slippers on.'

'Go and fetch 'em for me, I'm knackered,' he states, fishing the tea bag out of his cup, where no doubt I'll find it down the side of, rather than inside, the bin liner tomorrow; a pet peeve of mine.

I huff but fetch them anyway. When I come back from the hallway he's sat in the lounge, cuppa in hand, and the television is on.

I stand in the doorway. He's transfixed by the pixellations.

'Night then.'

'Night, Love.'

Another sigh escapes me as I leave the room.

I get my pj's on, check Joe is settled and get into bed. I check my Inbox through my phone. There's a private message from Monique;

Ring me, asap.

I pick up the house phone and call her. 'Is everything okay? Did you have a good time?'

'The film was great, and you missed out on my fabulous company which is a sin in my book,' she says. 'Anyway I need to talk to you about Loser Liz.'

'Mon,' I say, shocked. 'That's a bit blunt, even for you.'

'Yeah, well after tonight I've a new name for her – Besotted Bettina'.

I laugh. 'Yeah she was a bit taken with Niall.'

'Not with Niall, with you.'

'What?'

'I know we couldn't talk while the movie was on, but every other bit of conversation was about you. When you met Niall, how long you'd been married, were you happy, had you ever cheated, did Niall resent the fact you didn't work, how long had I known you? It went on and on. I asked her what the twenty questions was about and she said she was trying to fill in the years she hadn't known you. She was worried about seeming nosey and didn't want to ask you directly, but it was so weird, Lo. She was going on about the grief you'd caused her today, and how she was sure you hadn't meant it, but it

70

really upset her. She was asking if you'd ever done anything to upset me.'

'I'm sure it's nothing more than getting all the gossip on me from my best mate, and she was really shaken up this afternoon. With what she told us about her husband, it doesn't surprise me. Honestly, don't sweat it.'

'Well I don't like her, she's odd. Sorry for putting on you like this, but please don't bring her for coffee or anything again.'

'You feel that strongly about it?'

'There's something very off about her, Lo. You need to watch her.'

'Okay, okay.' I say.

'I'm only going on cos I love ya.'

'I know hun, love ya too, BFF,' I say. 'Sleep tight.'

'I certainly shall. I shall be thinking about Ryan Reynolds in that film.'

'You saddo.' I laugh and put the phone down.

I lie back in bed and think about what she's said. What else would Bettina talk about? She had nothing much in common with Monique apart from myself? Monique has such a strong personality I don't think she realises sometimes how difficult it is for others to converse with her. She doesn't really have any other friends than me. I also think that maybe I pushed Bettina into going out tonight. I should have just driven her and Tyler home. After what happened with Danny she must feel so insecure about everything, and she's only been around me for a couple of weeks, which isn't really long enough to trust anybody. I still have to see

Bettina, she's Tyler's mum, so I resolve I'll just meet up with them separately for a while.

Saturday morning rolls around. I get up and head to the kitchen while Niall takes Joe to his swimming lesson. I'm pleased we have no pre-arranged plans for the weekend and that when they get back we can just chill and have some family time. It's a lovely day, and I decide that instead of taking Joe car booting, I'll make a picnic. There's a large park within a twenty minute drive of the house we can go to. I prepare the food, sit at the table and boot up Niall's laptop to check my eBay account. Out of the forty items I've listed, nineteen of them have sold overnight. I look, staggered by what I'm seeing. Three different bidders have bought several items each, and they've all paid by Paypal, so the money is in my account already. I leave positive feedback, praising them for being prompt payers, and then make my way upstairs to prepare their purchases for sending. The local Post Office is open on a Saturday morning, so I'll be able to get them sent quickly. I like to be punctual in posting, in order to maintain my one hundred per cent feedback rating. Hopefully I might get some regular customers. If that happens, I can up my game and regularly look for items, rather than just visiting the odd charity shop or car boot. I feel really energised and positive.

The guys get back from swimming and Joe is in a strop. 'He must be tired after his late night with Tyler,' says Niall.

'I've packed a picnic for us,' I say. 'Do you want to get the bikes out and we'll go to Rother Valley?'

'Are you joking, Love? We've just come back from swimming. He's in a right mood and I just want to have a sit down. I've been working all week.'

'I thought it'd be nice for us to have some family time.'

'What's this then? Are we not a family now?'

'You know what I mean; going out, having fun.'

'Well, let's compromise. We'll have the picnic in the garden and I'll kick a football around with Joe for a bit. He'll like that.'

'You can do that,' I say, thinking about the dwindling stock on my eBay account. 'I'm going to have lunch and go to the car boot this afternoon.'

'Oh, Joe'll enjoy that.'

'I'm not taking Joe, he's tired, remember? I'm going on my own.'

'Here we go.'

I walk into the kitchen before I throttle him.

I eat lunch, and gather my boot stuff together. I take three fold up cotton bags that fit inside each other and a small handbag with lots of loose change. I've learnt that people doing car boots never have change and always run out of carrier bags before the end. As I go to get in the car I see a shadow cross the concrete. I turn quickly with my keys turned out, ready to stab in self-defence.

'Hey steady on. Gosh, you haven't changed one bit, Lauren,' says Danny Southwell.

CHAPTER SIX

I back up against the car. I see the same lad I knew from school, only now he has lines on his face, grey flecks in his hair and stubble. He's small for a man, only about an inch taller than my five feet seven, but as he stands wide-legged, with his hands in his pockets, his demeanour makes me wary.

'What are you doing here? Do I need to shout for my husband?'

He grins. 'You look like I'm about to kill ya, Lauren, mate. Calm down, I'm here about Bet.' His eyes focus on my face. 'Gosh you really haven't changed much since school. It's weird us being older, innit? I still feel about fifteen.'

My jaw is clenched and my shoulders are fixed. I feel like I cannot move. Is Danny here to hurt me or for a school reunion? 'How did you know where I live?'

He clasps his hands tightly. 'After the police accused me of kidnapping my son, I rang her mother. She said you've been a good friend to her. A little digging on the internet got me your address, so I thought I'd come and see what the score was.'

'Have you any idea how psycho that sounds?'

'Lauren, I'm not without resources now and seriously, an eight year old could find out where you live on the internet these days. Anyway,' he nods towards the house, 'nice looking place you've got. How ya been doin' all these years?'

I feel myself start to loosen as memory takes over and I'm back just talking to Danny from school. He has a small scar on his lip which I know is from where he fell off his skateboard in Year Seven, and he has the tiniest hint of acne scars. I'd always had a soft spot for him at school, he was a loveable rogue. Not that our paths crossed often, but he'd been in a few of my classes.

I straighten up and move nearer to speak to him. 'I'm alright, Danny. Yesterday was a misunderstanding. She'd forgotten I was picking the kids up. What did the police say?'

'They rang and said they were on their way round to check out the house and I had to stay there until they arrived. Not long after that call, they phoned back to say he'd been found. How the dozy cow managed to lose him at school I don't know.'

'Like I said, it was a misunderstanding.'

'Bet's mother said, but I've got a right to know what's going on. He's my son too.'

'Yes, and I don't mean to be funny,' I state, 'but I don't think Bettina would like you round here. I know you have visitation rights over Tyler, but that's just at the weekend isn't it? She was so frightened yesterday—'

'That's what I want to talk to ya about. I wanna know what she's been saying about me, which is probably a load of crap. I can tell with how her mother talks to me that she doesn't exactly get the truth.' Danny runs his hands through his hair, his face looks pained.

'Look, I'm trying to be a friend to her, so I don't want to know the ins and outs of your marriage. I'd rather not be involved.'

'Well, you see, that's the problem,' says Danny. 'Like it or not you are involved.'

My forehead creases. 'How?'

'Why did she say she came back to Sheffield?'

'To be near her mum.'

'Well she's lying. She came to Sheffield for you.' He points his finger at me.

'What on earth are you talking about?' I'm starting to get exasperated and check my watch. If he doesn't go soon it won't be worth me going to the car boot, and I really need more stock now I've sold so much stuff.

'Has Bettina told you she was having some problems? Had to see a psychiatrist?'

I look at him and remain silent. I'm divulging nothing. I look back at my house. Niall and Joe haven't noticed that I'm still here. I wonder how long I'd lay dead for before they discovered me, probably not until the evening meal didn't turn up, or maybe not if they gorged on chocolate and bits from the fridge. Perhaps it might get to Monday morning when they had no clean shirts for school and work. I think I must be accidentally putting on Harry Potter's invisibility cloak rather than my jacket when I leave the house.

'Lauren, listen to me. Just hear me out and then I'll be getting off.'

I look back at him. 'I'm listening.'

'When Bettina left our school she was mad at you. She thought you'd dissed her, left her to the clutches of Jodie and the gang. Her mother pulled her out of school after they'd waited for her one night and threatened to do things to her with a broom they'd had in their hands. I saw them and broke it up, but it was the final straw for her mother. Bet was grateful to me and showed me in more ways than one; that's how she ended up pregnant,' he looks at me, smiling, but he doesn't find it reflected back.

I fold my arms around myself. 'And?'

'One time when we were talking about school days, she was having a right go about you. I stuck up for you, saying that I'd always thought you were alright and that it wasn't you who'd bullied her anyway. She went mad, accusing me of fancying you and saying I was only with her because I was forced to be. She developed a bit of an obsession about you, saying you'd let her down and that all this was your fault, that you were ruining her marriage.'

'What?'

'I know. I told her she was being ridiculous. We tried for another baby and got our Tyler. She calmed down for a bit after that.' He sighs. 'A couple of years ago I had an affair, first of a few to be honest. I don't attempt to say it's okay, but she weren't right when she found out. Alicia had blonde wavy hair and Bet went ballistic. Said I had it bad for you and was shagging your lookalike. She threw a hot drink over me; I had to go to hospital. I thought that was just temper until the crazy bitch stabbed me in the hand.' He wipes a drip of sweat from his forehead with his t-shirt sleeve. 'I got the police involved and she had to go to counselling for a while. She came through it though, said she was fine and then the next minute she's left and come back to Sheffield and taken Tyler away from me.'

I go and sit on the front step trying to take in what he's saying to me. How am I supposed to know who to believe? Did she stab him? Is he twisting things to get me on his side with Tyler? Maybe that's what was happening now. I'm at a loss for what to do and what to say. I put my head in my hands feeling like it's about to explode. Then I think about what Monique said to me about Bettina's constant questioning and I feel my mouth go dry.

I lift my head back up. 'What is it exactly you want me to do? Do you want Tyler? Is that why you're here?'

'I love my kid, course I want him back, but that isn't why I'm here. When she walked out she told me I'd pay for what I'd done to her, and believe me I have – I am. She's doing everything in her power to make sure my contact with Tyler is as brief as possible. If she had her way I wouldn't see him at all. But that wasn't all she said and I thought you needed to know, now you're hanging round with her.'

There's a pause. 'Go on then, what else did she say?'

'She said she was going to destroy you, slowly, one part of your life at a time, until you knew how she felt.'

CHAPTER SEVEN

When he's left I get in the car and sit there for a few minutes, thoughts whirr through my head. There's no way I'm going to go to the car boot now so I drive to my favourite coffee shop and let out a silent prayer that my favourite sofa will be free, even on a busy Saturday afternoon. By a miracle it is. I toy with ordering a hit of espresso before deciding I'm shaky enough already, so I stick with a large decaf black coffee. I sink down into the sofa's cosy depths, close my eyes and think of everything I've been told over the last few days. Is it really possible that Bettina is out to get me? She doesn't seem crazy and yet how do I know what crazy looks like? Why would she be obsessed with me over one incident that happened when we were younger? How can I not believe it when my best friend and Danny have both warned me? My breathing feels ragged and unsteady and I feel the first tingling of a panic attack, something I haven't had for years. My heart starts racing and I begin to feel sick. I have an overwhelming urge to rush home. I remember my training and push through it, breathing steadily and remember that it's the fast breathing that causes the dizziness, while the stomach churning is caused by adrenaline. It takes a few moments but I feel my heartbeat calm down and relax enough to take a sip of my coffee. I need to decide how to handle this information, but I just can't take it all in. Danny seemed okay, but then I've only seen him for ten minutes out of the last God knows how many years. If Bettina's telling the truth then he's trying to destroy her, and what better way to do it than to turn her only friend against her? On the other hand Mon only has my best interests at heart, so she has no reason to lie. I make a decision to keep my distance from Bettina for a while. It'll be difficult with the kids and the fair, but I think it's the best course of action for now. I think of when I'll next need to see her. If I ask Tanya to get Joe from school again on Monday, then I can turn up as late as possible on Tuesday. I can sit with Seb at the fair meeting, and she can't really take offence at that seeing as it's her fault we're doing the sponge stocks together. I figure I just need a couple of days to assess the situation and get my head around things. In fact that's an idea, I'll have a day off from everyone; Monday I'll have another day to myself at home. I need some time alone, to work through my foggy brain. I take my phone out of my bag and text Mon. Soz can't meet u Monday, something came up.

A few minutes later I get a text back asking if everything is okay.

`Yes, just busy, sold lots eBay. Catch up FB soon.`

When she replies to say that's okay, I feel relieved. I reckon we'd have spent Monday talking about nothing but Bettina, and to be honest, right about now I feel like I've had a belly full of it. All I want at this moment is Niall and Joe. It's the weekend and I want to be with my family, whether they go out with me or we just share the same time zone. I leave my half drunk cup of coffee on the table and head straight home.

When I get back, it's no surprise that Niall and Joe don't realise I've returned empty handed. I was going to tell Niall about Danny's visit but decide that I can't be bothered going through it now. When I work out what's going on I'll tell him. Right now I want to forget about it. I walk through the house and out of the patio doors, removing my shoes and walking barefoot along the grass towards Joe, who is happily bouncing around on his ten foot trampoline. 'Hi mum,' he waves. 'Are you coming on?'

'Sure am hun,' I smile and climb through the netting that keeps him safe.

'Mum you aren't allowed on without socks.'

'I'll be okay this once.' I realise how hypocritical I'm being to go on barefoot when I'm forever telling Joe to make sure he has socks on but I don't care. I want to break the rules and I don't want to miss being with my son for one more second today. We bounce around the trampoline. I pretend to try and get off and Joe drags me back by the arms and pulls me around the floor of it, then he bounces over me, as if he might fall on me like a mini wrestler. As we look at each other, with our hair raised with static electricity, we start giggling and my heart is full to bursting with the love I have for him. I feel someone watching and look up to see Niall in the dining room. He smiles and waves, whilst taking a sip of a cup of tea. I wave back and return to Joe, diving on him in a wrestling move and listening to him giggle uncontrollably.

'Did you bring me anything back mum?'

Damn. 'No love, there was nothing decent. It was nearly all Traders this week.'

'Oh well, I'm glad you're back.'

'Me too.'

Monday turns out to be the perfect day for lounging around. I return soaking wet from dropping Joe off at school. Typical British summertime has returned; pouring rain and six degrees outside. I shrug my coat and shoes off at the door, and to make sure I'm toasty I switch on the central heating. Wearily, I pad upstairs in my slippers, walking on the only carpet in the house, the stair carpet, and enter the bedroom. I let my clothes drop to the floor and dig out my Christmas pjs from the bag on the top of the wardrobe. They're made of fleece and really snuggly. I realise this is all completely over the top but I don't care. I quickly dry the ends of my hair and fringe with the hairdryer and get into bed. What the hell. I climb under the duvet, designed to feel like duck-down and check out the clock. Tanya has offered to give Joe his tea so I have until six pm all to myself. It's not even nine. Glorious. I snuggle down inside the bed and go back to sleep. When I wake, it's lunchtime.

I eat chocolate for lunch with a coffee. When I'm stressed my diet is the first thing that goes out of the window. I'm usually so meticulously organised with what we are eating for breakfast, lunch and evening dinner and have it balanced so we eat a good diet, but this past week I'd been slipping; chip shop, pizza. I'd felt guilt after each convenience meal but not guilty enough to cook properly for us. I'd thrown food away this weekend and felt guilty about that too. I hated waste. As I lie here, I wonder what to do next. Having rested I need an activity. I look at my wardrobes and an idea forms.

I spend a few hours rearranging my wardrobe into ready to go outfits. I'm especially pleased with a blue gingham shirt and white jeans that I put the teacup necklace with and decide I must wear that very soon. Feeling better, I spend the next two hours making a chicken pie for tea and an apple crumble for dessert. The cooking completely relaxes me. While I bake I seem to go into another world, just one of sensations; feeling the ingredients as I rub them together, taking in the smells that permeate the room as it cooks. I'm rolling the pastry when I hear a knock at the door. Groaning at the interruption I wipe my hands down my apron, walk to the front door and look through the spy-hole. It's Bettina and Tyler. What the hell are they doing here when it's obvious I wasn't around to fetch Joe? I hear Bettina through the door. 'She doesn't seem to be in. I hope everything's okay. Stay there and I'll have a look around the back.'

God, if she goes to the back window she'll see my half rolled pastry. I have no choice but to answer the door.

'Hi sorry, I was caught short.' I shake my hair.

'Just wondered if you were okay, only I haven't heard from you for a few days.'

'I'm fine, just been having some family time and I've had a bit of a dodgy stomach today.'

'Oh, Tanya said she was getting Joe as you had a backlog of work to get through?'

'Well, yes, that was the plan before my stomach started.'

'Well I came to tell you that they've moved the summer fair meeting to tomorrow night. Same time though.'

'Oh right, thanks for letting me know. Hopefully I'll be okay by then.'

She looks at me as if she expects to be invited in. I feign a cramp and whimper. 'You must excuse me, it's happening again. I'll catch up with you tomorrow.' I close the door on them and rush upstairs where I peek out behind the curtain of Joe's room and watch them walk away. Bettina looks back at the house before she strolls off. I'm not entirely sure she hasn't seen me. I realise then that I'm still wearing the apron, smeared in flour.

Twenty minutes after I've got Joe back home, Niall comes through the door. 'Something smells nice.'

'Chicken pie and apple crumble.' I say

'My favourites. Come on what do you want?'

'Your body,' I state giggling. For some reason Niall doesn't laugh back, instead, he turns to Joe and asks him how his school day has been.

'Fine,' says Joe, his stock answer for a school day. Niall and I roll our eyes at each other and I head to the kitchen to finalise the dinner, whilst he heads upstairs to get changed.

We have a relaxed evening, and for once Joe is really tired and fast asleep by eight. I climb onto Niall's chair and move onto his lap to snuggle up.

'That's not very comfy, Lauren.'

'I just want a snuggle.'

'Your bony elbows and butt are digging into me, it hurts.'

'For God's sake, why do I bother?' I shout and walk out of the room, back to the retreat of my bedroom.

I power up my laptop, switch to my Facebook tab and see that Monique is online.

'Hello, did you miss me today?' I type.

'Course I bloody did. You aren't allowed to ditch me again. EVER.'

'I won't. Missed you too, although spending the morning sleeping was fun.'

'You ditched me to sleep? You prefer sleeping to my delightful company? I AM INSULTED.'

'Hey shouty caps, I've said I won't do it again. You'll be proud of me tho, cos I spent the afternoon making up outfits.'

'Well obvs I'll need to see if they're acceptable first, seeing as I'm convinced ur colour blind.'

'Cheeky. What's been going on with you then?'

'*sulks* Well you'd know that if you hadn't bailed on me.'

'Forgive me?'

'Maybe, if you buy the coffees next Monday.'

'Done.'

'Did some overtime at the weekend, wasn't much else to do. Yoga class was cancelled due to illness. Oh, and I had 'lunch' in the disabled toilet with Dr Love as there's no other staff around on a weekend ;)'

'Filth. Please stop, I do not wish to be tainted by association.'

'What? Don't you have 'lunch' with Niall?'

'Not even getting a snack at the mo :('

'What's up with him now?'

'God knows, he just doesn't seem up for it.'

'Oh well, at least you have sexy Seb to look forward to on Wednesday.'

'Don't you start. Anyway it's been changed to tomorrow O.O.'

'So that's why you've been working out outfits...'

'No it was NOT, found out after. Confess though, little bit excited re potential flirt.'

'You seen Bettina?'

I wonder whether to mention the few minutes at the door earlier but decide against it.

'No. I've avoided her after what you said. I'll see her tomorrow at the fair meeting, but I'm going to sit with Seb and keep my distance.'

'Any excuse.'

'Well, he can be my bodyguard lol.'

'How's the business empire?'

'Brilliant, I sold loads this week.'

'Oh yes, you said when you were blowing me out, but ended up *sleeping*. Well done Branson. Did you get a lot at Saturday's boot? It was a lovely day wasn't it?'

'A few bits, but not as much as I would have liked.' God now I'm lying to Mon as well. 'I'm off to read for a bit now, finish my day off with an early night.'

'Ditching me again? Watch it, I'll have my revenge.'

'Scared.com.'

I feel so much better the morning after. The sun is out again, though there's a cool wind. I grab my gym kit and sling it in the back of the car and do an hour's swimming and a yoga class. I have bags of energy, maybe from doing bugger all the day before. I grab a fresh juice at the gym and spend ages in the shower and the changing rooms, making sure I don't resemble the sweaty mess that emerged from class. As silly as it sounds I seem to have even more energy after this. I head home and spend some time on eBay. I've received a few more orders so I get the parcels organised and ready for the post office. I can drop them off before going to school. As I'm heading out the door later I realise I've not checked my phone. I eventually find it right at the bottom of my bag, which may be why I've not heard the twenty-seven missed calls I have on it.

Twenty-seven? I check, and every single one of them is from Bettina. There are also four texts. I open them up.

'Where are you?'

'Are you not speaking to me?'

'Have I done something wrong?'

'Why are you not answering?'

I ring her straight back.

'Bettina, is everything okay?'

'Where the fuck have you been?'

I hold the phone away from my ear. 'I beg your pardon?'

'Oh gosh, I'm sorry, Lo.'

Lo? She called me Lo? That's Monique's name for me, not even Niall calls me that. My voice is low, measured. 'I don't appreciate being sworn at.'

'I'm sorry. I've just been really worried that you were avoiding me for some reason. My mum told me Danny's been snooping around. Has he said anything to you?'

'Nope, I haven't seen him, why would I?'

'My mum said he was asking about you, she thought he might try to get in touch. I just wanted you to know.'

'Well thanks, if he turns up I'll get Niall to sort him out.'

'You wouldn't want to do that, he's not right, Lauren.'

'Well, I haven't seen him, and if I do I'll tell him to get lost.' She pauses and I wonder if she's thinking of when I wouldn't let her in earlier. 'There's nothing going on Bettina. I've been ill, you saw that for yourself. I told you I'd see you at school later and there's the fair meeting after that. I do have a life away from you, you know.'

Her voice breaks up on the phone and I feel heaviness, like dark clouds are working their way over my head. She's choking back tears. 'I'm sorry, I know I overreact, but he frightens me. And I know we're not really friends, but I've enjoyed spending time with you. I just wanted to make sure he wasn't poisoning that.'

I relent then as the guilt washes over me. 'We are friends Bettina, but I can't be available to you all the time. Listen,' I hesitate. 'Are you still in touch with your doctor?'

'No, I'm on a waiting list here,' she sniffs.

'Well I think you need someone to talk to about Danny,' I say. 'Someone impartial who can guide you on how to deal with it. That's not me Bettina. I can't take that on.'

'I understand,' she says her voice going quiet. 'Thank you for saying we're friends. It means a lot. I'll try not to bother you so much. Probably see you later.'

She hangs up and I feel like the worst person on earth.

CHAPTER EIGHT

I have absolutely no enthusiasm for the summer fair meeting whatsoever, and only turn up because Joe is excited that his mum is part of the team, that and he wants to pelt me with a sponge. I've put my swimsuit on under my clothes so his dream can come true. I've brought a change of clothes and some towels to be on the safe side though. I see Bettina sitting in the corner. As I move closer I see her eyes are rimmed with red and are slightly bloodshot. She sees me looking.

'Hayfever.'

'Look, I'm sorry about our conversation earlier, but I've been feeling crap and fed up myself.'

This seems to animate her somewhat. 'Why? What's the matter?'

I decide I'll put it on a bit about Niall. Maybe if I let her know my world isn't perfect she won't feel so bad, or if she is out to ruin me, it'll put her off. 'Me and Niall aren't getting along so well at the moment.'

'Really? I didn't pick that up from him in the car. Maybe he's just tired from work.' She hesitates a moment. 'You don't think he's having an affair, do you?'

'No.' I am shocked by this statement. 'Nothing like that. He likes to watch TV all evening and Joe's getting to sleep later and later these days, so it's just hard.'

'Or not as the case may be,' she sniggers.

I smile. The lack of sex in my life seems to have cheered her up a bit, at least. Great, glad it's of use to someone.

'You can join my boat. Danny's put me off men for a long time. So right now, the only one getting any is Monique with Dr Love.'

'That she is, lucky bitch,' I state.

'So how is Monique by the way?'

'I've not seen her for about a week.'

'Oh? That's not like you.'

'I was poorly yesterday, remember? So couldn't make it to see her.'

'Such a shame. I know you love your coffees.'

Mrs Sullivan comes in at that point wearing a black suit and red shoes. 'Get her,' says Bettina.

'Right, last minute checks ladies and gentlemen,' she says. 'If you can set up your stalls as much as is practical. We'll do it here in the hall though rather than outside. Should the weather turn against us we'll have to bring it indoors anyway.'

I glance around the room looking for Seb, but he's not here.

I spend the next half hour dragging out the stocks, setting them up and practising opening and closing them. I get a sponge and pretend to throw it. Our posters are finished and there is nothing left to do. We're ready for the fair. I put everything away and check to see if Bettina needs any help but she doesn't. Her books just need boxing up for display, and she's done a great job of sorting them into genres and alphabetical order for easy selection. The rest of the meeting passes quickly. We say our goodbyes and head home.

As I walk to the car I feel let down and disappointed. I look down at my outfit, black skinny fit jeans, a red bat-sleeved cotton top and black ballet slippers. I'd tied my hair in a side ponytail. I look casual, yet cool, but it's been a waste of time. The person I'd hoped to look attractive for; the one person I could count on to boost my confidence, even if he was a bit of a man slut, wasn't there. I open the car door to go home.

'Did you miss me?'

'Arrrrrrrrrrgh.' My heart beats frantically. 'Oh my fucking God, you idiot,' I screech, and smack my fists into Seb's chest.

He lifts his hands. 'Sorry, sorry, I didn't mean to scare you.'

'Scare me? You've taken ten years off my life expectancy at least. What did you think would happen if you snuck up on me?'

'I didn't think I was sneaking up on you. I thought you'd seen me and were ignoring me.'

'I looked up the road before I crossed to see if there were cars coming. I wasn't paying attention to bloody pedestrians.'

'Well you should, one of them could be an attacker and you wouldn't be able to give a description.'

I thought back to Danny surprising me in much the same way on Saturday and decided I wasn't getting in my car again without an attack alarm firmly in my hand.

'Where were you tonight then?'

His cool brown eyes bore into mine. 'I'll tell you if you drive us to the pub.'

I hesitate, the keys swinging in my hand. I think of the alternative, going home and talking to myself. 'Oh, go on then.'

We walk into the Queen's Head and I insist on buying the drinks as he bought them last time. I don't want to feel I owe him anything. At the bar I try and stand so my backside sticks out a little and I add a little wiggle to my walk as I return with the drinks. We sit in the same seats as before, and I think how much calmer he is now compared to the idiot I had spoken to in here just two weeks ago.

'So what happened to you tonight then?'

'Truth? I couldn't be arsed. I'd had enough of school today, the kids were total twats. I practically ran out at home time. I told Mrs S. I'd got a migraine.'

'I had to lug all the sponge stocks around to set them up cos you didn't show.'

'You keep making out you're an independent woman, Mrs Lawler, I'm sure you were fine.'

'That's not the point.'

'You missed me,' Seb beams at me.

I feel my cheeks flush. 'Don't be stupid.'

'You did, you missed me,' he jumps up and does a twirly dance. 'She missed me, she missed me.' It reminds me of when Tom Cruise went bonkers on Oprah. The other pub residents either try their best to not look, or give him a dirty look to indicate it's not suitable behaviour for this class of establishment.

'Seb, sit down,' I hiss.

He does and grabs his pint. 'How long have you been with your husband?'

I feel a whoosh like a popped balloon as I realise that is where I should be, at home with my husband, not here with Seb acting like some teenager with a crush. I decide I will tell him just how much I love my husband and go home.

'We've been together twelve years,' I say. 'We met when I was nineteen and he was twenty-nine, in a bar in Sheffield City Centre. I thought I was grown up and he still acted like a kid, so the age difference didn't matter. I found out I was pregnant with Joe at twenty-two and Niall said he was about to propose anyway, so we eloped to the Registry Office.

'Weren't your parents mad?'

'I have nothing to do with my parents, and that's a subject that's not open for discussion. Ever.'

'Okay, sorry. So you and Niall have been married ten years?'

'It'll be eleven in August, not long after my thirty-second birthday. How old are you anyway?'

'How old do you think I am?'

'Twelve.'

'Ha ha. I was thirty-five last November. Now stop changing the subject.' His voice lowers huskily, 'Are you happy Lauren? I can't work it out. You say so, but then you're here with me.'

'Yes. I love my husband. If you're waiting to hear that I don't, you're going to be disappointed.'

'I'm disappointed.'

My mouth curves at the edges. 'You are so good for my ego, Seb Kingsley.'

'I could be good for a lot more.'

'Don't.' I put my finger across his lips. They are soft to the touch and he looks at me. The feeling is too intimate. He opens his mouth and my finger falls onto his tongue. He closes his lips and sucks lightly, circling my finger with his tongue. I feel a pulse between my legs and butterflies in my stomach. I withdraw my hand.

'You're going to go now, aren't you?' he says.

'No,' I reply. 'I'm not.' I take my finger and run it around the rim of my glass. I don't know which of us is more surprised by my answer.

We chat for another thirty minutes or so, and then I say that I really will have to leave. Outside the pub, Seb offers to walk me to my car, his own being parked nearer to the school.

I look up at him. 'No, I can walk back myself.'

'You don't have to be scared of me, Lauren.'

We end up walking beside each other as we pass houses, some with curtains open. Some of the kids from school live around here, and I feel like I'm on display. I waffle on about complete nonsense the whole way to the car, trying to diffuse the tension between us.

He runs his hand through his hair. 'Well night, Lauren. Thanks for coming for the drink.'

I sigh. 'I just don't know what to do with you. I like you, you could be a good friend, but nothing else Seb, nothing can happen between—'

I'm not finished as his lips touch mine. I thought feeling sparks of electricity were a cliché but I feel them zip through my body. Seb runs his hands up the back of my top, causing me to shiver. He takes this as I'm feeling cold and wraps his arms further around me. I should be protesting, I should be backing off, but his warm mouth feels so good against mine, and I've missed this kind of tender touch. I need it. Seb backs me up against the car door. His tongue fights to get between my lips and I allow it. A small moan escapes me and I kiss him back, my tongue entwining with his. He breaks the kiss, backs away from me and smiles.

'Friends then,' he says, 'I'll see you around Mrs Lawler,' and just like that, he leaves me hanging.

CHAPTER NINE

I sit in the car, unable to drive as adrenaline takes over and I begin to shake. I can't believe what I've done, but I can't lie, at the moment I don't regret it. I feel alive. I relive the kiss in my head over and over and feel the wetness pool between my legs. I wanted to carry on kissing him, it was divine; like sucking on the most succulent strawberry. I pull down the windshield and look at myself in the mirror, expecting to see a bedraggled harlot, but I look exactly the same, with only a few wisps of hair out of place. I re-tie my ponytail, start the engine and begin to drive home. As I turn at the end of the road I see a parked Mazda five at the corner on the opposite side. It's him. He flashes me twice with his indicators and I roar off, leaving him behind.

When I get home, I pop my head around the door. 'I'm back,' I state breezily.

'You're late; you missed Joe going to bed. Thought you'd be back by seven thirty-ish, it's nine.'

'Sorry, some of us went to the pub after. I should've called.'

'Nah, don't worry. We had a good time together, played scrabble. He's getting quite good at it now.'

'Well I've got some stuff to sort out on the computer so I'm going straight up.'

'You've had a busy day with the school and the little empire,' he laughs. 'It must be exhausting.'

I bristle at his stab at humour and go upstairs to bed where I continue to replay the kiss in my head until I fall asleep.

It's a few moments after waking before the memories of the night before hit me. I berate myself for what I did. What an idiot I am. I turn over and see Niall laid next to me, his head on the pillow with his mouth open, dead to the world. Strange snorting noises come out of his nose. His elbow is pointing out from the pillow, an annoying sleeping habit of his that drives me mad. If I turn around in sleep I'm often awoken by being elbowed in the face. I lie there for several minutes, looking at my husband and wondering why I've felt the need to kiss another man. It can't be justified by the fact that I have an overwhelming need to be adored, to feel that someone cares. Niall provides for our family, showing he cares every day. I am being selfish wanting more. I lay back and stare at the ceiling, wondering what I'm going to do about my actions, but I'm interrupted by the buzzing of the alarm clock. I switch it off and get out of bed, back to the morning routine.

Back from school I text Monique.

`Emergency.`

She texts back.

`I have some time owing. I can get out for twelve-thirty.` We arrange to meet at Etta's. I spend the next three hours watching the clock go round.

'So what's the great emergency, then? Better not be because you've forgotten my rules and bought eight identical v-neck t-shirts in different colours.'

I stick out my tongue. 'You're so funny. Thank God you could meet me.'

'I was bored out of my brains. I'd have met you if you were just hungry.'

'Well, I wish I was just hungry.' I took a deep breath. 'I snogged Seb.'

Monique starts laughing. 'Is that all? This is you, Mrs needs attention, who hasn't been getting any, then a cute guy comes along and wants in your pants. I'm not the slightest bit surprised.'

My face falls. 'I've not done anything like this before.'

'That's because Niall generally comes around and there isn't a stud muffin waiting in the wings. Did you nearly have sex?'

'God, no.'

'Well then, what's the problem? It was just a snog.'

'The problem is that I feel guilty about it, but don't regret it. It was amazing,' I snap.

'And this is Joe's teacher next year? Shame Joe's an angel really. You won't get kept back after school.'

'Can you not take anything seriously?'

'I'm trying to balance you, you take things too seriously. Look, are you going to snog him again?'

'Certainly not.'

'Well then, no harm done, and you've had a bit of fun. Can we eat now?'

Sometimes Monique can be really supportive and other times, like today, she just doesn't understand. I wonder what her relationship with Toby was like. She doesn't talk about him much, but I'm guessing it made her build walls because she's kept every relationship since really light. Our cheese and onion toasties arrive. I'm ravenous and dive straight in. Monique smells hers and pulls a face. 'This smells weird,' she says. 'I'm not eating that.'

I pull her plate towards me and have a smell. 'Mon, there's nothing wrong with it,' I say. 'It smells fine.'

She takes a bite and pulls a face. ''I'll get some crisps.'

'You are beyond weird,' I state. 'Were you perhaps drinking with Dr Love last night? Mon?'

'Sorry, I was miles away. No. He was working yesterday afternoon and the same tonight. I might not see him until Monday. Absence makes the heart grow fonder and all that. Actually I'm starting to feel a bit shit, I think after here I'll go to bed.'

'You okay?'

'Yeah, fine, its working at that damn hospital with all those bloody bugs.'

I finish my sandwich and we leave, Monique gives me a peck on the cheek and a hug. As we part she whispers, 'One more snog wouldn't hurt.'

I get home and clean the house from top to bottom, pushing my body through scrubbing at marks on walls and floors, and ignoring the fact that if I wasn't feeling so guilty I wouldn't be doing this. I wonder if I'll see Seb when I fetch Joe from school. I don't usually but will he make it happen? I bet I'm another notch now, just one he had to work a bit harder for, and now he's cracked it.

I crash onto the settee throwing off my cardigan as I'm so damn hot from rushing around. I grab a hair tie from the coffee table and fasten my hair into a bun at the back of my head. My chest is pumping up and down through the exertion. I grab the laptop and log on to catch up on mail. I have a Facebook friend request from a Mr Uri Kent. I fire a message back. 'Your name is offensive. Do I know you?'

Later, I log back on to find another message from Mr Kent. 'I think you know me quite well, especially my tongue.'

Jesus, it's him. I accept his friend request and set up a private group between us. 'For goodness sake post your messages here where no-one can see them.'

'A secret group? So I can say what I want and no-one but us knows? I like it.'

A few minutes passes.

'Are you anticipating my messages?'

I squirm on the settee, guilty.

'I loved the feel of my tongue in your hot mouth. Entering your warm parts and feeling you writhe against me. You had goose bumps on your arms.'
There's another pause then,
'Did you feel me get hard as I pushed you against the metal? You revved my engine.'
He logs off.

Monique calls me later, unusual after we've seen each other so recently. 'Are you feeling alright now?' I ask.
'Yeah fine, not sure what that was all about,' she says. 'Anyway what are you doing Friday night and Saturday day?'
I stretch my unoccupied arm. 'Nothing much, I've kept them clear cos the school fair's on Sunday and I know I'll be busy.'
'I've found a cheap London break, only sixty pounds each, including travel. Wondered if you fancied an overnight?'
I smile. 'Oh my, yes, that would be fabulous. Let me check with Niall.'
I go downstairs and ask Niall, who has no problems with it. 'Abandoning me again to spend my money, eh?'
My jaw sets. 'I'll not go if you don't want.'
'Don't be daft, I'm joking. Get yourself off.'
I rush back upstairs. 'I can go. What time are we leaving?'
'Train station at eleven. I've taken annual leave for Friday, so we can have all of Friday afternoon and

come back on the two-thirty train Saturday. You'll be back in time for tea.'

'I can't wait,' I say, suddenly excited by a couple of days away from Sexy Seb and the maybe Bonkers Bettina.

'I know, we haven't been away for ages,' she says. 'Get ready for ...'

'Chaos,' we shout in Unison.

All of our previous minibreaks have endured some drama or another. Monique blames me every time. She says that for all my organisational skills, when it comes to mini-breaks, I lose the plot. She says I attract chaos like Uri Geller bends spoons, it's a phenomenon. The last time we went away, I realised at the station that the tickets had been booked on a card that had expired. After a trip to Customer Services, who said I had to ring the ticket issuer, we got the tickets with three minutes to spare. Then there was the time we went to a country retreat and I attempted to turn the car around, not realising it was on a one way system. It was winter, and I got the car stuck partway in a drainage ditch, causing the traffic to come to a halt until the site tractor could pull us out. We term these moments my 'chaos'. I am determined this time there will be no such thing. Monique has booked the trip this time after all, so I'm cleared for that.

Thursday morning though, I begin to throw up. Damn Monique, she obviously had a bug yesterday and passed it on. I throw up three times before collapsing back into bed. Niall drops Joe off at school and says he'll try and finish early so he can pick him up. After lunch I ring Monique. 'I'm sick. I don't think I can go.'

'There's no way I'm going without you. Get plenty of water down yourself, I need this night away.'

'But I feel terrible.'

'So did I yesterday, but I still came out for lunch with you. When were you last sick?'

'A couple of hours ago.'

'Right so it's probably out of your system now. Get some sleep, there's nearly twenty-four hours until the train. We're going, and that's that.'

'Jeez you're so bossy and mean.'

'Sleep.'

The next morning I feel wiped out but drag my stuff together and drop Joe at school. I buy a can of red bull from the corner shop, and then book a taxi to the train station as I'm not in the mood to catch a bus. I make myself a slice of toast and jam, the first food I've had since yesterday's breakfast. I catch sight of myself in the kitchen mirror. Under my eyes are dark circles. My skin looks sallow and my wrinkles all seem really prominent. I look five years older than usual. I grab my make-up bag and launch for the Touche Eclat. I need the big boys if I'm not going to go for the 'extra in Thriller video' look.

I arrive at the train station at eleven sharp. Of course Monique looks like she's stepped off the cover of InStyle. She's dressed in a V-neck knitted purple tunic, with a tan belt at the waist and some slightly flared indigo jeans. This is set off by a pair of tan ankle boots that make her look taller than ever. She has a matching purple Samsonite spinner and a little shoulder purse in tan, no doubt carrying just the bare essentials. This girl knows how to travel. I, in contrast, have my 'free with a catalogue' navy wheeled holdall, my Levi's, one of the V-neck tees she is always taking the piss out of me for in red, my black footglove flats (they're comfy) and a large fluffy black cardi, even though it's quite warm today. I feel a bit pants still and want a material hug.

Monique looks at me from top to bottom for a few minutes. 'Well, it could be worse under the circumstances,' she drawls. 'Let's go.'

When we are on the train she fetches me a coffee and gets a water for herself. She passes me a Berocca. 'The coffee ain't decaf,' she says.

At twelve she fetches me a bacon butty and I'm ready for it. I scoff it greedily. 'You not having one?'

'I ate a good breakfast.'

I sit back satisfied, and feeling a lot better, though if someone passed me a pillow right now, I'd marry them. Monique opens her shoulder bag and brings out a small carrier bag from Accessorize.

'You owe me eleven pounds for the repair kit'. She takes out a comb and sidles in the seat alongside me. 'Right, let's sort that bloody mop out.'

She plaits my hair and twists it up onto the back of my head, fixing it in place with grips. She sprays it with an industrial strength mini hair spray and curls up a few tendrils around the front of my face.

I point to the carrier bag. 'Is that a small carrier bag, or the Tardis?'

'I just know how to shop, and you do realise I've carried a plastic bag for you? The sacrifices I make.'

'It's like that bag Hermione had in Harry Potter, where she could reach in it over and over and get out whatever they needed. What else you got in there?'

She pulls out some black beads and fastens them around my neck, then hands me a pair of black drop earrings. 'Get them in.'

'Yes, Boss.'

She looks over me appraisingly. I feel like I'm about to be introduced to my future husband as part of an arranged marriage. 'Much better,' she says, and heads back to her own seat.

I take out a copy of Good Housekeeping magazine from my Betty Barclay.

'What the fuck is that?' Monique grabs it and throws it down the train. It narrowly misses an elderly gentleman's head and lands on an empty seat. She moves down to the luggage rack and opens the front compartment of her case, taking out issues of Grazia and Vogue.

She rolls her eyes at me. 'Read one of those. At least you can appear to have some style.'

'God, are you going to be like this for the entire journey?' I snap. 'I know I'm not looking my best but I've been sick and you're being a right bitch about it. What's got into you?'

'A fucking baby, that's what's got into me,' her nostrils flare. 'And being sick's not an excuse because I've been puking for the last three days now and I look divine.'

CHAPTER TEN

'Fuck.'

'Yes, well that's how it usually gets in there.'

'You know what I mean.'

Monique sighs and fiddles with the bag the jewellery came out of. 'This is why I wanted to come away, so you can help me decide whether I'm keeping it or not.'

My voice softens. 'You think you might?'

She shrugs. 'I've no idea what I'm going to do.'

I touch her hand. 'Why didn't you tell me before?'

She withdraws her hand and crosses her arms. 'Because I only confirmed it a week ago and to be quite honest with you, lately it's been Bettina this, Niall that and Seb the other.'

I lower my gaze. 'I'm sorry, I have been a bit me, me, me.'

'Yeah, well it's typical that the one time I needed you was the day you decided to cancel.'

I ignore the mean streak she's displaying as she's in shock and hormonal. She's just hitting out and I'm the nearest target. I remember pregnancy mood swings well enough, even if it was over nine years ago.

'What did Dr Love say?'

'I've not told him yet, and I don't know if I'm going to. If I do decide to keep it, I do not want a significant other interfering.'

'You'll need support, Mon.'

'I've never needed anyone, and if I want some support I've got you.'

We don't speak as the train pulls into St Pancras. *Chaos*, I think.

We get off the train, but I notice a few magazines left on seats and run back on to get them. I pick up my Good Housekeeping, which is now minus its cover, having been ripped off whilst flying over the seats. Monique just rolls her eyes at me again as I get off at the other end of the carriage armed with five magazines. 'I'm recycling,' I pout.

We arrive at the hotel to see if we can check in early, bearing in mind its only fifty minutes off the check in time. The hotel is a converted house in Bayswater. It looks nice from the outside. Several storeys high, it's a white painted building with a wrought iron railed basement. We walk inside. The reception area is light and airy, although I notice the couch for visitors has a large rip across its red leather.

'Your room is available now, Madam,' says the Receptionist, a young blonde lad, who gains an icy look from Monique who believes she should be addressed as Miss. He hands Monique a room key and points. 'If you follow the corridor to the first turning on your left and then take the stairs down.' We do as instructed and walk towards the basement.

We enter the room. It smells of damp.

'What the fuck is this?' Says Monique.

I just gasp. I swear to God that I have never seen anything like it in my life. It's a small room, containing a double bed with plain white sheets and an itchy looking beige blanket folded across the bottom. I pick up the blanket. It's covered in hair.

'Aaarrrrgh'. I drop it as if it's scalding hot and wipe my hand down my leg.

The window is made of etched obscure glass that resembles the squared graph paper we had at school for drawing angles, but there is no mistaking what's behind it as we recognise the whirr of a generator. We look at each other.

'Monique, open the bathroom door.'

She approaches it as if we are hiding from terrorists. She carefully opens the bathroom door and I see a green bathroom suite. She checks out the loo and nearly barfs. A look of complete fury crosses her face and she storms out of the room, swiping a box off the side table on her way out. I follow her back to the reception.

'That room is completely unacceptable,' she screeches at the receptionist. He takes a step backwards. 'I am pregnant, and I do not wish to share my bed with umpteen other people's pubic hairs, and as for this ...' She slams down the cardboard box and the tea and coffee sachets fly across the counter. 'I am fully into the concept of re..cy..cling.' I see her spittle hit the guys shoulder as she enunciates every word. 'However, I think for the purpose of holding my tea, coffee and sugar sachets, you could at least have the decency to *find a plate or a bowl,* and not make it out of a piece of cardboard that won't even hold together.' She waltzes off and sits on the couch, avoiding the huge rip. 'We shall wait here,' she announces, 'until you find us another room.'

The receptionist goes rushing into the back room, his chin trembling. A few minutes later he comes out with another key. 'This is our best room,' he states, pointing at the opposite corner of the reception room. 'Please, enjoy.'

The new room is quite spacious and has two single beds, no hairy blankets in sight and a huge window overlooking a park that looks green and serene. It appears really nice. We are unpacking about fifteen minutes later when I suddenly realise there's a small problem. 'Mon?'

'Mmmm, hmmmm?'

'Where's the bathroom?'

We look around the room; bed, dressing table, window, wardrobe, no bathroom. 'We must have to share the one along the corridor,' I state, heading for the door at the same time Monique opens the right sided wardrobe door to hang up some clothes.

'The bathroom's here, behind the wardrobe door.'

It's true. One side of the wardrobe is exactly that. The other side covers a small recess which houses a tiny sink and a shower. To say it's small, it is actually quite clean.

I begin to giggle. 'I'm not moving again.' I walk around to the desk and pick up a bowl containing the tea and coffee. 'Look,' I state. 'It's otherwise perfect.'

She narrows her eyes at me. "All I could think about was that bloody cardboard holder.'

'Our room is *not* acceptable. We do *not* have a bone china tea holder.' I guffaw as I collapse on one of the single beds. 'I'm done in. I'm having a kip.'

'Yes, me too,' Monique abandons packing and flings herself on the other bed. By half past three we're both fast asleep.

'Lauren. Come on, it's gone seven. We're not sleeping in any longer.'

'Nnoooo, go away,' I put the covers back over my head. The next minute they are entirely on the floor. 'Up.'

'God, were you an Army major in a past life?'

'I'm starving,' she says. 'I need to eat something so I can throw up later.'

After splashing my face with cold water and reapplying some lipstick, I put on my black Monsoon mini-dress and get ready to hit London. Bayswater is a lovely area, brimming with little cafes and restaurants. We pick a chain we know well and head there for some pasta. We both eat like it's the Last Supper. The sleep and food reinvigorate us and we head for a small shopping complex where I buy a pair of black silky pyjamas with a matching dressing gown, it's sexy, but doesn't look like I'm trying too hard; some new pants, a few pieces of jewellery, and a lovely ornate headband.

Monique eyes my stash. 'Good gracious, we've only been out ten minutes.'

'I was born to shop,' I reply. I smile; I'm starting to enjoy myself.

'Who are the new pants for?' Monique asks and winks.

'All of this is for me *personally*. I figure if I start feeling better about myself, I'll stop trying to lean on other people. Like you for instance.' I throw my arms around her and give her a hug. 'I still feel bad for not being there when you needed me, but I'm here now. Tomorrow we'll have a good chat and a think. Tonight should be about fun, so how about we go back and watch Big Brother?'

'Sounds like a plan, and don't laugh, but I'm really sleepy again.'

The next morning we head down to breakfast where I'm informed by Monique that due to the hotel's religious beliefs there will be no bacon, but an alternative made of turkey. I walk downstairs to be served a green coloured egg yolk, some unidentifiable turkey/bacon substitute and an equally green looking Monique. 'Let's eat out,' I state.

We return to the shopping mall, to the diner we'd spied yesterday that served breakfast. I peruse the menu and ask the guy behind the counter for two decaf coffees and two croissants.

'Just toast,' he says.

I peruse the menu again which details approximately fourteen different breakfast options you can have. 'Toast?'

'Toast.' He repeats.

I point to the picture. 'Not a croissant?'

'Toast.'

I look at Monique. She shrugs. I turn back to the man.

'Okay, toast.'

'You sit. I go there.' He points outside. 'Fifteen minutes, yes? I get croissant.' He gestures to the central seating area and walks off.

'I spied a Patisserie Valerie on the way past,' I whisper to Monique. We give the guy time to leave and then escape.

We are ensconced in one of my favourite cafe's, and all Monique keeps repeating is toast and chuckling.

'Oh God, I just thought, we could have gone with the alternative of … bread,' I say. We cackle together causing the other breakfasting patrons to look at us, some frowning, some with eyebrows raised and half smiles on their faces.

'Enjoy your breakfast,' says the waitress as she puts down two huge mugs of coffee, a cake stand containing a dozen mini fruit scones, little pots of jam and two small pots of cream.'

'Still think I'd have preferred toast,' I say and we laugh.

After breakfast I take Monique to Harrods toy department and let her walk around whilst dozens of overexcited children run amok around her feet. She looks scared to death. 'If you can survive this toy store hell, you can survive your own baby,' I state. 'The mothers here don't know what to do when the nannies and au pairs aren't around, so they bring them here and fling money at them in the vain hope they'll behave.'

'Can we go to the pet department?'

'Yep, can I just look at these Barbies first?'

After Harrods I take her to the National History Museum. We wander around all the stuffed animals and end up at the giant dinosaur skeleton. 'Look at all this history that you can pass onto another person,' I say.

'Google can do that. I don't need to.'

'I give up. Let's get lunch.'

'We hole up in Costa for one of their delicious toasties. I have a glass of fresh orange juice whilst Mon orders milk. 'Heartburn'.

'Okay,' I say when we're settled. 'Time for baby chat. Why, when you were with Toby, did you adamantly not want a kid?'

She fidgets with her glass. 'I just never did. I still don't think I do now. I love being by myself.' She pauses, rubbing condensation from the glass. 'Toby knew to give me my distance, we led quite independent lives. He had lots of sporty friends and I did my yoga. I had lots of quiet time to myself. He started wanting more, I couldn't provide it so he moved on.'

'So why the hesitation now?'

'Because it's here inside me, a real thing. I could dismiss a thought, but I'm not finding it so easy to dismiss a real baby. I'm scared shitless, Lo, but I know at my age that if I don't have it, that it really is my very last chance.'
'I think you should have it,' I say
'Why?'
'You have lots of love inside you, I know cos I get some of it. I really think you could do it Mon.'
She gives me a half smile. 'If I do, will you be there for me?'
'You need to ask?'
'Even if Bettina and Sexy Seb want your attention?'
'I'll ditch them. I'm all yours,' I joke. 'Although I do still need to see my husband and child.'
'Well obvs, but at least Niall is a good egg. He'll let you come when I need you, like this weekend.'
'Mon,' I say my eyes widening. 'Those pregnancy hormones must really be getting to you. You've just given Niall a compliment.'
'Fuck,' she says, 'So I have. This parasite's making me soft.'

We arrive back in Sheffield at quarter to five. Monique heads off for the bus and I go to entrance of the short stay car park. Joe comes dashing out of the car and runs towards me like we've been separated for years. 'Mum, dad's bought me five packets of series seven Lego figures,'
'Someone's been spoilt,' I say
After a huge hug he looks at me from under his fringe. 'Have you got me anything?'

I laugh, 'What about four packets of series eight Lego figures?' I say getting them out of my pocket. 'London's a bit ahead of us.'

'Wow, thanks mum,' he runs back off towards his dad. 'Mum got me series eight.''

'Sorry,' I mouth at Niall as I get to the car.

'Bloody fickle children,' he pretends to flick Joe's ear and then drives us home.

I've been home a while and then it hits me. Tomorrow is the school fair. I call Bettina,

'Hi, just a quick call to say see you tomorrow.'

'Hey stranger. I tried you at home but Niall said you were away? You feeling better? Niall said you were ill again.'

Oh crikey, I'd told her I had a bad stomach the week before, obviously karma had given me the sick bug. 'Yep, had another bug. Must be run down. I've been away with Monique. She made me go, even though I wasn't fully better, the bully. Anyway I feel okay now.'

'Oh good. Listen I've been given some extra books by a few neighbours. Could you pick me up in the morning and help me get them to school?'

'Course I can. I'll see you in the morning then.'

'See you then.'

Niall is gobsmacked by my news about Monique. 'If she rings, don't mention it. I said I wouldn't tell anyone.'

'No secrets between us, love. She must know that. Do you think she'll keep it?'

'I've no idea, but I said I'll be there whatever.'

'Course, not a problem, you know if I'm around I'll take care of Joe if she needs you.'

'Thanks, Love,' I say, and reach up to give him a kiss. Its familiar and I breathe in the remnants of his aftershave.

'Do you want to come upstairs?' I say.

'Would you be offended if I said no, only I've been playing football with Joe and to be honest, I've pulled my groin.'

I reach out and stroke his cheek. 'I could kiss it better?'

'No, honestly, it really hurts,' he says moving my hand away. 'Do you want to sit on the settee with me and watch CSI?'

'No, you're alright, I'm tired from the trip. I'll go on up. I need an early night so I'm ready for tomorrow.'

'Oh yes, how could I forget. Me and Joe have a quid each ready to smack you upside the head with a sponge.'

'I feel you are getting rather too enthusiastic about this.'

I power up the laptop to check all my messages. I am inundated with emails and Facebook notifications after ignoring them for thirty-six hours. I ignore them all and click into the secret group for Seb and I. I've named it 'eBay queries'. I figured if I left it on by accident that would be too boring for Niall to click into. I read the list of messages.

'Where are you luscious Lauren?'

'I feel all alone :(.'

'I'm tapping my fingers on the keyboard, still waiting.'

'Bored now, gonna have to think of something to do.'

'Oh, my hands have found something to play with …'

'Hmmm right now I'm thinking about your hot tongue snaking around the inside of my mouth again. Now I'm imagining it somewhere else ...'

There were no more updates. I caught up with the rest of the emails and wondered what in the hell tomorrow would bring.

CHAPTER ELEVEN

We couldn't have asked for better weather for the fair. It's a bright day with sunshine, accompanied by a cooling breeze, so everyone who attends can join in without feeling like they're going to melt. We arrive an hour before the start to make sure everything is in place. I spend the morning filling up balloons and tying up banners. Seb is there, dressed in black and grey stripy pyjamas, he smiles at me as I arrive and carries on with what he's doing. I'd dressed myself as planned, with my swimming costume underneath my clothes. I'd just gone for black jogging bottoms and a black baggy tee. Not ideal clothing if it turned hotter later, but at least if it got wet I'd still look respectable.

I think back to when I used to take Joe to fun sessions at the local swimming baths, many children were almost left to drown by their dads as my costume barely fit my 36Ds. I had to go to M&S and buy a more respectable swimsuit, more akin to what a sixty year old would wear. My current costume has a decent bra bit to it, and the black makes my waist look a lot slimmer than it really is. It suits my figure, makes it look a bit fifties pin up, but that doesn't matter today because I'm neither swimming nor bathing, so no-one will be seeing it.

Bettina is busy setting books out on her stall. Her blonde hair is loose and she must have used some tongs as it's lightly waved. She's wearing a floaty summer hat in pale pink and a vintage type tea dress with soft pink roses and bluebells on it; a dress I'd have killed for. With pale pink peep toe sandals and nails, and a large blue shopper style bag which matched the bluebells on the dress, she looks exquisite, and I feel dowdy and lifeless by comparison. I'd had to tie up my own hair in a bun, and had left my make-up off as I figured water didn't mix very well with blow dried hair and a face full of slap. I walk over to her.

'I really do adore that dress.'

'I know, you said when you picked me up, but thanks,' she twiddles with a piece of hair.

I watch as she pulls an embroidered tablecloth out of her bag, its patchwork, with loads of different vintage style squares of pretty florals. It's divine, and I touch it. 'Where did you get this from, it's delightful?'

'I've had it years,' she says. 'You're not the only one who does vintage you know.'

I take a step back. 'Well, of course. It's just that I would have liked to get some for my shop if they'd still been around. I'm sure they'd have sold amazingly fast.'

'I think I'm just about there with the stall.' She looks away.

I gather I'm dismissed, so I head over to the kids canteen where the school cooks have kindly volunteered to cook us a breakfast before they start serving teas and coffees to the patrons of the fair. I turn back to Bettina but she doesn't look up. She's smoothing out the tablecloth. I watch her rip off a tag hanging down from it. I recognise it as a Dunbar's tag, a store not too far away in Derbyshire – a store that opened last year.

Breakfast is so tasty and appreciated. Fried egg, fried bread, bacon, beans and fried mushrooms with a slice of toast and butter, and all washed down with a coffee. Why does it taste so much nicer when it's cooked for you?

At ten-thirty Mrs Sullivan asks us to stand by our stations because some parents always turn up early in the hopes of getting the best bargains from the toy stalls. She is resplendent in a navy suit with a gold scarf, hair immaculate as always. She wishes us luck. I head over to the sponge stocks where Seb has pulled up two child-sized chairs to one side. I can barely sit on mine but it's better than standing all morning.

'You're quiet,' he says.

'I've went to London with my friend. It was a nice break, I enjoyed it.'

'You didn't reply to my updates.'

'You seemed to be doing okay by *yourself*.'

'Would've been better if you were there.'

'Oh I know,' I wink at him, warming up to the idea of tormenting Seb for entertainment.

A young girl comes up with her father. 'Morning Mr Kingsley,' she says quietly.

'Hi Deborah. Let me guess, you want to hit me with a wet sponge?'

'Yes please,' she giggles.

The sight of Mr Kingsley in his pyjamas is a target for all the young lads in the school, who can't wait to turn their nerdy teacher into a soaking wet victim. However, without his glasses, and with his hair becoming wet and unruly, there's a sudden surge of mothers drawn to the stocks. I watch as he peels off his pyjama top and replaces it with a dry one. He gives us all a quick reveal of his ripped body. The tattoo of a dragon stretches across his skin. Its body and tail snake around a muscled left arm, whilst its head comes to a stop just above his left nipple, sitting atop a defined pec. I swear some mothers actually swoon. I get so hot I imagine the dragon could have scorched me with its breath, and toy with the idea of switching the hose pipe we've been using to fill the bucket onto myself to cool down.

'Hey mum.' Joe is here and I sweep his gangly body up into my arms. I am so pleased to see him.

'Put me down, that's so embarrassing.'

Oops. Mother mistake made already. Hugging child in front of others at school. 'How about a free go of the Sponge Stocks then? You can salvage your integrity?'

'Don't know what that word means, but can I have the sponges?' he says.

Whilst I'm getting them ready I ask Joe where his dad is. 'Oh, he's gone to get a couple of coffees, says you'll be ready for one by now.'

My husband is so right, I am desperate for a drink, and I could do with a wee too, listening to this water sloshing around is not helping.

I head over to Seb and ask him to put me in the stocks. 'Oooh kinky,' he whispers.

'Shut it, Joe's over there. He doesn't need to know his future teacher's a total lech.'

He mimes a stabbing in his heart. 'I am wounded.'

I hate it in the stocks, I feel so vulnerable. I know it's only a pretend thing, and I could break out of it if I wanted to, but I feel trapped and claustrophobic. I'm not a good swimmer and can hardly bear water on my face. I swim breast stroke with my head so far out of the water, I always have a bad neck when I've done; however this is for Joe, so I try to calm myself. 'Okay. I'm ready.'

The first four sponges miss completely, although some spray still splashes me, but the fifth hits me squarely in the face. I can't stand it. I shake my head and desperately want to wipe my eyes, but my arms are in the stocks. Niall has come up and I ask him to wipe my face with a towel. He knows how much I hate water, but tells me that would be cheating and then pays Seb a pound for another five sponges. I'm frustratingly unable to see what Seb makes of Niall as I'm stuck in these things. Niall walks in front and guides Joe's hands to show him how to throw more accurately. 'I'll do the first one,' he tells Joe, then raises his arm in an overhand throw as if he's playing cricket and I'm the wicket. Whoomph, straight in my face.

'Yeeeeeaaaaaaaaahhhhhhhh,' he does a sad dad dance and slaps Joe's hand in a high five. I find it remarkable that Joe is so caught up with the perfect shot that he lets his dad off with one of the most embarrassing jigs ever. Joe takes the next four shots and two of them are right on target, straight in my face.

'Hey, what's all this? Pick on your mum time?' Bettina strolls over to us.

'Shouldn't you be on the book stall?' I splutter, drips fall down my nose from my fringe.

'One of the other mum's is having it for ten minutes. I'm having a quick walk round and a coffee. I need the loo too. I just couldn't resist seeing the always well put together Mrs Lawler looking like a drowned rat.'

'You want to see her at home,' chips in Niall. 'She walks about in leggings and a tee shirt all the time, you know.'

'Niall,' I shout.

Bettina giggles. 'Tell me more of her secrets while she's locked up in the stocks.'

'I'll tell you what,' says Niall, handing Seb another quid. 'For every sponge you get in her face, I'll tell you something embarrassing about her.'

'Niall, no,' I squeal. 'Seb, let me out of the stocks.' I wriggle, but it hurts my neck and wrists.

'They've paid their pound fair and square,' he says, then I feel him at my back, touching the stocks where my arms are, as if checking them. He whispers. 'Your husband's a moron.'

Of course, Bettina gets four of the five sponges right in my face. She does a girlish twirl, like a ballerina on the top of a music box, and asks Niall and Joe if they want to join her for a quick coffee so they can tell her four of my secrets.

'I know some too,' says Joe. 'If you buy me a penguin biscuit, I'll tell.'

Seb releases me from the stocks. My hair and the top of my tee shirt are soaking but will be fine with a towel down and ten minutes of sunshine. As I reach for a towel, I fail to see Tyler run up out of nowhere. He picks up the hose pipe and turns it on Seb. 'I dare, I dare'. Bettina goes to knock it out of his hands, which turns the hosepipe towards me and before I know it I am absolutely drenched from head to foot, but worse than that, the water is freezing, so I scream.

'Tyler Southwell,' shouts Mrs Sullivan. 'What on earth is going on?'

'They dared me, Miss.' Tyler points to a group of giggling schoolchildren.

'Do you do everything you're told to do? I think your mother needs to take you home.'

Bettina looks horrified.

'No need,' I say shivering. 'Boys will be boys. If all their parents stick a couple of quid in the tub, we can let him off.'

'That's very understanding of you,' says Mrs Southwell. She then turns to Bettina. 'I realise you are on a stall, but you also need to be responsible for your son.'

Bettina looks at the floor. 'Of course, Mrs Sullivan. He can stay on the stall with me for the rest of the fair.' She digs in her bag and brings out a five pound note. 'That's Tyler's contribution. It can come out of his pocket money.'

'Muuum, that's not fair,' Tyler harrumphs. She drags him over to her stall and her furious face leaves no doubt about the fact that Tyler will be lucky to be given any more pocket money this month.

At least she didn't get any inside info on my life, I think.

Mrs Sullivan decides that the sponge stocks have been a success, but in the circumstances it's time for them to finish. We can dry off, get changed and have a wander around the rest of the fair ourselves. I spied some delicious looking chocolate cupcakes on the cake stall earlier and hope there's still one there with my name on it. Niall tells me he'll find me in a bit and heads off with Joe. I grab my plastic Tesco bag, containing my changes of clothes, hairbrush, towels, hairdryer and spare plastic bags for the wet clothes (Monique would throw a fit but hey she isn't here) and head into Seb's classroom, which has been set up as our changing area. He follows me in.

'Erm, excuse me. I need some privacy to get changed,' I tell him.

He leans against the wall. 'I don't think you do. I think you'll need some assistance getting out of those wet clothes, *and* I can help you dry off,' he replies.

'Seb, my husband and son are outside.'

His tongue wets his lip. 'That makes it even more fun, don't you think?'

I'm trying to pull my t-shirt over my head but it's so wet it rolls up and gets stuck. I sigh in frustration. He comes over and helps me take it off. Struggling with a wet shirt isn't exactly like the clothes ripping off scenes you get on TV, but my nipples visibly harden under my swimsuit. I flush. 'It's the cold.'

'No it's not, Lauren.'

I realise at this point that I can take my gear with me, go and find Niall and we can go home. There he'll no doubt re-enact the sponge stocks in the garden with my kitchen sponges and state that whilst I'm wet I might as well let them have another turn. I inhale deeply. 'Lock the door.'

'I already have.'

He comes towards me and grabs my wrist, leading me towards the storage room at the back of the classroom. As his classroom is at the rear of the school we are unlikely to be seen anyway but it's good that he's thinking of things like that, my own sense seems to have disappeared. He pulls me into the cupboard where he strips his pyjama shirt off and throws it to the floor. I put my hand against his chest and feel the cold, damp skin underneath my fingers. I stroke around the head of the dragon, tracing my fingertips around the outline. I've never seen a tattoo up close, the black ink is like a trail of temptation, of darkness. Seb's breathing intensifies.

I move my hand to his cheek and touch his face. I can feel the beginnings of stubble. I pause and look at him. His eyes darken as his pupils dilate. I can still leave, I remind myself, but instead, I lean into him, raising myself up on tip toes and lick the side of his neck, he tastes of water and salt.

'You started it this time,' he says, his voice gruff.

'And at any time, I may well end it,' I say, trailing tiny kisses down his chin. He catches my mouth with a groan and his tongue is strong and insistent between my teeth. He helps me remove my leggings and they join his shirt on the floor. I stand in just my swimsuit. Seb's eyes appraise me as he takes in the curve of my breasts, with their slight swell over the top of the swimsuit. He places his body oh so closely next to mine, and then his mouth is on mine again. My breathing is getting raspier and I can feel his heart beating against my chest. He drops the strap of my swimsuit and runs his hand over my breast, caressing an erect nipple. I arch my breast into his hand, savouring the touch. His other hand moves down my back, grabbing my ass and pulling me towards him.

'Put your hand here,' he moans, showing me the opening of his PJ bottoms, which had been fastened previously, but now give me a tantalising glimpse of what lays beneath.

I start to trail my hand over his stomach, touching the fine hair there, and move my hand lower.

My phone rings. Loud and shrill, playing the Star Wars theme tune, it reminds me that my son and husband are just outside. I leap for the phone whilst

Seb tries to grab hold of me and keep me close to him.

I shake him off. 'Hello?'

'We're done here and ready to go. We walked up this morning, so thought if you were nearly ready we could get a lift back with you?' says Niall.

'Yes, of course. I'll just be a few moments. I'm just changing into some dry clothes.'

'Don't get too dry, I've promised Joe we'll make our own sponge stocks at home.'

'Yes, I thought you might.'

'I'm allowed to be a little predictable at my age aren't I?' he laughs.

'Of course. Well I'll see you in a few.' I end the call.

I daren't look at Seb's face. He comes over to me and lifts up my chin. 'It doesn't matter to me, Lauren. I just like spending time with you, though you're driving me mad,' he indicates the bulge in his trousers. He sighs, 'Go on.'

I grab my things and leave to find my husband. As I get to the door he whispers,

'I'll contact you tonight, on Facebook.'

'Please don't,' I say. My eyes beg him not to, before I close the door behind me.

I ruminate all afternoon. I can't believe what I did. I feel guilty, yet it was exhilarating to be that naughty and abandoned. Why can't it still be like this with Niall? After re-enacting the sponge stocks in the garden I go upstairs to shower. Niall comes in to use the loo.

I peer around the shower curtain. 'What's Joe doing?'

'Building a Lego train we got at the fair.'

'Well, come and get in here.'

He looks at me. 'I'll get wet.'

'That's the idea, idiot. Come on. Let's have a quickie whilst Joe's busy.'

'Don't be ridiculous, Lauren. What if he comes up?'

'He won't. Once he's in Lego world he's lost for ages.'

'It's not very responsible though, having sex whilst our child is downstairs. Maybe later eh?' He slaps my wet bottom. 'Damn, I've got my bloody sleeve wet now.'

He walks out. I am left frustrated. I close my eyes and feel the force of the shower on my shoulders, waiting for it to work on my muscles and release the tension. It doesn't work, so I pad out of the shower, trailing wet footsteps and droplets everywhere, and reach into the back of the wardrobe. Returning to the shower, I switch on the bullet vibrator and place it between my legs. I lean against the tiled wall of the shower, remembering and repeating Seb's touch of my breasts, imagining he's here and we didn't stop. I run the bullet over my clitoris again and again imagining it's his fingers until I come in a delicious wave, the tension leaves my body instantly. I sit down in the bath and let the shower wash over me.

The temptation that night proves too great and I log into Facebook and click on our group. The green button indicates Seb is online.

'I'm here.' I type.

'I'm pleased.'

'I shouldn't be though.'

'Why are you then?'

'I don't know.'

'I want to finish what we started.'

I feel between my legs get slick again, and the pull from earlier returns.

'I can't do that.'

'Look, if it's virtual, it can't count right?'

'I suppose not.'

'Imagine what we were doing before your phone rang.'

It doesn't take me much to imagine it. I've thought of little else all day. I'm brimming with lust again.

'My hand is on my cock and I'm pretending it's yours. Tell me what you were going to do.'

'I can't do this.'

'Your hand's here, I can feel it. Oh, God, tell me what you want.'

My mouth is dry. I need to decide whether to turn off the computer or stay. I close my eyes for a second and breathe. All it does is make me focus on the heat in my core. I begin to type. 'I trail my hand down your stomach and dip below the waistline of your bottoms. I grasp you within my hand. You feel cool to the touch but I move my hand around and your cock soon warms up and gets hard.' I feel silly typing for a minute.

'Good. Now I have moved my hand from your breast. I'm sliding it down your stomach, below your navel and it is going inside your knickers.'

My embarrassment wears off quickly. I feel myself getting ever more slippery between my legs and my breathing gets faster. I move my hand exactly as he says.

'Now imagine I'm touching you there, stroking you, first quickly and then slowly until you are begging for release.'

I can barely type. 'God, yes, and I'm pumping your cock with my fist. You want to fuck me but I won't let you. You have to come in my hand.'

'Christ, Lauren.'

'I need to finish.'

'Me too. Now think of this afternoon and how we could have ended it. See you soon.'

I lean against the bed and imagine that indeed my hand is his hand, that this is a continuation of the earlier afternoon and that he's stroking my breasts while bringing me to a climax. I rub myself faster and faster, until I feel the pressure building and I come in a fierce explosion all over my fingers.

I quickly switch off the page and lay back against the bed feeling sated.

When Niall comes to bed at two in the morning, he disturbs me. I cuddle into his back which he welcomes, holding on to my arm that I've wrapped around him. Now feeling guilty, I move my hand down to his stomach, but he grabs it and tells me he's tired. I move away sitting up in bed, tears in my eyes. 'What's going on Niall? You're constantly turning me down.'

He huffs like I'm being a nuisance. 'I've just got a few things on my mind at the moment.'

'Well tell me about them for goodness sake, because I can't go on like this.'

He sits up. 'I was thinking about seeing the doctor about a vasectomy.'

'Oh. Okay.'

'I really don't want any more kids, Lauren. I love Joe to bits, but I feel too old to start again.'

'That's fine with me, Niall.'

'Really? You're still only young. I thought you might end up wanting another.'

'Really,' I say. 'We've discussed this before. Joe's nine. I'd have changed my mind before now don't you think?'

He sniffs. 'One of the guys at work's wife has just got pregnant. Claims it's an accident, but he's not so sure. They're both in their early forties. He reckons she's had a last minute panic attack about getting older. I've been worrying about accidents and ending up in the smelly nappy zone again. I'm just too old. I feel settled, Lauren. I like how we are.'

'I said it's fine. Arrange the vasectomy. I have enough with Joe. He's perfect.'

'Oh thank God.' He exhales deeply. 'That's such a weight off my mind. Now Monique's pregnant I thought you might get the idea of pushing prams together.'

'Do you know, I just can't imagine Monique with a baby.'

'Me neither.' He pats my arm and turns over. In seconds he is asleep. I stay awake most of the night.

CHAPTER TWELVE

The post school run finds me in a quandary. I'm supposed to be meeting Monique as usual, but Niall has woken in a happy mood and wants us to spend the morning together as he's on a late shift. I don't want to ruin Niall's good mood when he seems genuinely upbeat for the first time all month, and maybe if we spend more time together I'll stop my stupid behaviour with Seb. As I'm not due to meet Monique until ten-thirty this morning anyway, I delay telling Niall I'm going out, put the kettle on and begin to fix us breakfast. I hope he'll understand that I still need to see her though.

Brrrriiiiiiiiing. The doorbell cuts into my thoughts.

'I'll get it,' says Niall. 'Morning Bettina,' I hear. 'I'll get her for you.'

I throw the croissant packet down on the side. What does she want?

I wander into the hallway. 'I wasn't expecting you, was I?'

Bettina stands at the door in jeans and a blue cotton blouse with flower trim, her hair is in a ponytail. I expect her to burst into a country and western song any minute.

'Lauren, it's rude to keep visitors on the doorstep,' she replies and walks past me into the house.

'Did you put the kettle on?' says Niall, from the lounge.

'Yes, Love.'

'Oh fab. Coffee, milk, one sugar, please.' Bettina moves through into the dining room and sits on one of my comfy brown tub chairs.

'Two things,' she says, brimming with cheer. 'I saw Mrs Sullivan this morning. The fair raised three hundred and seventy-three pounds. She said that about forty-six of that was from your sponge stocks. The book stall raised seventy-eight.'

'That's fantastic,' I say, hoping that my enthusiasm has reached my eyes. Inside I don't give a stuff, and just wish she'd go away. It's now a quarter past nine and my quality time with Niall is being eroded by her presence. My arms are folded and I tap a finger against my left arm.

'I know, and loads of mums at the school have said morning to me today. I feel like I'm actually starting to get settled in now. I've arranged to have coffee tomorrow with one of them, so don't worry, I could be out your hair soon.'

'Don't be silly, I like hanging out. It's just I have a lot on.'

'Like Monique? Which is understandable, cos she's your best friend after all.'

'Even Monique has to take a back seat sometimes. Family comes first.'

'Don't you usually meet her on a Monday?'

'I'm not sure if we're meeting today, I need to ring her.' I take a sip of my coffee and then it comes to me. If she knew I was meeting Monique, what is she doing at the house? 'So, you said two things?'

'Oh yes, I just wanted to apologise for Tyler again. I think he was just trying to look cool in front of the other kids. It's hard being the new boy.'

'There was no harm done, it's only water. If the weather had been any hotter I'd have quite enjoyed it.'

'I'll be honest,' she whispers, looking over her shoulder to check Niall is out of earshot. 'It looked pretty hot from where I was. Mr Kingsley still pursuing you?'

I look away. 'Nah, he flirts, but I've put him straight on that score,' I lie. 'Look,' I say finishing my coffee. 'I've got stacks to do today, but how about we meet up on Wednesday? There's a lovely little market at Chesterfield if you fancy it?'

'That'd be great,' she says, rising from her chair and picking up her bag.

The telephone rings. 'Excuse me a moment.' I lift up the cordless.

'Lo? It's me. Are you coming over?'

'I was just about to ring you, I've got a bit held up at home and so I thought I'd just pop over for an hour this afternoon before I fetch Joe home, is that okay?'

'I need you now Lo,' she sniffs.

'Well, it's just a bit tricky right now.'

'I've lost the baby.'

I gasp. 'Oh my God. When? Are you at the hospital?'

'I'm at home, but I need you. Please?'

There is just the sound of sobbing at the other end of the line.

'I'm on my way, Mon.'

I sit on the sofa. I feel the blood drain away from my face. Poor Monique, the decision was made for her in the end.

Bettina shouts. 'Niall, come quickly, something's wrong.'

Niall comes rushing in. 'What's the matter, is it Joe?'

'Monique's had some bad news,' I eye Niall, trying to transmit what I can't say out loud to his eyes.

He nods and says, 'Well you'd better get over there.'

I start to gather my things together. Bettina asks if there is anything she can do and I shake my head.

'Well I'll just have my coffee if that's okay with you?' she says, sitting back down on the chair. 'Only I'm food shopping next, so it might be a while before I get another.'

'I'll make a fresh pot shall I?' says my husband, in such a sarcastic tone that I can't believe she doesn't hear it.

'Fab,' she smiles. 'I'll keep you company for a bit whilst Lo's out. You don't mind if I borrow the company of your husband for a bit do you, Lauren?'

'Erm, not at all. If it's okay with Niall, it's fine with me.' He looks at me and I see his nostrils flare.

'You're so lucky to have such a trusting relationship. I couldn't have left Danny with my friends.'

I stop and look at her. 'I'm very grateful for what I have.' I think of Monique as I say it. I am so damn lucky to have Niall and Joe. I feel tears welling up behind my eyes. 'Well I have to go. I'll see you later.'

'Give Monique my love. I hope she's okay.'

I give Niall a peck on the cheek. 'I'll see you tonight.'

'See you later, Lauren.' He tucks a piece of hair behind my ear.

Bettina clears her throat. 'Hey, audience here you two. Anyway Niall, while Lo's out you can tell me her secrets. I believe I'm owed some from yesterday.'

I get in the car, closing the door a little stronger than necessary. I take deep breaths. What is wrong with that woman? Is it me or does she have no social boundaries? I decide my frustrations may be more about Mon. Bettina's not to know what's going on.

I set off. It takes me fifteen minutes to drive to Monique's as the traffic lights decide to turn green for me today.

I rush up to the main door and ring the buzzer. Today she doesn't come to meet me, she just buzzes me in.

Her door is slightly ajar and after removing my shoes at the entrance, I walk into the lounge to find her curled up on the sofa weeping quietly. The curtains across the patio door are drawn, casting the room in dim shadow. I pull them open to let in some light and sit next to her on the sofa, putting my arm around her. She turns and collapses against my chest, her sobbing gains momentum. I feel uncomfortable, which makes me feel guilty. Monique's always been there to listen to my problems, but we've never been at this stage of raw emotions needing physical comfort. I'm not a hugging type of person, except with Joe. I'm at a loss to know what to do, so I just let her weep.

After a few minutes she lifts up her head and sits up and away from me. She smiles weakly at me. 'I don't know why I'm so upset, I was considering getting rid of it anyway.'

'Yes, but you'd not decided and it's a loss, Mon, don't try and minimise it, you need to grieve.' I walk into the bathroom and grab some toilet paper for her nose and pass it to her. 'Do you feel up to telling me what happened?'

She sniffs, wiping the tissue under her nose and her voice quivers. 'I got a lot of pain yesterday afternoon and then I started bleeding. I passed this huge clot.' Her eyes go huge. 'It was so frightening. I went to the hospital and they did an ultrasound but the baby was gone. They said there was nothing they could do and just to go home.' She starts crying again. 'I felt so alone.'

'Why on earth didn't you ring me?'

'You had the fundraiser and I know how hard you'd worked on it and how Niall and Joe were looking forward to getting you with the wet sponges. I didn't want to spoil that. It was the longest day of my life. I'm so pleased you're here today.'

'I'm here until school time and I'll come back tomorrow. I presume you're staying off work?'

She nods her head.

'Right, I'm going to run you a bath.'

'I can't have one, in case of infection.'

'Oh right, okay then.' I drum my fingers against my arm. 'Do you have a hot water bottle?'

'Bottom right cupboard in the kitchen.'

I walk into the kitchen. There are a few pots in the sink. I can tackle those later. I put the kettle on with enough water to make us both a drink and fill the hot water bottle. I have to smile as I lift it up. It has a fluffy leopard print cover, truly Monique. That makes me think of how she didn't argue when I passed her the toilet paper, she didn't demand a leopard print tissue. I sigh. Whilst I'm waiting for the water to heat up I walk into Monique's bedroom. The curtains are already closed. I check the bedding. There's no bleeding on the covers, but I change them anyway. I light the Yankee candle she has on her bedside cabinet and fluff up her pillows. Back in the kitchen I sort out the hot water bottle and drinks and carry them through to her room.

As I walk back into the lounge, Mon's eyes are drooping like she's struggling to stay awake. 'Right, let's get you in your room,' I say, and help her to her feet. I settle her down in her bed and we sit quietly while she drinks her coffee.

'I just want to sleep; I want it all to go away.'

'I know, Honey.'

She puts her head down on the pillow. I pull her duvet up, close the door and leave her to sleep. I go and tidy the few pots and put the old bedding into the washing machine. For a while I sit on the sofa and look out onto the patio, feeling helpless and wondering what I'll do when she wakes. It sounds selfish but I can't wait to see Joe, to hug him and be grateful that he was born so perfect. Once again I reflect on how lucky I am.

I leave it until the last possible moment before I leave to collect Joe from school, but Monique remains asleep. I don't want to wake her because I'm a firm believer that sleep aids recovery. I write her a note to say I'll be back in the morning, but to call me if she needs anything, and then quietly close the door behind myself.

I meet Bettina in the school yard. 'How's Monique?'

'Not good. I can't go into details but she's really upset about something. I need to spend some time with her. Is there any chance you could have Joe after school tomorrow? I could get Niall to pick him up and I could stay over at Mon's.'

'Joe can sleep over, it's cool. Tyler would love it. I'll take them to school Wednesday morning and you won't have to worry about being back. Spend a couple of days with her.'

'We were having coffee on Wednesday.'

'So? Don't worry about that, your friend needs you.'

'I feel like I'm letting you down though.'

'Well don't. You can't look after everybody you know, and sometimes we are more than capable of looking after ourselves.'

'Sorry,' I shrug. 'Thank you. I'll meet you here in the morning and bring you his stuff.'

'No probs. You want to have a bath or something tonight and take care of yourself for a change, instead of everyone else.'

'I might just do that,' I say, knowing full well that I plan on spoiling Joe to death with attention tonight.

Joe is in his element that evening. I've built a den in the lounge, something I haven't done since he was little. I set it up in front of the television and give him his tea in there. I slide in alongside him and stick his current favourite film, 'Iron Man 2,' on. I watch his face more than I watch the film. I see his eyes light up at various points, his chuckle and the amazement when Iron Man does something demonstrating his amazing strength. Later I bring in a few small bowls with different chocolates in them. He hugs me. 'You're the best mum ever.' I break out in a huge smile and wonder why I don't do this stuff more often. I'm always on the computer these days. I realise that as much as I've been blaming Niall for just sitting around, that I am to blame myself. I've turned boring and disappeared into a virtual world. No computer tonight I decide. Iron Man finishes. I tell Joe he needs to change into his pyjamas and head upstairs. 'Awww is it bedtime?' he pouts.

'Nope, time for Monopoly,' I say. The world's longest game that I usually refuse to play, protesting I don't have time, but in truth find so boring.

'Awwwwweeesssooome,' Joe yells. He jumps up to give me a huge hug before bounding upstairs.

Niall comes home just before ten to find Joe tucked up in bed reading and drinking a hot chocolate topped with squirty cream and marshmallows. 'Someone's projecting,' he half smiles. 'He'll be up all night with that sugar rush.'

'Button it with the psychobabble. We've had loads of fun.'

'I've seen the evidence of that fun all over the kitchen and living room.'

'Yeah well once we settle Joe down I'm going to tidy up and then get a few things together. Bettina's going to have Joe overnight tomorrow so I can stay with Mon.'

Niall frowns. 'Let's talk about that downstairs.'

Joe looks at him. 'I can go can't I, Dad? I can't wait. Tyler's got loads of Ninjago.'

'Yes you can go,' he says. 'Poor dad left all alone,' he mock cries. 'You best give me some hugs tonight, enough for tomorrow too.'

'What? Am I two?' says Joe and we all collapse into giggles, then Joe jumps on Niall and gives him a cuddle.

Downstairs I quickly tidy up. Niall comes into the kitchen and follows his usual routine of getting home and sticking the kettle on whilst mooching around the cupboards and fridge for snacks. He's in luck tonight as the remainder of four packets of chocolates remain. I see him eyeing them greedily. 'They're all yours,' I state.

'I should think so. I do of course provide the money for such snacks.'

'Watch it,' I elbow him. 'Right what was with the face up there?'

He points towards the dining room tub chairs and I go and sit down.

'Look, I don't want you to take this the wrong way, but doesn't Monique have some family of her own to look after her?'

'Niall, she's lost the baby.'

'I know. Now hear me out. Are you absolutely sure she's actually lost it and not just got rid of it? She's never been maternal.'

I draw a breath and close my eyes for a few seconds. These two have never seen eye to eye and for a moment it really gets to me.

'If you could have seen the state of her, you wouldn't ask me that.'

'Well that's just it Lauren, I don't see her do I? She likes to have you for herself?'

'Are you jealous of the time I'm spending with my friend?'

'No, I just think that sometimes, when you're in full Florence Nightingale mode, you forget your loyalties are to your own family.'

My voice rises, 'How can you say that?'

'Easily. You've known Bettina for two minutes, and let's face it, you can barely stand her half the time, but now she's having our son overnight, and might I point out that *none* of this was discussed with me in the slightest. I might be easy going Lauren, but I am certainly no pushover. You need to rein it in with Monique. She needs to stand on her own two feet, which is just how she likes it, and you need to be home with Joe. He's your responsibility, not her.'

I'm shocked. I don't remember Niall ever having spoken to me this way. I want to rage against him but deep down I know he's right. How can I abandon my friend though, when she's always been there for me?

'I do hear what you're saying, but she really is in a bad way.'

'Where's her family?'

'They all live in Suffolk and she's not close to any of them.'

'Does that not tell you something?'

'Yes, it tells me that at this moment in time she needs me.'

Niall sighs. 'You're still going then?'

I look at him. 'I'm going tomorrow after school and staying until Wednesday. It's all arranged now, but I swear I'm listening to you, and when I'm back my attention will be where it belongs, with you and Joe. I promise.'

'I hope so,' says Niall, who gets up, moves to the lounge and switches the TV on.

I stand in the kitchen, thoughts swirling around my head. I feel like I'm outside myself looking in. I've been so busy with my friends, eBay and Facebook, that some of what's happening between Niall and myself really is my own fault. I assume he sits in front of the TV all night cos he's tired from work.

But is it possible I've spent so much time the past year on the internet I could be partly responsible for this? He's right about Bettina too. I don't know her that well, and if I listen to Monique and Danny, she's bad news anyway. Tonight with Joe showed me the fun I'm missing out on and before long he'll be too cool to spend time with me and I'll regret the missed opportunities. I whizz up a quick pancake batter ready for the morning and stick it in the fridge. Then I take out a stew from the freezer, and stick a post-it on the front saying 'enjoy, love Mum xxx'. I pop that in the fridge as well. Now I don't want to go. I feel so mixed-up and unsettled.

That night I know it's going to be impossible to fall straight to sleep and despite all my new resolutions I switch on the computer. There's a message from Seb.

'I've thought about you all day today. I couldn't get you out of my mind.'

I think of the previous night. I feel dirty and I'm appalled at myself.

I message back. 'I'm sorry, some things have happened at home that make me realise just how much I love my husband, and these silly adolescent games I'm playing with you have got to stop. You totally rock, you know that, and if I was single it'd be different, but I'm not and I need to grow up. I'll leave this message on until the morning and then I'm deleting the whole group from Facebook and yourself from my account. Please don't try and stop me. You need a woman who can be all yours Seb. I am using you to replace the void I felt I had with

Niall, but recent events have shown me I need to spend time with my husband and son. I hope you understand.'

I sign off and close the computer. I head back downstairs to Niall. He's sitting in his favourite chair.

'I've been thinking about what you said and you're right. We need to spend more time together as a family, and I need to make more of an effort to be around.' I place my hand on the waistband of his trousers. 'Because you are so clever you've won a reward.' He shuffles to let me pull down his trousers and pants and hutches forward to the edge of the chair.

'Is it my birthday?'

'Ssshhh,' I tell him as I take him in my mouth. For once he doesn't complain about missing a programme.

CHAPTER THIRTEEN

I'm back at Monique's by half nine the next morning, having first made sure to delete the secret group and Seb, aka Mr Uri Kent, as a friend from Facebook. He'd very simply put :(underneath my statement. I felt a little disappointed that he had no more to say than that, but let the thought go. Today is about Mon. She buzzes me in and I am surprised to see her up and dressed. She's wearing black Sweaty Betty yoga pants, a Carrot Banana Peach fitted yoga tee and some slipper boots with little pompoms at the back of them. She is fresh faced and her short dark hair lies flat. She looks about fourteen.

'How are you doing?'

'Um, okay, I suppose. Thanks for yesterday. I felt a lot better after that cry and sleep. I'll make us a drink.'

'I brought our pastries.' I dangle the Asda carrier bag at her, but she doesn't bite.

'Great,' she moves into the kitchen. It's a small galley kitchen, so I leave her to it as when two people are in you can't move around very comfortably.

I pull the coffee table up to the sofa as it's not warm enough to sit outside this morning; there's been some slight drizzle and it's quite cloudy and windy. I holler, 'Have you got a large plate and some bowls?'

She brings some crockery through. 'Here, you go. I'm not sure I'm all that hungry though.'

'You need to eat. Do you want me to sort out drinks?'

'No, it's okay.' She returns to the kitchen.

I empty out the rest of the carrier bag: a selection of magazines including a fashion weekly, a couple of gossip magazines and a monthly that was on offer. I place the pain au chocolats on the plate and empty the mini croissants and little brioche into the smaller bowls, and bring out a small pot of jam. I also have three girly DVDs.

Monique returns with the coffee and sees the stash. 'You spoil me,' she says, and I shrug.

We spend the morning quietly, as you can when you've been friends for a while, watching one of the movies and steadily working our way through the food. I pause it partway to make fresh coffee.

I bring it through. 'God I love coffee, it sorts me out. I feel all warm and happy when I've had one.'

'Perhaps you can get me a barrel-full then?'

'Oh Mon, I wish I knew what I could do to help.'

'You're already doing it. Just being here. I'll be okay. Just need time.'

I nod. 'Well, it's stopped drizzling out so let's go and get some fresh air. You need some time out of this flat.'

She agrees and goes to get her trainers. I relax a bit as she seems to be coping a little better today.

The local park is just five minutes' walk from Monique's apartment. It's a lovely park with a cafe, a playground for the kids and a large duck pond. If you walk further through there are a few pieces of outdoor exercise equipment for adults. There's a lovely leafy walk alongside a stream that after an hour or so leads you up to a fishing lake and another cafe where they sell the most amazing butties. This fresh weather is perfect for such a walk. 'If you can manage a walk up the Dam Cafe, I'll buy us a chip butty and some coke.'

'How on earth do you manage to remain so slim Lauren? Pastries, and then chips and coke?'

'Well it's not every day is it? I just feel like spoiling you right now.'

'Oh enough about me now,' Monique straightens and lengthens her stride. 'I'm fed up being pathetic. Tell me what's happening with sexy Seb?'

I tell her some of it, leaving out the Facebook group stuff, and just mention that he'd kissed me in the classroom.

'Oh my God Lauren, did you kiss him back?'

'I did at first, but I stopped myself.' I rub my nose, it feels itchy. 'I told him it was a mistake. I love Niall, so that's that.'

'Yes, but that's twice you've kissed him now. I'm having a hard time being convinced you're not going to go for round three, so how's he going to be feeling? What if he won't give up?'

'I'm sure he will. He'll get nothing further from me and I won't see him so much now that the fair's over.'

'Until September. You'll see him every day then.'

I sigh. 'I'll have to cross that bridge when it comes. Its ten weeks away, hopefully it will all have settled down by then.'

'So how are you and Niall?'

'Loads better. We've talked about stuff. Hey, guess what? He wants the snip. Apparently he's been avoiding nookie cos he was paranoid I was going to get pregnant.' The words are out of my mouth before I think about what I'm saying. I gasp and cover my mouth. 'Oh my God, I'm so sorry. It just came out.'

'Lo, you can't avoid the subject; there are lots of babies about. Look.' She points to a pair of yummy mummies strolling with their buggies.

'Yes, but I should be thinking about what I'm saying.'

'It's fine, carry on. What was the hapless idiot thinking this time?'

'He's decided he's too old for any more kids and thought at the last hurdle I might panic and want another, which I don't. So now he's okay, and going to get the snip.'

'So the old love life's back on track?'

'We're getting there slowly.'

'I thought you were on the coil?'

'I am, but he's paranoid because of a workmate's missus.'

'I'll not have helped.'

'Don't be daft. He was being like this long before your situation. Thinking about it, maybe in some ways you even helped. Maybe that made him bring the conversation up? Anyway who knows? At least the end is in sight and I can get back to some shenanigans.'

'I'm surprised though. You'd think he'd want a brother or sister for Joe after having such an angel the first time.'

'He grew up with three brothers. Never a moment to himself. He can't cope with the noise kids make. Even if Joe has a friend round I can see the tension get to him after a while.'

'Seems like Joe might suffer for that.'

'I've never particularly got on with my sister. I just make sure Joe goes to lots of social events, sports groups, and has friends over. I think it's enough. He seems to like his own company, just like his dad.'

'Which is great cos then you have more time for me,' she smiles and jogs up to the cafe.

On the way back the drizzle starts again, getting heavier until the rain is pouring down. Monique's short hair looks fine wet, but I can feel mine hanging in strings with water running off it, reminding me somewhat of the sponge stocks. Monique takes one look at me and giggles, 'Now you'll wish you listened to me about waterproof mascara, you look like a clown.'

'Thanks friend. I'm going to shake myself out all over your Yankee candles when I get back to yours so they won't light.'

'Evil witch.'

'Troll.'

It's heaven to get back to Monique's. Her apartment is furnished throughout with a navy blue, thick pile carpet. I can feel my feet sink into it as I walk. I nip in the shower, then Monique does the same. We sit back on the sofa in our pyjamas with towel turbans on our heads. Spa time I shout, and out of my travel case I bring out face packs and a French manicure kit.

'Yay,' says Monique. 'It's like being on a minibreak. I'm going to call my flat the Coffee Rocks hotel.'

'Well I think I need to sample some as Hotel Inspector to check if you are deserving of such status.'

I'm given coffee and an accompanying caramelised biscuit. 'I give the Coffee Rocks Hotel the full five stars,' I declare. 'In fact I shall award six as the bathroom is not in the wardrobe.'

I go to make the evening meal around five.

'I'm able to fix a meal you know.'

'I told you, I'm spoiling you, so sit down and line the next movie up.'

I'm making a simple spag bol. I chop up the onion, first topping and tailing it and then I cut it through the middle and slice it up. I used to like growing onions. They fascinate me. I like that they're complicated. No matter how neatly I try and dice them they always fall apart. Sometimes I find the inside layer is bright yellow or green, something different to what you expect. Occasionally the middle is rotten and I have to throw it away. It's not often that onions make me cry, but the power of an onion, that as you cut through the layers it can do so, is an amazing thing. Somehow it reminds me of people and life.

The rest of the evening and the following day passes quickly. We have had a pleasant time, although there were some occasional tears and silences on Mon's part. Monique hugs me as I leave.

'Thank you. I can't tell you how much I needed that.'

'You're welcome. I was glad to spend the time with you.'

'Do you think Niall would let you come up for the weekend?'

I step back. 'I doubt it, Mon, he'll expect me to be with him and Joe. I've already spent two days away this week.'

'Course, I'm being stupid, sorry.'

'Don't be daft, it's understandable, you just don't want to be on your own. I'll try and sneak over at some point for an hour, okay? But I need to spend time with my family, especially now me and Niall seem to be getting on a lot better.'

'Well, anytime you can get over will be great,' she says.

As I pass the main school doors on our way home, Seb crosses my path. 'Could I have a quick word Mrs Lawler? It's about the fundraising?'

I step to one side, out of the way of the streaming crowd of other parents, carers and children, and tell Joe he can go on the play equipment. As he's usually banned from this before and after school he thinks it's amazing and runs off.

'I get what you said on Facebook Lauren, but can't I just see you occasionally? I know you felt something too.'

I look at the floor. 'There's absolutely no point. So, please, just leave me alone? Nothing happened thank goodness, so let me be.'

'That's not entirely true though is it?'

My shoulders slump and I feel a bit teary. The last couple of days have left me feeling raw and emotional. 'Seb, I'm asking you to leave it, please.'

'But I know you feel something for me.'

I touch his arm. 'The truth is that I think of you so much and I shouldn't.' I feel the heat of him through my touch and move my hand away. 'I love Niall. I've never cheated and I don't intend to. It hurts because I'm so tempted to see you, that's why I closed the internet page, because I knew I'd not be able to keep away.' I rub the middle of my forehead with my fingers; I can feel a headache brewing. 'I have to though, Seb, for my marriage which I value, and for Joe.' With that we both look at him playing happily on the frame.

He sighs. 'I'll try and leave you alone,' he says. 'But only because I care for you so much.'

'Oh please don't say that.'

'Is everything okay here, Mr Kingsley? You look a bit upset, Mrs Lawler.' Mrs Sullivan has appeared.

I step back. 'Yes, it's fine. I was just chatting about Joe being a bit behind with his maths and I got all emotional, silly really.'

Seb adds. 'I was saying that next year I'll make sure he gets some extra help if its needed.'

'Well don't forget my office door is always open Mrs Lawler. I understand Mr Kingsley is Joe's next teacher and you worked together at the fair, but the first route for concerns is to Joe's current teacher, and then me.'

'You're right. I apologise for monopolising your time.' I state to Seb. 'Joe,' I shout. 'Time to go home now.'

Of course, as I'm walking down the drive wanting to hurry home, Bettina calls out for me 'How's Monique?'

'We had a really good time thanks, she's feeling a lot better. Thank you for helping out with Joe. I hope you don't feel I'm putting on you. Niall thinks I'm taking advantage.'

'Oh I think we're okay now that he knows me a little better,' she replies. 'You'd forgotten to pack Joe some clean pants so I popped over to yours last night. I thought Niall was bound to have not eaten so I called to the fish shop on the way. We all ate together before I brought the boys back. I think he was a bit narked that Joe still wanted to come back with me though.'

'You had tea together?'

'It was a right laugh. You have some lovely crockery, it seemed a shame to put chips on it, but I can't eat them out of the wrapper.'

'Niall always does.'

'Well he didn't yesterday. Oh and your bedroom is so pretty. I'm thinking about doing mine a similar colour.'

I grit my teeth. 'You were in my bedroom?'

'Oh God, don't look so panicked. I wasn't seducing your husband. I just asked for a guided tour.'

I give her a beaming smile. 'Well, I must get back, thanks again for having Joe.'

'Any time you need me to mind him, it's no problem. It was a pleasure yesterday, he's a lovely boy.'

I ask Joe about everything on the way back. 'We were only there ten minutes, Mum, eating our chips. Then dad said he really needed to get on with some jobs whilst we were all out of the house and we went back to Bettina's.'

'Okay darling,' I say. Once again I'm reading too much into things. So what if she took the kids to our house for tea, she was just getting Joe stuff I'd obviously forgotten to pack in my rush to get to Monique's. *Failing as a mother again*, I hear in my head. I've a bit of a nerve worrying about Niall when I consider what I've been up to with Seb.

All thoughts of Bettina are forgotten as I enter the house. Monique's okay, business is good, and I'm looking forward to seeing my husband when he gets in from work. Therefore I'm surprised to find Niall already at home and in the lounge.

'What're you doing home this early?'

'I took some time owing. I had something I needed to do.' His face is frozen into a tight mask. He turns to Joe. 'I've charged up your DS, it's on your bed if you want to play for a bit before your homework.'

'Cool,' Joe goes running upstairs, it sounds like a stampede, not the small feet of a nine year old boy.

'What's wrong?' I ask.

'This came in the post today.' He hands me a piece of paper.

I unfold it. It's typewritten in capital letters and says YOUR WIFE HAS A SECRET. TRY 19, 5 AND 2. My brow creases. 'What? ... I don't understand.'

'Letters of the alphabet. Didn't take much working out,' says Niall. 'It spells Seb. What secret do you have with Seb then?' He spits the word Seb out like a venomous snake.

My heart is pounding. 'Niall, there is absolutely nothing going on between me and Seb Kingsley.'

'You've had plenty of opportunity with those fair meetings.'

I thrust the paper at his chest. 'I have opportunities to cheat all the time while you're at work and Joe's at school.' I feel air pumping out of my nostrils. 'That however, does not make me a cheat.'

'Well you'll not mind if I check your laptop,' he says. 'You're always on that bloody thing, I'm going to see what you spend your time doing.'

'I'm running my business.' I feel myself tremble. 'If you do this, you're showing that you don't trust me, Niall. That's a heavy weight to put on our relationship. Do you really want to do that?'

He hesitates. 'If it's not true then why would someone do this?' He waves the paper around. 'Why would they go to the trouble of posting a note?'

'I have no idea,' I say, but then it comes to me.

'Oh my God, it'll be her, Bettina.'

'What?'

'She's trying to ruin things for me. She told me she turned up for tea last night and you were all cosy together. She turned up at the house the other day when she thought I was out. It's just like Danny said, she's trying to ruin me.'

'Danny? *Danny Southwell*? Her ex? When have you seen Bettina's husband?'

'Last Saturday. He turned up here as I was about to set off to the car boot. He came to warn me about her. Told me that she's nuts and was out to get me. Oh my God, it's true.'

'That psycho turned up at the house? Where was I?'

'In the house with Joe.'

'So you're telling me that Danny Southwell was outside our house, that you didn't shout for me or come and tell me, and you didn't bother telling me afterwards that he'd been?' He shakes his head from side to side. 'Did you even go to the car boot that afternoon Lauren? I thought it was funny you returned without anything.'

So he had noticed.

'You talk about trust,' he looks at me with a sneer, 'where was it that day?'

I'm silent. I don't know what to say that at this point that won't make things worse. How can the day have come to this when I was so positive about everything? I can't stand seeing Niall look at me this way.

He folds his arms across his chest. 'I want to see your computer, Lauren,' he says. 'So go and get it.'

CHAPTER FOURTEEN

I open the computer with my password and hand it to him. I walk away, open the back door and sit on the doorstep. I often come out here to think. I breathe in the cool, fresh air and listen to the sounds of traffic passing the busy parkway near the house. It was going to be such a nice evening.

Niall will find nothing of course, thanks to my fortuitous deleting. I had ensured all comments to Monique were deleted too, so all that remained was our usual chat about life in general with inane comments about shoes. If he came across some crass comment in there about himself, well it served him right for reading my private stuff.

For some reason, even though I know full well I kissed Seb, I am damn angry that Niall was so quick to think I would cheat on him. He didn't trust me at all. My teeth are clenched and I feel the need to hit out at something. Over in the corner of the garden, behind the shed, is an old tin bath that we haven't got around to taking to the tip. I stand up and walk over to the garage, unlock it, then heave the door open over my head and walk to Niall's shelves where I grab a large hammer. I stride to the back of the garden and take great heaving swipes at the bath. It reverberates loudly, how I imagine standing next to a church bell would sound. The bath begins to dint and I feel my anger pouring out like an overflowing red hot bath. Bang. Bang. Bang.

Niall comes running out of the house and I notice his first thought is to look up at the neighbours' windows to see if any of them are watching. All reason leaves me and I throw the hammer, watching as it sails through the shed window. The plastic cracks, and it leaves a gaping wound.

'For God's sake what are you doing?' He yells as he runs up to me and grabs my arms.

'What does it look like?' Tears stream down my cheeks. I begin to smack my fists into his chest. 'You think I'd have an affair? You're a total bastard. I hate you.'

Niall wraps his arms around me so that mine are trapped and drags me into the house whilst I kick him in the shins the best I am able. 'Stop it, Lauren. Calm down.'

'Calm down?' my voice gets even higher.

'Think of Joe,' says Niall. 'He's just asked what's wrong with you. I've told him you're sad and angry about something that's happened with Monique.'

I am shaking, I take some deep breaths for he is right, I will be frightening Joe.

We are silent for minutes, each not knowing how to get past this.

'How could a note do this to us? You didn't believe me ... after all these years?'

'Well, it wasn't just that,' Niall puts his hands in his pockets and shrugs his shoulders. 'When Bettina came over with the kids the other night, she kind of warned me about him. Said she felt he was really into you and was flirting while you were arranging the fair.'

'*So what*? He flirted with me, big deal. At least he paid me some attention, which is more than you've been doing lately.'

'I suppose I deserve that.' He adds quietly. 'Did you flirt back?'

'I had a bit of banter yes, but nothing major, just like how you are with nearly every female you ever meet. I'm not going to apologise for it. I'll tell you right now that it was nice feeling that someone found me sexy. It made me feel good about myself. Like I said, this is all down to Bettina. Well good for her, she's managed to drive a wedge between us, score one for Bettina.'

'She was just looking out for you.'

'You're going to stick up for her, even though I told you about Danny coming to warn me?'

'He's supposed to be a bloody psycho; I wouldn't rate anything he said.'

'Yeah? Well Monique warned me weeks ago that she thought Bettina was shifty. That night she went to the cinema with her, apparently she never stopped asking questions about me.'

'She was like that in the car on the way there with me too. She just seemed nervous and we didn't have anything else in common but you. It was probably the same with Monique. You can't assume from a small piece of conversation that she's out to get you. She's had plenty of opportunity to kick your arse if she wanted to.'

'She's going for a less obvious way instead.'

'It doesn't appear that way to me. Lauren you're being paranoid.'

'I had a fucking poison pen letter sent about me today, I think I'm entitled to be a little bit paranoid.'

'Look,' Niall runs his hands through his hair, 'I overreacted big time, Lauren, I'm sorry. It was just the thought of that nerd having his hands on you.' His own hands ball into fists as he speaks.

'Sorry doesn't really get us anywhere right now though does it?' I reply. 'Like you said, I've broken your trust.'

'I'll get over the thing with Southwell.'

'Yes, but you didn't trust me in the first place.' I walk over and pick up my laptop and put it on the side to take upstairs. 'That's going to be a lot more difficult to fix than the shed window.'

I go into the kitchen to start the evening meal.

I speak when I need to. Inside I feel wrecked, like I've just heard news of someone's death. I put on smiles when Joe is talking. Niall is over exuberant. He thinks I'll immediately put it behind me, like I do with our usual arguments, and move on. Life is short, but I don't feel that way this time. When Joe goes to bed I run myself a bath and immerse myself, topping it up with warm water every so often. I stare at the white tiles on the bathroom wall as if I am drugged with anaesthetic, too numb to do anything but lie beneath the water. I let my skin wrinkle up until it's too uncomfortable to stay in it any longer. I wrap myself in my towelling robe, looking at it as I do so. Its purple colour has faded, there are pulled threads hanging down from it all over. It has seen better days. It needs renewing. I feel at one with my robe. I place my feet in my slippers and pad into the bedroom where I dry my hair without being bothered to comb it through, knowing full well it will frizz and resemble tangled wool. I leave the hairdryer plugged in and on the floor, pull on my pyjamas and get in bed, pulling the duvet up to the top of my neck, seeking immediate sleep that will take me away from my problems. Luckily my body complies.

I wake in the night as Niall gets into bed. I wait to see if he gets on my back to cuddle in, but he turns the other way and I let myself drift back to sleep.

Thursday I ring Monique and ask how she is. She seems a lot brighter, but obviously picks up the tension in my voice.

'Is everything alright, Lo?'

'Yeah, just a bit fed up today. Nothing to bother you with, you've enough on your plate.'

'Lauren Lawler, what is going on?'

'I don't want to put on you Mon, it's not fair.'

'I'm a big girl and can decide what's fair, tell me what's going on, I'm getting worried now.'

I fill her in on the note and Niall's accusations.

'Jeez, Lo,' she says. 'It's got to be her hasn't it? What a bitch.'

'Well apparently I'm overreacting.'

'It's a bit suss that she just happened to mention Seb, and the next day, poof, here's a letter stating you're up to no good.'

'Did you really just say poof?'

'It's an official magic term.'

'Joe would call you lame, don't you know it's "booya" now,' I scoff.

'Is that a hint of a smile I can hear in your voice? See you need your Monique,' she says.

'I do,' I agree.

'Well get your ass over here then. I'm bored. Let's talk this thing through.'

I mull it over but I don't feel like going anywhere.

'Thanks Mon, but I just feel like moping.'

'You can mope just as well here as there.'

'No. Thanks for the offer but I'm just going to lounge about at home til schooltime.'

'Suit yourself, you know where I am if you change your mind.'

'Thanks Mon, and sorry for putting on you.'

'Will you leave it with the sodding guilt trip. Go forth and eat chocolate.'

'You've read my mind,' I state.

I take myself off up to my bedroom armed with a mug full of decaf and a share bag of Minstrels that I have no intention of sharing. I stick on my latest Private Practice box set to see what Addison and Co are up to, and lose myself in the drama of Oceanside Wellness for an hour or two. The phone disturbs me mid-afternoon. I look at the screen thinking that if it shows an unknown number, or anyone I don't want to speak to, I'll ignore it. 'Niall mobile' flashes on the screen. I hold the phone in my hand, hovering over the answer button. I decide to let it go to the machine.

'Lauren, if you're there please pick up, it's an emergency.'

I press the green button, all annoyance temporarily forgotten. 'What is it? What's happened?'

'I'm in the hospital car park. Someone's just run into the back of the car. Then they've come round and played hell with me and said I reversed into them. I don't know what the hell's going on. They've someone with them who's saying they're a witness and that it was me. I was reversing, but I stopped when I saw them coming towards me. It was them. There's no-one else around to witness it and they're phoning the police.'

'Calm down Niall, surely there's CCTV?'

'Oh, course, I didn't think of that. I'll mention it to the police when they get here.'

'What are the people like, do they look rough? It's only a car. If they look like they might stab you, don't make a fuss.'

'It's a bloody doctor. I've seen his badge. Dr Matthias Bailey.'

'Are you all right? You're not injured?'

'I feel shaky, my legs are wobbly, but I didn't do anything Lauren, I swear.'

'Is there much damage to the car?'

'It needs the boot sorting, it's crushed. It went with a right bang.'

'Just wait for the police Niall, they'll sort it out.'

'Okay, obviously I don't know how long I'll be, I'll see you as soon as I can get away.'

The line goes dead. I sit back on the bed. I'm not surprised at this doctor saying it's Niall's fault. No-one in this world seems to tell the truth anymore, or stands up and admits when they've made a mistake. I hope the CCTV's working so justice can prevail. I feel my anger return. I wish I could turn up to the car park with a baseball bat and knock seven bells out of the git who's blaming Niall. I bet he's a cocky doctor who thinks the sun shines out of his arse. I notice it's time to get Joe from school and think that now, if Niall's car needs repair, he'll take mine, and I'm the one who will end up inconvenienced. Annoyed I stomp to the car.

I say hello to Tanya in the schoolyard and let her twitter on about pointless rubbish whilst I wait for Joe. She's looking at me weirdly and I realise she's waiting for me to answer a question.

'Oh, err, what did you say?'

'I said, you don't seem with it Lauren. Is everything alright?'

'I'm sorry. Niall's just had an accident in the car, my minds wandering. I didn't mean to seem rude.'

'Gosh, don't worry about it. Is he okay?'

A hand clutches my arm and makes me turn, as if defending an attack.

'Good God Bettina, you made me jump.'

'Sorry, did I just hear Niall's been in an accident?'

'Yes, someone's just reversed into him in the hospital car park.'

'Is he okay?'

'Just shaken up, thanks.' I fidget from side to side and turn to the school Portakabin windows. 'Is this bell ever going to ring? I just want to get home so we can get things sorted out.'

'Do you need me to do anything, Lauren?' says Bettina.

The tight wiring of the coil inside my body bursts free. 'I think you've done quite enough lately, thank you.'

Bettina backs off, shocked, and her face sets like stone. 'What the hell are you talking about? I've not banged into the car.'

'I'm on about your little chat with Niall about Seb. He accused me of having an affair with him yesterday.'

'I only said he was flirting with you. I felt he should know. Niall adores you and don't think I haven't seen you flirting right back. You want to stop having a go at me and look at your own behaviour.'

Tanya walks over to the other mothers, raising an eyebrow at them. It seems Bettina and I are now sparring in a ring with all the spectators looking to see who will win the next round.

'How dare you judge me? You keep coming around to my house and having cosy little coffees with my husband. Go and get your own. Oh, I'm sorry, you can't can you? He won't have you cos you're a bloody psycho.'

I feel the slap hard against my cheek; it jars my head and stings. I clutch my face.

'You've no idea what I've had to put up with.'

172

'Unfortunately I do, Bettina, cos you keep bringing it to my door. I had the pleasure of your lovely husband's company after you *forgot* I was collecting your son'.'

She's silent for a moment, her mouth open with the sharp breath she's taken. Then her eyes narrow. 'I made a mistake. Have you any idea what it was like for me, thinking he'd taken my child?'

'But he takes him every other weekend you thick cow. Anyway thanks to you, Niall and I are hardly speaking. Did you post the note through the door and then decide to say it to his face instead, or was the note a back up to make him believe you?'

'What note?'

'Oh come off it, the cryptic note that you stuck through the letterbox saying to watch out for Seb.'

'I don't know what you're talking about, or what you're accusing me of, and if anyone round here's a psycho then you want to take a good look at yourself, Lauren, because from where I'm standing, the only loony is shouting at me right now.'

Brrrrrrrrring. The school bell goes.

I jab a finger towards her face. 'I've not finished with you, stay away from me and my family.'

'With pleasure.'

I feel shaky and hot and guide Joe back to the car. As the mobile classes are away from the main classrooms, I am only gawped at by the parents from Joe's class and the one next door.

Tanya comes running up. 'Are you alright? What was that all about?'

She's only interested in getting some gossip for the rest of the parents, so I point at Joe and mouth. 'I'll tell you later.'

I get behind the wheel of the car and burst into heavy, noisy sobs.

'Mum, what's the matter?' I turn to see Joe's face all scrunched up in concern and looking like he might cry himself. 'I saw you and Tyler's mum arguing. I can still play with Tyler can't I?'

'Course love,' I stroke my thumb down his cheek. 'Mum's just being silly, take no notice. Dad's had a little bang in the car.' Joe tears up. 'Oh he's fine honey, but it upset me a bit and then Bettina said something to upset me too, and I lost my temper. I was silly, I'm a grown up and should act better. I'm sorry Joe, you shouldn't have had to see that.'

He wipes away my tears. 'We all make mistakes mum.' I hear my own words reflected in his own. 'Remember what you tell me and just walk away, okay?'

'I will, I promise.' I smooth his hair behind his ears, this wise boy who is right now looking after his mum when it should be the other way around.

'You'll need to say sorry to Tyler's mum tomorrow.'

'I don't think it's as simple as that son,' I shrug.

'Why not?'

'It's grown up stuff.'

'Aaarrrgh, I hate it when you say that. Are you okay to drive now cos I'm starving? Can we stop for a sausage roll?'

Niall gets in at six. His face is grim. He has shadows under his eyes and his skin looks sallow.

'What did the police say?'

'They took both our statements, breathalysed us.'

'They thought you'd been drinking?'

'It's standard procedure. They said they'd contact security to see about the CCTV and get back to me.'

'What about the witness?'

'Still adamant it was my fault.'

'Are you sure you weren't just tired and didn't realise?'

'Lauren, don't go there okay? I didn't reverse into that car.'

'Okay, don't bite my head off. I'm just thinking you probably didn't get a lot of sleep.'

'I was stationary.'

'Don't argue with mum again,' chips in Joe. 'I hate it when you argue and you did it for ages yesterday. Anyway Mum'll be losing her voice if she does anymore. She's already fallen out with Tyler's mum today.'

'What?' Niall looks at me.

'We had words in the school playground.'

'They were arguing really loud, Dad, I couldn't tell what they were saying, but I thought they were going to have a fight.'

'What were you arguing about?'

'The note.'

'Oh Lauren, you don't know she had anything to do with that note.'

'Well I had a go at her for saying things to you about Seb.'

'But I'm glad she did Lauren, because you weren't going to.'

'Are you talking about Mr Kingsley?' says Joe.

We both look at him. 'Erm. Yes. Yesterday we were arguing that we thought he should have worn his clothes to the school fair, not his pyjamas,' Niall says.

As a spur of the moment excuse it's the worst I've ever heard, but Joe takes it seriously.

'He did look stupid, but he was probably trying to save his clothes for best.'

'Gosh, we never thought of it like that, I guess you're right,' I say.

'You grown-ups are so lame sometimes. All that arguing, and I could have told you that yesterday.'

'We're very silly,' I agree, 'let's get some tea and then how about a game of Tumbling Monkeys?'

'I'll go set it up.' Joe scampers off into the living room.

Niall follows me into the kitchen.

'So you had a catfight in front of the entire school?'

I throw the bag of pasta onto the worktop. 'Not the entire school, just the Portakabins. I'm considering calling the police cos she slapped me.' I touch my cheek. 'I shouldn't let her get away with violence. Hey that's a thought,' I say, warming up to the idea. 'They might phone her shrink and get her back into some kind of therapy. That's what she needs for posting poison pen letters.'

'Have you heard yourself Lauren?' Niall takes me by the shoulders. 'You sound obsessed. You have absolutely no proof that she sent that note. It could be anyone from that school. Maybe one of them's got a thing for the nerd and took umbrage that he has an eye for you?'

'It just fits in with what Danny said. She's come back to Sheffield for some twisted revenge against me.'

'Or maybe she left a bad marriage and just wanted to be near her mother.'

'Why are you sticking up for her all the time?' I slam the pan on the top of the cooker and watch water spill onto the gas flame, which goes out. 'Sodding hell.' I move the pan to another ring and light it. 'Do you fancy her or something, Niall?'

'Oh don't be so pathetic.' Niall's face is twisted in fury and he slams his hand against the wall. 'Look, I don't want to argue any further cos it's affecting Joe. Let's just eat our meal, play the game and sleep on everything. I've had a hell of a day.' He walks out of the kitchen.

'Yeah, you're not the only one,' I state quietly to his retreating back.

I'm dreading school the following morning and tell Joe that I'll drop him off at the school driveway. I just can't face seeing anyone. I've not had a shower and my hair looks like I've sprayed cooking oil down my centre parting. I look in the windscreen mirror and think that I must get my roots done soon. On my return to the house I walk round slamming cupboard doors. I pull everything out of one of the bottom kitchen cupboards and listen to all the tins slam out over the floor. I look at the dates on everything and opening the back door, throw anything out of date outside with a satisfying surge of adrenaline. I tidy the rest back up and potter into the living room. My mobile rings, its Monique.

'How're you doing today babe?'

I sigh. 'I don't know.'

'Are you going to come over?'

'Nah, I just feel like being at home.'

'Yeah, well open your front door. I thought you'd say that, so I'm here.'

I go to the front door and sure enough Monique is standing there, looking resplendent in a blue and green silky blouse and jeans. I feel wet on my cheek and gulp to hold it in, but she puts her arms around me in a hug and the dam bursts again.

'If they complain about a water shortage this year, they should come find us two. I think we've provided enough over this last week or so to see England through the summer.'

I retract myself from her hug and walk into the kitchen and lift the kettle. 'Coffee makes everything better.'

'And bacon sandwiches.' Monique holds up a material bag with a peacock design on it complete with feathers and sequins. From inside it she brings out the familiar green logoed supermarket carrier bag. 'Bacon and breadcakes. I thought the hard stuff was needed.'

I smile. I feel like a rainbow is peeking out from a thundery cloud. 'I'm a mess.'

'Well you can rectify that by sticking yourself in the shower, Stinko, and I'll fix the butties.'

I turn the shower up extra hot and welcome the feel of the almost burn as the water touches my skin. I spend time lathering myself up in a vanilla scented shower gel and give my hair a really good wash. I dress myself in some clean clothes, a red Topshop sweater and some three-quarter length black skinnies and head back downstairs to the tempting smell of freshly cooked bacon. Monique has put it on the dining table and is seated, and partway through her butty. 'Sorry, it smelled too good to wait for you.'

'That's okay; I couldn't get out of the shower once I got in.'

'You feel a bit better for it?'

'Yeah, I feel clean. I need to stop wallowing and do something.' I take a bite out of my butty. 'Mmmmmm.' I realise I feel ravenous and wolf it down. 'Is there any more bacon left?'

'Yeah, and another two breadcakes.'

'You want another?'

'Nope,' she points to her washboard stomach. 'This takes dedication and hard work.'

I point to my own stomach which has an extra podge around it that's been there since Joe. 'This affords me the occasional slip up.' I go and fix myself another butty.

'So what do you think we should do today?' Monique shouts into the kitchen.

I wander back out. 'Well first I need to check my eBay account, because I didn't do it yesterday with everything that went off. Then if I have any parcels to do, I want to get that out of the way, so this morning might be a little boring.'

'You can have an hour doing that while I catch up with the Housewives of New York, and then we're going out.' Monique passes me the TV remote. 'Put the TV on would you? I'm just going to visit the bathroom.'

I clear the dishes into the sink. I'll wash them later and clean down the dining room table. As Monique returns I head upstairs to get my laptop. I power it up at the kitchen table and log in. The first thing I see is my feedback rating. My lovely one hundred percent rating is no more and in the red column I have twenty-six negative feedback ratings. What? There must be some mistake. I feel like I've been caught cheating at an exam when I'm innocent. I click on the feedback to see what's going on.

'Horrendous product. Arrived broken. Do not use seller.'

'Covered in cat hair. Buyer beware.'

'Product cheap and nasty, not as described.'

The list goes on. Most of the feedback is from the two business sellers that ordered loads of items, but there are some from other recent buyers too. I am horrified. I feel cold and sick, and the room goes hazy, as if I might faint.

Monique looks over from Housewives. 'Christ Lo, what's up? You look like you've seen a ghost.'

'My business ...it's...' I can't form words and just point to the machine.

She hurries round to look at the screen. 'Oh my God, how has that happened? It must be a mistake, just contact eBay. They've obviously put someone else's feedback on your page.'

'It's not Mon, look.' I open one of the orders on screen. 'Those are mainly the items I sold in the big orders that I thought might drum up more business for me in future. It's all ruined, what am I going to do?'

'Surely you can complain to eBay about them?'

'It's my word against theirs. eBay won't do anything and anyway, others have posted negative feedback too.'

Monique looks more closely at the feedback. 'Your feedback rating is still high. Why don't you just offer an apology and offer to refund them or something?'

'I could do, but they spent close to two hundred pounds. That's just such a lot of money.'

'But that and a nice quote from you saying sorry they didn't like your stuff should bring your page round, clear up the negative stuff. You'll soon make it back.'

I slump back into my seat and look up into Monique's face. 'Why is this happening? I can't take much more.'

I put my head in my hands and bring my palms down to rub over my face and eyes. 'God, it's got to be, Bettina? She's set me up. I bet all these accounts are hers.'

Monique looks at me carefully. 'I have to admit, this does looks like a set up.'

'I'm not giving a penny back.' I clench my teeth. 'I'm going to get that bitch.'

'Oooh. Are you going to kick her ass? Can I watch?'

'I can't be that obvious after yesterday.'

'Why, what happened yesterday?'

I fill her in on the details of the spat, her eyes widen as my tale goes on.

'Lo Lawler, get you. You're a wildcat. I wouldn't want to be on the wrong side of you.'

'Yeah well she's going to regret it,' I say. 'I'm just not sure how yet.'

I turn back to the computer and start adding the same feedback to each comment. 'I am sorry you have found this product unsatisfactory. I send items as I would expect to receive them, and yours was sent in excellent, 'as new' condition. On this occasion I can assure you your item was sent in immaculate condition.' I sign off and put the computer to sleep with a satisfactory click.

'Right, any idea what we should do next? I'm ready for getting out of here. I feel like I could hit the gym or something,' I say.

'You're hitting Bella's. I called them while watching Housewives and made you an appointment for eleven-thirty. Those roots are appalling, and I'm not being seen in public with you until they're sorted.'

I smile and check out my reflection in the living room mirror. 'Excellent, first line of defence, look absolutely amazing. When I see her this afternoon at school she'll wonder why I'm so happy. I don't know what revenge I'm going for yet, but she'll not be ready for it.'

'Now that sounds more like the Lauren I know. I'll see if I can think of anything you can do. I'm getting my nails done whilst you're having your hair sorted. Hey, we should get claws.'

'I'm not dragging you into this, Mon, you've been brill, but you've had enough of your own problems. By the way, I'm paying for your nails.' I put my hands up before she can interrupt. 'No. I insist, you've been fab.'

'Okay. Gosh there's more action here than in today's episode of Real Housewives.'

'Come on, let's get to the hairdressers.' I stand and run my hands through my hair. 'I need to get armoured up.'

CHAPTER FIFTEEN

I feel better after my haircut, and my new soft highlights make me look golden skinned and healthy. I'm naturally blonde, but my hair goes darker as the years pass, so now I require a blonde 'top-up' every six months. I say goodbye and thank Monique for turning up and dragging me out of the doldrums, with a promise to ring her tomorrow.

I have twenty minutes before I need to pick up Joe. I slam the car in gear and head to Bettina's house.

It's a detached house, on one of Handsworth's better estates (we couldn't afford one). Determined, I march up the driveway, and ignoring the doorbell, pound on the door. I can see her moving behind the glass panel. She opens the door and looks at me warily.

'What do you want, Lauren?'

'I came to ask you to just stop it. You've probably ruined my business now, so there you go. You've created more trouble for me than I ever did for you at school, so please can you just leave us alone? I don't know how you managed the different eBay addresses, whether you had me send the stuff to relatives or what, but enough's enough. Can you retract your feedback so I can at least get on with my life, and I'll let you get on with yours?'

Bettina fold her arms across her chest. 'What on earth are you rambling on about? Do you want the number of my psychiatrist, Lauren, because you seriously have some kind of mental issue.'

I hold up my hands. 'If that's how you want to play it so be it. I'm just letting you know that it stops now, because I'm not putting up with any more of your nonsense.'

'I'd like you to leave now. I need to get Tyler from school. We're away this weekend.'

'Not a problem. I'm going.'

'You need to sort out your issues and stop dumping everything at my door. You're not the only one with problems, but all anyone ever hears about is me, me, me; poor old Lauren with my terrible life.'

I glare at her. 'How dare you? You were the one who moved back to Sheffield, you didn't have to be near me.'

'You don't own Handsworth, Lauren. My family is here, which is more than can be said about yours. They ditched you long ago didn't they?'

I stagger back. I feel like she's slapped me. I try not to think about my parents, the dad who walked out on us and my mother. She couldn't be bothered with me, or get rid of me fast enough once I was old enough to cope on my own. It's one of those things schoolchildren know about each other, but I thought I'd left my school years behind a long time ago.

I walk away. It's started to pour with rain and my lovely new hairstyle is gone. My new armour failed the practice round. I head for the car.

Her voice comes from behind me. 'Lauren, come back, I'm sorry, I shouldn't have said that.'

I look back at her. 'But you did. I believe Danny, you're obviously no friend of mine. You are definitely one psychotic bitch, so go rot in hell.'

'You're making a mistake,' she shouts after me.

I ignore her, I need to get to school.

Despite what she has just said, she hasn't finished. 'By the way, just so you know, Seb asked me out. I was going to say no because I didn't think you'd like it, but sod it, he's not yours.' Her mouth twists up at one side and whilst I'm looking at her with my mouth wide open, she walks back to her house and slams the door.

At home Joe rushes off to play and I sit on the settee. I can't even be bothered to put the kettle on. All the mess of the past few days runs through my mind, the note, the car, the argument at school, my eBay business and now she's targeted Seb. I don't know how true it is or whether she's just said it out of maliciousness, but I need to find out. I have his mobile number but can't risk phoning him at the moment. I pace the living room. Did she ask him, or him her? If he has done it, he's done it to make me jealous, I'm sure. He doesn't realise he's playing with a petrol fuelled bonfire. Why do I care? I accidentally knock a pile of Joe's magazines on the floor.

'For God's sake Joe, can you tidy these up?' I shout. I walk over to the stereo, put in my Rhianna CD and turn it up loud.

Joe walks past. 'Oh mum, I hate that CD.'

'Well stay in your room and you won't have to listen to it. Take the magazines up as you go.' Now I'm snapping at Joe. I need to sort myself out.

Niall comes in about ten minutes later, barging through the doors at warp speed. 'Turn that down can you love?'

He misses my glare. I stab the off button.

'Cheers. Okay, listen, they didn't have the cameras on in the car park, so there's no evidence to prove I'm telling the truth, so that's it, it's all on me.' He flops into the chair. 'At least we've got a courtesy car for a week or so whilst mine's being repaired.'

'Well that's something I suppose.' I want to tell him about Bettina, but then I remember what she just said, that it's 'me, me, me' all the time, and I keep quiet. I can't help thinking that it's yet another thing gone wrong. Another round to Bettina. I feel myself tense.

Niall smacks his hand on his thigh and stands up. 'Anyway, are you ready?'

'Ready for what?'

'We're going to see my parents this weekend, remember?'

Oh heck, I'd forgotten with everything that had been happening. I don't feel ready to see his folks right now. They are lovely people but they get in my space, and right now, I need people at arm's length. I need to get my head around what happened this afternoon, regroup and think of my next move.

'You've forgotten haven't you?'

I nod. 'Don't worry though, it won't take long to pack.' I pause, 'Actually Niall, would it be okay if I drive down tomorrow, only I'd promised to sort out some stuff with Bettina tonight?'

'You're talking again? Good. I'd rather you came tonight though, Lauren.'

'I know, but I don't want to ruin things when the situation is so delicate.'

'Well, can you be at Mum's for lunch tomorrow?'

'Absolutely. I'll aim for late morning, okay?'

'Okay, love. Can you get our stuff together then?'

'Of course. Is she doing your evening meal?'

'Yes, so no worries about that.' He heads to the bottom of the stairs. 'Joe, come on, we're going to Grandma and Grandad's.'

Joe comes rushing down the stairs. 'Yay, I love going there. How long are we staying?'

'Until Sunday. It'll be a nice break for everyone. I think I speak for me and your mum when I say we could do with a nice break and a change of scenery.'

A change of scenery. Suddenly I have an idea for Project Revenge.

'I'll pack your things,' I say, and leave the room with a smirk on my face.

They're safely on their way when I set to work in the kitchen. I have a new Pinterest idea to try for my project. When that's done, I dig my mobile out of my bag. I call Seb's number to get part one of my plan sorted.

'Well, you're one person I wasn't expecting a call from on a Friday night.'

'I need to talk to you. Can you come over?'

'Hey, I'm not going anywhere near your husband.'

'Him and Joe have gone to his mother's. It's just me. I need to talk to you about something.'

'Is this something called Bettina?'

'Just get over here and bring wine. Have you got my address?'

'I looked it up on the school computer a while ago.'

I sigh. 'I might've known.'

'See you in a few. What sort of wine?'

'As long as it's alcoholic, I don't care.'

My mobile rings a minute after.

'Yes?' I say.

'Hey girl, how'd it go at school earlier?'

'Oh, not great but I have a plan.'

'Oh yeah? Tell me more.'

'I'm going to have to ring you back Mon, I'm on with it all now and I'm in a rush.'

'Sure, okay. Catch you later then.' She sounds sullen but I just don't have time to worry about Monique right now.

Thirty minutes later he's at my door. He smells strongly of aftershave and looks as hot as a chilli pepper, dressed in a Guns n Roses tee and jeans. I can see a tiny bit of dark ink just below his collarbone and my mouth gets wet. He comes in and sits himself on the settee without asking.

'Guests usually remove their shoes in the hall.'

He throws them off and gives me a slow smirk. 'Anything else I should remove?'

'Look before you go there ...'

'I know, I know, you're not interested. Is that supposed to stop me from getting hard every time I see you?'

My eyes stray to his groin. I bite my lip.

'Just tell me why I'm here.'

'Give me a minute to get the drinks sorted.' I dash from the room.

Handing him a glass, I tell him about my past with Bettina and how I think she may be behind the note and the eBay saga. Seb listens without interruption; I notice his frown lines creasing as he ponders what I'm saying.

'So she took great delight in telling me you'd asked her out. That's not true, is it?'

He looks at the floor, avoiding eye contact.

'Oh my God, it is.'

'Not one of my better moves then? Shit if she's a psycho I can't afford to have anything to do with her.'

'Why did you do it anyway? Was it to get at me?'

'She seemed nice, a bit vulnerable. You know that's my type,' he half laughs. 'I admit it did cross my mind that it might wind you up, but I'd heard rumours from the schoolyard about us two and thought I'd head it off by making a play for Bettina.'

'This can't be doing your career any good.'

'Doesn't matter. I handed my notice in. I'm going abroad to teach for a while.' He looks at me, all wide eyes and honest desperation. I feel as if I'm seeing the true Seb, and not the ladykiller.

'I can't be around you and not have you Lauren. It'd be impossible for me to be Joe's teacher and have to see you every day. Meeting Niall at parents evenings, thinking all the while you're sat there about your amazing tits and the fact I want to fuck you over the desk.'

I sigh. 'What a mess I've caused. I'm sorry. You know if I wasn't with Niall-'

'Yeah, you said, but you are, and I feel a fresh start is just what I need. I'll cancel my date now anyway, if it helps.'

I take a sip of wine. 'That's what I wanted to ask you. It really will help, thank you.'

'I guess that's it then?'

I feel empty that he's going. It seems like we really had some chemistry and in another time and place we might have had something. 'Do you reckon we were together in a past life?'

'You say some weird shit you know.'

I laugh. 'So is Seb the ladykiller going abroad to devastate hearts all over the world, or are you actually going to be true to yourself and let some lucky lady see the nice guy you really are?'

'That will depend if I can meet another woman like you'. He winks. 'I suppose it may happen eventually, but until then, I shall be happy to be there for any unhappy lady that crosses my path.'

'You need to pick a happy lady, so she can make you happy.'

'Maybe. Anyway, as this is probably our last time alone together, let's have a toast to what might have been.'

'To what might have been,' we chink glasses.

Seb stands up, puts down his empty glass and starts to put on his shoes. I go and put the glasses in the kitchen sink ready to wash. I walk towards the window to draw the curtains. Seb walks up behind me.

'Can I have a goodbye kiss?'

It's my last chance. So, why not? He tips his head down and his lips touch mine. I can taste the wine. It starts as a sweet chaste kiss but though I want nothing more from Seb, I can't resist this final chance to touch him. I snake my arms around his neck and pull him towards me. Once again I've lost my control around him. The kiss lasts for minutes until finally we break apart, panting. 'Goodbye Seb.'

I turn to close the curtains, but really I'm turning away so he doesn't see that my eyes have filled with tears. I grip the curtains a little too tight as I pull them together.

'Bye Lauren. I hope you're wrong about Bettina, but be careful, won't you?'

'I will.'

I walk him to the door, and then as I turn to go back into the house, I see that my car has been keyed the whole way down the side. I go out to examine it and see there's a note behind the windscreen. 'Advantage me.'

Oh, it's like that is it? I've only had one glass of wine but it fuels my temper and I mutter 'Game on bitch.'

Driven by adrenaline, my hands won't stop shaking as I turn off the alarm I'd set for three thirty am and consider what I'm about to do; part two of my plan. I suck on my top lip, trying to get some saliva into my dry mouth. I push back the duvet revealing the black DKNY top and J. Crew trousers, chosen so I look hot if arrested. I imagined Monique's voice should I face the police dressed in Value jeans and so assembled an 'attractive assassin' combo. My armpits feel damp, and my heart races to the point that I can feel its thud within my neck, it reminds me of old movies when the monster moves slow before attack. I breathe deep, this is self-defence. I can barely tie the converse I slip on my feet, and for a moment I surrender. I lay down on the floor in child's pose, trying to regulate my breathing. It does no good. I must go now. I pull my wavy blonde hair back in a bun, grab my bag, slide on my D&G sunglasses and exit the house.

Behind the wheel of my faithful Nissan Micra, I drive to the bitch's estate and park around the corner, leaving the car obscured by a row of garages. I glance around checking for witnesses. Though I see no-one, I can hear the inebriated screams and laughs of people on their way back from clubs. I walk casually to her house, my posture

straight so should anyone see me they wouldn't
question my being there. As I arrive at the front
garden I appraise how immaculate it looks, planted
with symmetrical bedding in oranges and purples.
Box hedging as neat as a newly cut fringe ensures
my cover from the estate. She must either love
gardening herself or pay a fortune for someone to
keep it so pristine. As someone who has grown
vegetables from seed and tended to them like an
expectant mother, I hesitate before I put on the
rubber gloves. Can I really do this? Are things
really this bad? As I consider past events I feel my
jaw clench and my teeth grind. She deserves
everything she gets. I reach down, my fingers grip
the neck of the plants and I lift and smash them onto
the path where the soil parts from the roots and
spills out like spewed guts. I'm horrified to feel a
grin that I cannot stop form from my lips. I carry
on, full of energy, until the bedding plants are no
more and the piled up soil resembles a grave of the
newly buried. I move onto her dustbin, retrieve a
bag of food waste and push it through the letterbox
imagining the smell on her return, putrid and
decaying.

I open my bag, fixed together only with one stud,
extract weed killer and pour it over the meticulous
green lawn. I try and dribble it to spell out the word
bitch. Give it a few days and yellowing dead
patches will hopefully reveal my handiwork. I re-
check that no-one watches me and move around the
back of the house. I take a screwdriver from the
front pocket of the bag and use it to disable the

security light in order to prevent its on and off SOS. Pre-dawn light allows me to write WHORE in carefully disguised font across her white PVC door. For my finale, I empty fake vomit out of a plastic container, covering her patio furniture. I silently thank the person who posted the recipe on Pinterest. Back in the driving seat, I punch a fist in the air before I burst into tears. I turn down the visor and peer at my reflection, seeing the reasonably happily married woman turned revenge seeking missile. Ground down and exposed to my rawest state, if you looked closely you'd see every part of me, each individual cell, be able to look within the membrane to the protoplasm. See what's underneath ...

Back home I put my clothes in the washing machine and set them on a wash and dry programme. I put the weed killer and gloves back in the shed and wash out the fake vomit carton. Then I wash Seb's glass and put it back in the cupboard. I go to the computer where I bookmarked the page from Pinterest (I didn't pin it), delete it and clear my history. I'm too wired to sleep so I drink the rest of the bottle of wine and go upstairs to bed to read. At the top of the stairs I pause outside Joe's room. It's weird seeing his door open and his window with no blind down. I miss him already. Then the regret comes over me, what I've risked, how it could affect Joe. I begin to shake and feel sick. I just reach the toilet in time to bring up the wine I've consumed. I feel clammy and ill and cold, and imagine myself rotting in a police cell for causing criminal damage. I punch the toilet seat in disgust at myself. She's brought me to this level, so now I'm no better than her. I fold up a hand towel and place it on the bathroom floor, and that's where I wake a few hours later with my neck and back hurting like hell, and with a head that feels like someone has jumped up and down on it.

I groan and move to my bed. The alarm clock says seven fifty-two. I've got to set off to Niall's mothers in just over two hours. I open my bedside cabinet where I keep Calpol sachets for Joe. I swallow two of them like Joe's allowed. I'm too scared of liver damage to risk another and there's no way I'm going downstairs. I set the alarm for ten and pull the quilt firmly over my head. I ruminate over my actions and decide that she definitely deserved it, though I vow not to bother with her anymore personally, and just ring the police should anything else happen. I have a family to protect, especially Joe.

I finally drag myself out of bed at ten twenty-four and hit the shower in order to try and make myself feel more human. I take a couple of Ibuprofen on an empty stomach because I can't face food, get a breakfast bar out of the cupboard and a bottle of water out of the fridge for the car journey, and get on my way.

The drive to Brockton takes just short of two hours usually, but today I pull into a parking bay halfway and eat my breakfast.

On my way I periodically feel nauseous, but finally arrive at Niall's parents' village just before one. They live in a small village surrounded by farmers' fields and everywhere you turn there's a cow or a horse. I love this village. There's something about it that is so relaxing. Just down the road from Niall's parents' home is a small art studio that sells pottery. I like wandering down there, past all the pretty cottages with their gloriously tended gardens, admiring the beautiful flower beds and shrubbery.

I pull into Glen & Rebecca's gravelled driveway and slide my car in alongside Niall's courtesy car and Glen's BMW. They have a three bedroom bungalow with a bay window. There are overflowing red and yellow hanging baskets at either side of the door, with bees hungrily swarming around them. I leave my case in the car and ring the bell. I hear crockery clatter, and then Joe pulls open the door, with Niall coming up behind him.

'Muuum, you're here, hurry up you're missing lunch.'

'Well don't let yours get cold. Run back along and eat up.'

'You're late,' Niall says, 'but I suppose you'll have an excuse.'

I look up at him and I see him frown as he looks at my face, maybe he's noticed the blackness underneath my eyes and the white pallor of my face.

'Are you okay?

I shrug. 'Not really.'

'I gather it didn't go well with Bettina.'

'I have a lot to catch you up on,' I confirm.

Niall looks over my shoulder. 'What the *fuck* has happened to the car?' He goes running out to assess the damage down the side of the paintwork.

I stand alongside him and watch as he runs his hand along the groove. 'That's what we need to discuss. I think it was Bettina.'

'Lauren…'

'There's more to tell you before the car stuff, so don't give me any lectures about having no proof. Let me get inside and get some lunch and we'll talk this afternoon. Perhaps we could go for a walk around the village?'

Niall turns to me. 'This is getting serious Lauren. I think we need the police.'

'We've the rest of the weekend to figure out what to do.' I look back at the bungalow. 'I can't tell you how pleased I am to be here.' I realise that this is true. I've found Niall's mother quite stifling at times, but today her home is a refuge and the scent of summer hangs in the air, a slight breeze blows the scent of the flowers my way. I breathe it in. I'm now ravenous and head inside to get some lunch.

'I'm so sorry I'm late.' I greet Glen with a smile but Rebecca gets up and gives me both a hug and a peck on the cheek.

'We missed you last night. Are you feeling okay darling, you look awfully pale?'

'I've had a headache all morning. I've taken some tablets and I'm feeling a lot better. I'll be fine after this lunch I think.' I indicate the glorious spread of quiche, various salads including Waldorf and potato, jacket potatoes, nachos, salsa and large bowl

of chicken and bacon pasta, plus some garlic bread.
I sit beside my family and tuck in.

Afterwards we walk through to the garden. The
Lawler's have a stable door that leads out to the
patio through the kitchen. I love this door. For some
reason, even though we didn't have one, it reminds
me of childhood. I like the idea that you can open it
halfway and lean on it to chat to folks. Niall's
parents have a fat black cat called Tristan who must
be around eighteen now. He is laid out on the patio
looking like a comma, toasting his belly in the
sunshine. Tristan is so pampered that when I bring
him a tin of cat food he thinks that's a delicacy and
laps it up, finding his usual salmon to be completely
beneath him now. Later he'll come brushing around
my legs and wonder why the tin lady hasn't brought
his treat.

The patio consists of square grey flagstones that
extend from the outside of the kitchen door, all the
way to the end of the living room where there are
patio doors. We go to sit out on their furniture, a
green rectangular glass table with six canvas chairs.
Joe spots a new football lying on the tennis court
sized garden and he's off. Glen comes out of the
house carrying a glass jug containing what I guess
to be Pimms, judging by the fruit in the bottom. In
his early sixties, his dad is similarly built to Niall; a
tall, handsome man with wavy hair that has faded
from blonde to grey. He has the same crinkly eyes
when he laughs and I can tell by looking at him
what Niall will look like in twenty years' time. I'm

wondering if I can face a Pimms, when he pours and hands me one anyway.

'Kill or cure, Lauren. I reckon my Pimms Punch will put you straight.'

'Or on your back,' announces Rebecca coming out of the house with a tray of strawberry jellies, to which I know will have been added some rose wine as they're her 'house special.' Niall's mum is around the same height as me, five foot six, with short brown hair (topped up by the local hairdresser). She favours smart but casual, and is wearing some beige cotton trousers and a three-quarter sleeve silk top. Her reading-come-sunglasses are perched on top of her head.

We all take a seat around the table. I face out towards Joe so I can enjoy watching him run around the space, kicking his ball with abandon.

'Grandad, come and play.'

'That's my sit down finished already,' Glen says with obvious pleasure. He heads off to join Joe.

'Actually, I think I'll join them, looks like fun.' Niall is away too, and then there's just myself and his mum sitting at the table.

I lift my spoon and taste a bit of the strawberry jelly. It is refreshing and delicious, and I tell his mum this.

'Oh it takes no doing Lauren. It's one of those recipes that looks good and tastes nice, but only takes about five minutes of prep. I just can't be bothered with cooking these days.'

'Yes, well, make sure to pass me your mushroom soup recipe if you've stopped making it, because I can't live without that.'

Rebecca takes a sip of her Pimms, considering me over the top of the rim.

'So what's going on Lauren? Niall and Joe arrive without you and he says you're having trouble with some old school friend. Then you turn up today looking like, if you don't mind me saying so, hell.'

'It's complicated,' I reply. 'I wouldn't know where to start.'

'Well,' she leans over and puts her hand across mine. 'I won't pry but I want you to know that I'm here for you Lauren, if you need me. You've become the daughter I never had. I know you had a difficult childhood, and I just wanted to tell you that if you need a mature opinion or a chat, I'm always on the end of a phone.'

My eyes fill with tears. I've known Rebecca a long time now and she has always been motherly towards me, insisting on hugs and cheek kisses. I have always held her at a distance, being scared of letting a 'mother' figure into my life, for fear of being abandoned by another one. Now I look into her soft grey eyes and wonder why I've never let her in before. I need this person in my life right now. I put my other hand over hers, making a gesture of intimacy towards her that I never have before. Her hand initially jumps as I touch it but then she smiles at me. 'I'm scared,' I tell her, like it's bedtime and the monsters are hiding in my wardrobe.

I tell her all about Bettina, my history with her from school, how she's been hanging around Niall, the eBay business, the scraped car, the note, her telling Niall that Seb was flirting with me, Danny's warning.

'Oh Lauren. I really think you should phone the police.'

'That's what I want to talk to Niall about. He doesn't know about my business and the story behind the keyed car yet. I've been thinking the same myself. I thought I'd maybe look into if I can get an injunction or something. I'm just a bit nervous that I don't have any proof.'

'She's obviously been playing a very clever game. Well I know it's not going to help now, but when school breaks up you are more than welcome to come here for a week or two to have a break from everything.'

'I think we'd like that very much,' I say. I breathe in the fresh air. 'I love it here, it's so peaceful.'

'Not when the farmers plough the fields it's not, and getting stuck behind tractors on your way to the shops isn't a barrel of laughs.'

I raise my eyebrows at her.

She smiles. 'Okay, I admit it is lovely around here. We are very lucky. I do wish I could see my grandson more though. There's a hospital here, you know?'

I laugh. 'Very tactfully put. Look, I can't think of anything right now with what's going on, but I promise to consider it in the future okay?' I mean what I say.

She tops up my glass. 'Cheers to that.'

We spend another hour or so companionably chatting about this and that. She fills me in on village life, her local yoga class that I'd love, and the village festival they are putting on in the next week or so. It brings to mind the summer fair and for a moment, clouds threaten to challenge the sunshine for my soul.

'I've bought Joe a new Lego set, for after our evening meal,' says Rebecca. 'It should keep him busy for an hour or so, and then I'll help him run a bath. He loves our rolltop. There's a really pleasant walk around the village, and the Dog and Duck has a decent real ale selection. I think you and Niall would enjoy it tonight.'

'Thank you.' She's giving me the opportunity to catch Niall up with recent events on our own and I am extremely grateful to her for it. I feel my eyes threaten to spill over again, so I pick up the jelly glasses and carry them into the kitchen. I look out of the kitchen window, at Rebecca relaxed in her chair, looking out over the men and at them laughing and joking around. They're tormenting Joe with piggy in the middle and I wish I could stay here forever, wrapped warm and cosy like in an electric blanket. The other life, the hard life seems far away and surreal, and I wish I could toss it away like garbage and start anew here. I go to get my overnight case from the car and begin to spend time unpacking, feeling for the first time in a long time, as if I can relax.

CHAPTER SIXTEEN

After a dinner of thick vegetable soup with an array of different breads; followed by pork, stuffing and apple sauce sandwiches, Niall and I head out for a walk. It's still humid outside, the perfect temperature for a stroll and we meander around the village lanes, where quite often the pavement completely disappears and you have to keep a close watch for cars and cyclists. On the way to the pub we chat about how lovely the area is, and how spoilt Joe gets at his Grandma and Granddad's house. Inane stuff, as we are both aware we need a major chat and beer is required. The Dog and Duck is a small village pub, very spit and sawdust with brass plates on the walls and a landlord and landlady that have been there for years. Although we don't come here very often, Gary the Landlord, a robust, balding red cheeked man, who looks like he samples quite a few of his own wares, gives Niall's hand a firm shake as we approach the bar.

'Well you're definitely not the milkman's. I swear you're morphing into your dad, Niall, and you, Lauren, are looking as gorgeous as ever.' He lifts my hand and kisses it.

Thinking of the pasty and sallow face I arrived with, and doubting much has changed, I smile at the charmer. After how I felt this morning I can't believe I'm going to have yet more alcohol, but as I walked into the bar and smelled the real ale my mouth watered, so I ask for a half of Theakston's Old Peculiar, a drink I used to have long ago when Niall and I were first dating. We get ourselves a seat in a little nook that has a good window overlooking a little stream and flowered area. I take a sip of my drink, it's thick and treacly and I smack my lips after.

'Okay, well update time,' I tell him. I take a deep breath. 'Firstly, I know you won't be impressed with me, so I apologise right now for what I'm about to say, but things have been really difficult and I didn't want to get into it all yesterday with the car and going to your mothers.'

'Get on with it because I'm sure what I'm imagining is far worse than what you've done.'

'Right. Well, yesterday morning I went on my eBay account and it had been ruined with negative feedback from four different buyers, including two so-called business leads I'd had, so it would appear I've been set up.'

'Lauren, are you sure you haven't done something to upset someone, because this is getting disturbing.'

'Well, yes actually, I have. Bettina, but it was a long time ago, anyway, let me finish.'

He nods.

'So I contacted eBay, but I'm not sure what will happen with that. If they make me refund them I'll lose two hundred pounds.'

Niall huffs. 'That'll go nicely with the four hundred excess on the car.'

'Anyway, I went over to her house to ask her to stop it and leave us alone. She denied it all, as expected, and then when I said we should just avoid each other, she told me she had a date with Seb. You know, the same Seb she told you was mad about me? Well he's so obsessed with me he's asked Bettina out.'

'Are you joking?'

'Nope.'

He takes a gulp of beer. 'This is getting weirder. I'm starting to feel I'm on some wind-up TV programme.'

'Right, well anyway, last night I didn't go to see Bettina to sort things out. She said she was going away with Tyler, but with what happened after I'm not so sure I believe her. I phoned Seb, cos I had his number from the fair, and I told him about what she'd been saying. He was really shocked and said he didn't think he wanted to date her now. I said that was up to him and I hung up. I had a really bad headache so I went to bed early, and when I woke up the car had been keyed. I reckon she'd heard from Seb and did it.'

'I'm not very happy that you lied to stay at home and phoned that man.'

'I think we have more to worry about at the moment, Niall. What are we going to do?'

'I don't know.' I can see his tongue poking around the side of his cheek. 'Maybe we need to ring the police?'

'I wondered about an injunction.'

'I don't feel we've proof enough for that. I'll tell you what, for a start, I'll get a security camera fitted on the house. They're quite cheap now on the internet. If there's any more damage to the house we'll have surveillance footage.'

'That's a great idea.'

'Well hopefully that'll deter vandalism, and if she turns up at the house we'll have evidence for the courts to get an injunction, so I definitely think that's the place to start. You'll have to find some way of avoiding her in the schoolyard. There's only three weeks of term left so just get Joe to meet you at the bottom of the drive or something so you don't have to stand near her.'

I smile to myself at Niall's male solution planning in evidence.

'With eBay, I'd contact them and let them know what's happened, and that you seem to have been targeted maliciously. Hopefully with your meticulous feedback record they'll wipe the slate clean.'

'I hope so, I love my little business.'

'Now, without sounding like a jealous prick, no more talking to that Seb.'

I nod. 'Message received and understood. I shouldn't need to now anyway and by the way, he's leaving so he's not going to be around.'

'Leaving? Good. Well, I think that's all we can do for now, isn't it? I'll ring a garage on Monday and ask how much it is to get the keying covered on the car. I really don't want to put another claim in on the insurance or we'll lose our no claims bonus.'

'That's another expense then.'

'Yes, fate has decided we shouldn't have any money just now.'

'Fate or some spiteful cow.'

'Well she didn't blame me for reversing into her car, so we'll have to let her off that one.'

'Just that one.'

I let Niall have another pint and I have a still mineral water to help me hydrate. We consider sitting outside but the midges are hanging around the water and the moths around the lights, so we stay in the nook. We go back to normal conversation and it feels so nice here, to be away from everything and have this time alone with my husband. We need more of this sort of time, 'date nights', I've read it called in magazines. If we lived nearer to Niall's parents we'd have regular sitters.

'I've been thinking that I quite like it around here Niall. Would you consider moving out here with Joe?'

'Now where's that idea come from?' he says. 'You know I moved to the city to escape the quiet country upbringing I had. It can be a bit remote living in the sticks.'

'I think it's lovely, and it's away from the city fumes. It'd be so much better for Joe. Perhaps we could be nearer to Stafford town centre anyway. It doesn't have to be here, just near enough to see your parents more often.'

'I didn't have you pegged as a lover of my parents, Lauren, you normally try and avoid visiting them.'

'I know,' I giggle. 'I've realised today that I've resented your mum trying to be a mother to me. I felt like she couldn't bridge the gap of hurt I feel when parents get mentioned. What if I got close to her and something happened and she hated me? I couldn't go through that again.'

'My mother's not like that, Lauren. She's really maternal.'

'I guess she'd have to be with four of you.'

'I don't know, we were quite a handful. One thing I do know is that Mum took to you as soon as she saw you, the swan who thought she was an ugly duckling.'

'Yes, well today she made me feel like the swan, and I feel like I've made a breakthrough, that maybe I can feel loved by others, if I can trust them first.'

'You've no idea how happy that makes me feel to hear that. You can't let what your parents did to you torture you forever. You must be a good egg if I've stuck with you, being the golden child that I am.'

It's Niall's way of saying he loves me, and I grab hold of his hand. 'Shall we walk home now and snog on street corners and in doorways like teenagers?'

'Lead the way,' he says, downing the last of his pint.

We arrive home, Glen lets us in and we walk through to the living room, a spacious room painted beige with a traditional style brown leather suite and a brass fire with cream marble surround. I can't work out what's different and then it hits me. I look at Rebecca. 'Oh, I didn't bring flowers.' Usually these would have pride of place in the centre of the mantle shelf within five minutes of my arrival.

'Don't you be worrying about that Lauren; you've enough fetching and carrying after these two. I know they turned up without you last night, but I bet I know who packed.'

I grin as Niall pouts. 'I'd been working hard all day mum.'

'Of course, my darling boy, you provide for your family and that's an amazing thing.' She winks at me behind his back.

After a long game of Trivial Pursuit we head off to bed. I am by now absolutely shattered, and I'm aware that Niall is still in the en-suite as I feel myself drift off to sleep.

Morning starts with an array of breakfast cereals, sliced fresh bread, croissants and jam, and we are told in no uncertain terms by Rebecca that we are staying for Sunday lunch, and that she's bought an extra-large chicken and a gammon joint. I'm pleased to hear this as I'm in no rush to head back. After breakfast Niall, Joe and I go to our room to shower. Niall takes Joe in to supervise his, and I put my phone on to check for messages, having switched it off the night before. After a minute or so it starts beeping; I have seventeen message notifications. I open them in turn. They are all from an unknown number.

`'Enjoy what time you have left with your husband.'`

`'You are a selfish bitch.'`

`'It won't be long now.'`

`'Tick tock.'`

They go on, all warning in tone. I feel an icy chill up my spine and I tremble. I head to the bathroom. 'Niall, do you have a moment?'

He comes out of the bathroom drying his hands on a towel. 'What's up love? I'm just making sure Joe actually washes himself.'

I show him my phone.

'Right, that's it; as soon as we're home I'm ringing the police. They can come round tonight. If they can trace that phone we can find out who's behind it. In the meantime, turn it off.'

'I'll text Monique first cos I forgot to tell her we were going away.' I type a quick text that we're at Niall's mums and that I hope she's free for a coffee tomorrow as usual. I soon get a reply.

`'Of course, thought I'd got to report you as a missing person. Hope you're having good time. Usual place nine-thirty?'`

I type back yes and that I'm switching off my phone and will fill her in tomorrow. Then I turn it off and throw it to the bottom of my handbag as if it's made of dirt. I lie on the bed and await my shower, looking forward to the cleansing water and the feel of the heat warming my skin.

We set off back home around four with hugs from Rebecca and leftover food parcels for supper. Joe has a carrier bag full of toys he didn't arrive with. Rebecca reminds us that we are more than welcome to stay a week or two in the school holidays. It's been a glorious weekend. I drive down the country lanes with the windows open to catch the last of the country fresh air before the motorway clogs my lungs with fumes. Niall and Joe are in the courtesy car, which races me for a short while before disappearing off ahead.

I arrive at the house and I'm met with a stony faced Niall. 'I've phoned the police. Go upstairs and look, but don't touch anything.'

'Mum your bedroom's a right mess,' adds Joe.

I run up the stairs, enter my bedroom and see a scene of total carnage. What looks like my whole wardrobe is laying cut on the floor. Not cut to shreds, but cut enough to make it unwearable. My jewellery box is lying empty on the floor and all my trinkets, both valuable and vintage costume jewellery, are gone. The jewelled hooks I have on the side of the wardrobe to hang large necklaces on are also stripped bare. I lift up the duvet cover. Luckily my shoes and bags are hidden under the bed, saved by the king size duvet, they remain thankfully untouched. I think of my teacup pendant that I'd just bought and not had much time to wear yet, and I think of the sentimental pieces of jewellery I've had from Niall, including a diamond pendant he bought me when I had Joe. My wardrobe doors are open and there are only about ten items of clothing left hanging. Perhaps they got bored or ran out of time. I glance at my gold band, the only remaining piece of jewellery I have, and I'm thankful I never take it off.

I close the door on the scene, sit on the top step and cry. Angry tears pour down my cheeks, mixed with the total sorrow of things I can't replace. Niall joins me, sitting a few steps further down with Joe behind him.

'Dad says someone's broken in and been really mean to your stuff.'

'How did they get in?' I ask.

'They jimmied the kitchen window open, but they haven't touched anything else, only your stuff. I'm sorry, but your laptop's downstairs. It's been smashed.'

'Surely this proves there's a vendetta against me. It's got to be her.'

'Who mum?'

Niall frowns at me, clearly indicating I should shut up. 'Oh nobody you know, don't worry Joe. Someone's been a bit nasty with mum about her eBay business.'

Joe looks at me. 'I don't want to sleep on my own tonight.'

Niall folds his arms protectively around our son. 'No-one can harm you when we're with you. We'd kill them before we let anyone get you.'

'Can I sleep with you tonight though?'

I look at Niall, who nods, and I turn to Joe and stroke his cheek. 'We'll wait until we're allowed to clear up and then we'll put you in with us, just for tonight, okay?'

Joe's deer trapped in headlights look disappears. 'Thanks mum.'

It comes to me then. 'Niall, did the burglar alarm go off?'

'It was flashing when I got here. You know how it is though; no-one takes any notice any more.'

How come the autodialler didn't contact us? Oh damn ...' I think of my mobile phone lying switched off in my bag. 'It will have, but my phones not on.'

I turn on my phone and wait for it to load. There's a message. It's from the unknown number.

`Do you like your surprise? Everything you value is disappearing one by one, dignity, job. What next, husband?`

'Oh my God,' I squeal, but I'm drowned out by the sound of the doorbell. The police are here.

Niall takes Joe into the dining room so I can talk to the police about everything that's been happening. They ask for my telephone and look at the keying on the car and the mess in the bedroom, plus the broken laptop. They take notes of everything, and then PC Sheldon, a young slim guy with straight dark hair and a mole above his lip, indicates that I should take a seat in the living room. His colleague PC James goes to sit with Joe, allowing Niall to join us, and I hear him reassuring Joe that he's safe.

'Okay Mrs Lawler, so you believe that a Mrs Bettina Southwell has been committing these acts against you?'

'That's right. I'm hoping the phone tracing will prove that as I know I don't have any evidence.'

'We were called out earlier this afternoon to another property in Handsworth that was the scene of some criminal damage. It belonged to Mrs Southwell, and when asked who could have done it, she cited both her ex-husband and yourself.'

'More like she did it herself before or after she came here to make herself look innocent.'

Niall leaps to my defence. 'We've been away all weekend, so how does she reckon Lauren did that?'

'Yes, well Mrs Southwell also says that she has been away all weekend. We need to do some more investigating. I will be back to visit Mrs Southwell regarding this break in, but I have to say, from where I'm standing this looks very much like a dispute between you two ladies. You had a witnessed argument in the schoolyard, and on Friday afternoon, visited Mrs Southwell at her property and threatened her.'

I open my mouth to protest. 'I did no such thing. I went to ask her to leave us alone.'

'You can see the difficult position we are in, Mrs Lawler?'

'I can see that psychotic idiots are allowed to get away with anything. What's she got to do before you do anything to her? Murder me? What about her latest text where she's threatening my husband?'

Niall looks shocked. 'What text?'

'It came at the same time as the police arrived.' I ask the policeman to hand me the phone back and show Niall.

'Does this mean split us up, or is it a death threat? I don't think we should stay here tonight Lauren. We'll get a cheap hotel.'

'There's no need to overreact, Mr Lawler. I'll get someone to sit outside on surveillance tonight. Tomorrow you should fit the security camera your wife was telling me about. Hopefully we'll have more news for you by then.'

'I'll feel better if someone can stay outside for the night,' I say.

'I'll stay until ten, and then a colleague will be taking over my shift until six.'

'I'll be up by then to get things ready for school, so that's great. Thank you.'

PC Sheldon stands up and opens the door to his colleague, indicating that it's time to leave.

'Right, we'll leave you to it. We've got everything we need so feel free to tidy things up now, though you might want to take your own photos and keep items for the insurance company.'

'Yes, we will do. I'm going to have to take tomorrow off work now to deal with the car insurance, house insurance and key damage to the other car. This is just unbelievable,' says Niall.

'I'm sorry I can't do more. Please don't visit Mrs Southwell while we investigate.'

'But what about collecting my son from school?'

'I'll get the community bobby to stand with you. They often attend your school anyway. Goodnight to you both, and you Joe.'

'Niall brings our double mattress down into the lounge and I throw a duvet on the sofa for Joe. Niall makes Joe a hot chocolate whilst I go upstairs and clear up my stuff the best I can. I strip off the beds and change the bedding as the room feels defiled, and I open the windows for a while, as if I can let the bad out into the night. I sweep and mop the floor and dry it. I'm out of breath with the flurry of evening activity. I drag the black sacks of ruined clothing and dump them on the bed in the spare room. I'm desperate to talk to Niall and can see the frustration in his face; we can't speak freely in front of Joe.

At ten we're all back in the living room, waiting for Joe to fall asleep. After chatting excitedly for a few minutes, with the novelty of us all being in one room, we tell him he needs to settle. We wait. Our eyes accustom to the dark and we see him begin to twitch. We know he's dropped off enough to not be disturbed by our low murmurs.

'I hope the police find something from the phone.'

'What if they don't, Lauren? They're affecting Joe with all this now. He was scared to death tonight. What if I go and see Bettina's mother?'

'No. If we need to contact someone I'll find a way to get in touch with Danny. He can ring her doctor and get her admitted. He's the money to sort it.'

'Well we've got to do something. I can't just sit and take all this.'

I run my hand down his clenched jaw, stroking his face and trying to free it of tension. 'We'll sort it, somehow, we're strong.'

I turn around and curl up into his body. He spoons protectively around me and if I open my eyes I can see Joe. 'We'll be alright. We're a team.'

I was nervous about taking Joe to school with Tyler being there, but I saw Bettina's mother dropping him off. She smiled as she passed us in the car, so was maybe unaware of what was going on between us. I was pleased to drive away from the school and stuck an old Sugababes CD in the player and turned it up loud, singing along to 'Hole in the Head' as loud as I could. When it finished I'd enjoyed singing along so much I pressed repeat. I had a few strange looks from drivers and passengers in other cars, but just smiled and carried on singing. Maybe I was verging on hysteria by then? Who knows?

I pull into Endcliffe Park's car park near the coffee shop and find Monique already there. She gestures to the waitress and then gives me a hug, 'I've already ordered, so it shouldn't be long now.'

'Thanks, I'm so ready for it.'

'So how was your weekend away?'

'Loved it. Just what I needed, time away from the psycho, except when I got back the house had been broken into, my clothes were shredded and all the jewellery's gone. We had to phone the police.'

Monique's mouth drops open. 'What? Lo, oh my, that is sick, what did the police say?'

'Looking at evidence, going to talk to her, will let us know. Anyway, if it's okay with you can we talk about other things? I'm so fed up of thinking about it all.'

'No problem. Let's get this coffee quick, and then do you need to look for some new clothes?'

'I was going to suggest we did that. I don't have a lot left to wear.'

We wander around the shops and I find a couple of pairs of trousers and some tee shirts. They aren't my Levis or j brands though, and I hope the insurance doesn't take long to sort out. I know my attachment to clothes is a little pathetic, but it's something to depend on. I feel naked without my nice things.

'How are things with Dr Love?' I ask.

'Oh, we're pretty much done there, I think.' Monique carries on looking through the racks and holds up a silk khaki top. 'That'll suit you, try it on.'

'Never worn that colour in my life. Won't that cling round my bust? How come this one's on his way out?'

'Try it on, and then moan if it doesn't look nice, which you know it will, cos I am a stylista extraordinaire. He's started to bore me, and after the whole miscarriage thing, I've not been that interested in nookie, so his attention has waned somewhat. Anyway, I'm more than happy right now with my own company, and that of my fairy godfriend, Lo Lawler.'

'Why thank you,' I wave an imaginary wand. 'You shall be rewarded with further coffee and a sprinkled donut from the new cake shop and cafe across the street.'

'Lo! Cheating on your favourite coffee shop?' Monique pretends to swoon, placing her hand across her brow.

I pout. 'I'm just testing it out to see if the competition's any good.'

'Is that what you were doing with Seb?'

'Ha ha, you're funny you, aren't ya?'

She rifles through some belts. 'What's happening with the eBay stuff?'

'I've not heard anything yet. I have to use Niall's laptop now. I've lost so much stuff.'

'Are there any summer fetes coming up you could do?'

'I don't have any more booked. Anyway, I've lost my mojo with it at the moment. Until things are settled I'm forgetting about the business.'

Monique sighs. 'She's messed you up good and proper hasn't she?'

'She's done exactly what she set out to do. Hopefully the police are on the case and she'll stop now.'

'I hope so Lo, cos if she does the same to your shoes and bags, I'm going to have a breakdown looking at the state of your clothes.'

'It's not my fault she only left me with my George specials. Anyway, at least they're comfy.'

'Please, stop, I'm only jesting. If only you were my size, I could lend you some of my things. I feel so helpless.'

'You help just by being around Mon,' I say. 'Now come on. Donuts and sprinkles.' I wave my imaginary wand again.

The community policewoman, PC Smith, is a young enthusiastic brunette with her hair tied back in a ponytail. She meets me at the bottom of the drive. She is on a bicycle, 'Easier for getting around.'

She accompanies me to the Portakabin. All the other parents and carers try to look as if they aren't staring, even though they couldn't be more obvious if they tried. Once again its Bettina's mother who is there to pick up Tyler, so I needn't have worried. 'We'll be fine now,' I tell PC Smith and she cycles away.

Joe comes out of school. 'Mum. Mrs Sullivan wants to see you.'

I bet Joe's mentioned something about the break in. We walk around to the school entrance and I press the buzzer. I walk in and report to the receptionist. She asks me to take a seat in the waiting room. There's a box of baby toys in the corner that Joe starts playing with, despite the fact that they are years too young for him.

Mrs Sullivan appears from her office, dressed today in a black power suit with a white and black spotty blouse that reminds me of spilled ink. 'Joe, are you okay to wait there? Mrs Tweedy will keep an eye on you.' She beckons me into her office, a small room fitted with a glass partition that overlooks the school office and path to the dining room and classrooms. It's fitted with a blind for privacy. She closes it and the door.

'Mrs Lawler, please take a seat.'

I sit myself down on the blue fabric covered chair facing her as she takes a seat behind her desk. I feel like a pupil in trouble with the headmistress.

'I have a couple of issues to talk to you about, the first I'm afraid, is that a complaint has been made about you.'

I sink into the seat. 'What sort of complaint?'

'I've received an anonymous letter that states that you have been having an affair with Mr Kingsley, and that some of it took place within the school building. As it's anonymous, I am not going to go down any official route, but I need to know if it's true?'

I sit up straight. 'I would never cheat on my husband. And the only time I've spent with Mr Kingsley has been at the fair.'

'That's what he said, so your stories corroborate. What I'd like to know is why you think someone would send such a letter.'

I feel I have no choice but to fill her in with all the things that have been happening.

'That must have put you and your husband under a terrible strain, but also brings me to the other thing I wished to talk to you about. I understand you and Mrs Southwell put on quite an exhibition last week.'

My face goes red. 'I must apologise for that.'

'Just…no repeats of it, please. I trust that your problems are now being handled by the police. I must ask you to act courteous and adult in the school grounds. You set an example to the children here; we cannot have parents fighting in the yard. If there are any further problems between you then you must come to me, and I'll see what I can do. As there's less than three weeks of the school left, I'm hoping we can manage until then?'

'I'm sure it'll be fine,' I say, 'thank you.'

I'm about to walk out of the door when I turn to her. 'Seb Kingsley seems like a really nice guy. He deserves a good reference.'

She smiles a slow smile. 'Thank you for that, it's nice to hear, although I'm well aware of Mr Kingsley's strengths and weaknesses.'

'Sorry, I didn't mean to tell you how to do your job.'

'Oh, it's not that,' she says. 'Seb is my son.'

CHAPTER SEVENTEEN

'Seb is what?' I walk back into the room and stand with my back to the door.

'My son has spent much of his adult life wandering around the world, not quite knowing what to do with himself. He trained to be a teacher and it's suited him, being able to move around, but with a vocation. I asked him to come here because he'd had a bad time of things lately and needed to get back on his feet. We agreed not to tell people that he was my son. I felt it would cause embarrassment for him, so please don't say anything.'

'I won't mention it.'

She sighs in obvious relief. 'I know he's not a bad lad, but he does try and get by more on his charm than his intellect. I was hoping he'd leave that side of his personality aside working with me, but alas, it seems not.'

'I think you'd be surprised. I got to know him a bit at the fair and I'd like to think I saw some of the real Seb, kind hearted and quite vulnerable. Yes, he could do with losing the ladies man patter, but I reckon in a couple more years he'll settle down. I do believe he wants that, eventually.'

'Well, time will tell I suppose. Anyway, I won't keep you any longer, Lauren, you have your own lovely family to get back to.'

'Yes I do,' I smile. 'There's a lot of stress going on for us at the moment but at least we're in it together.' I walk over and shake her hand. 'Thanks, Mrs Sullivan, and I promise to keep things away from the schoolyard.'

'Appreciated.'

I collect Joe from the waiting room, thank Mrs Tweedy and we head home. Pleased to be back through the door, I kick my shoes off in the hallway and sag down onto the stairs as Joe goes running through to greet his dad. I hear a female voice and wonder if it's the policewoman, so I put my slippers on and head into the room.

I am greeted with the sight of Bettina on the settee, looking pale, red eyed and dishevelled with a tissue in her hand. I look at her and she flinches.

I turn to my husband. 'What is she doing here, Niall?'

'I think you'd better sit down, Lauren, Bettina's had quite a lot to tell me. Joe, Tyler's in the dining room on the Xbox.'

'Wow cool, can he stay for tea?'

'Probably not son, just go and play for now.'

'Aww, please?'

'Joe...'

'Oh okay,' he goes off to find his friend.

We're left all together. I want to grab Bettina off the settee and throw her out of the house, but the silence is pregnant with some untold tale, so I place myself on the floor with my head resting near to the bay window and wait for her to say whatever it is she needs to say. 'Right, what's going on?'

Niall is the first to speak. 'Bettina has a cast iron alibi for not breaking into the house over the weekend. She was with Tyler in Leeds.'

I look at Bettina. She is struggling to catch her breath between quiet sobs. 'So you have absolute proof you didn't trash my room?'

Niall answers for her. 'Yes, she has proof. She had to deal with some issues with Danny. She's come to tell us today, as it's about to break in the press. Danny is in police custody, on suspicion of manslaughter.'

I hug my knees with my arms so I'm tightly curled up, grateful that I'm already sitting on the floor. *Danny? Manslaughter?* I know he had a reputation for being a hard case, but manslaughter? I feel my stomach flutter, if Bettina was away this weekend then who damaged my car? Who broke into our house? I start laughing, I have no idea why.

'Oh my God, what is happening?' I rock slightly backwards and forwards. There's silence for a moment, then I bite my lip and turn my head towards Niall. 'How do we know she didn't pay someone else to do it? She's not without money.'

'Lauren, please?' Her voice cracks as she turns to me. 'I've come here because I'm desperate, I can't take any more. Just hear me out and then I'll be gone.'

'Just give her a chance, Lauren love, okay?'

I nod.

Niall disappears into the kitchen and returns with three glasses and some sherry. 'Medicinal.'

I turn to Bettina. 'Let's hear it then.'

She takes a deep breath. 'Niall's told me about all the trouble you've been having. I honestly had no idea. I'm not the one behind it, but if you want to believe that I am, please yourself, because the police know it's the truth. Anyway, I wanted to come and clear things up for Tyler's sake.' She takes a drink of her sherry. 'I told you Danny had a nasty side, and he's got an extremely volatile temper, for God's sake he stabbed himself in the hand. Tyler was brought up in that household, he heard our arguments and he's spent the past couple of years thinking he has to look after me. I don't want that. I'm the mother,' she trembles. 'It's my job to protect him. That's why I didn't want Danny having any custody of Tyler, and why I was so scared when I thought he'd taken him from school. I've been trying to get his access stopped.'

'So what happened?'

'He was arrested Friday lunchtime for punching someone in his local bar. The man hit his head and died on route to hospital. I'm torn between feeling sorry for that man's family, and being grateful it wasn't me or Tyler,' she wipes her eyes with the tissue, then sits up straight.

'When you came to the door on Friday afternoon, I was just getting everything ready to head to Leeds. The police wanted me to come and talk to them, and I thought I might be able to get the rest of our stuff from the house, clothes and Tyler's toys. Danny didn't let me have anything when I left. I thought he may have thrown our stuff out, but no, it was there to taunt me, or maybe it was there in case I was stupid enough to go back.'

I rub my forehead. I can feel a headache coming on. 'I'm sorry. I believed Danny. What he said seemed plausible at the time.'

'Niall said Danny told you that I came here for you. I moved to be near my mum, so me and Danny had some stability, some security. I'm not lying, Lauren. I do have issues from school. What happened there affected my life. You were a potential positive in my moving here. I'd mentioned you to my doctor and she'd said if I could come back and make amends it would help deal with some of my childhood issues.' She snorts. 'Well that went well. I'll be able to keep her employed for years after this.'

'Bettina, I wasn't to blame for you leaving school. You got me into trouble.'

'I don't have the energy to go there now, Lauren. To be honest I'm starting to believe with what's happening now, that a schoolgirl spat wasn't much in the scheme of things.'

I look at the floor and pick at some flaking nail polish on my toe. There's more silence for a while as she worries at her tissue and I find my feet more and more interesting.

Niall breaks it. 'What've you got to do now then Bettina? What did the police say?'

'I'm free to do what I please. He's my ex-husband. I've no ties to him anymore beyond the large one,' she looks towards the dining room door. 'I'm going to give up my rental. I've got a while left on the lease but I'm going to look for something larger to share with mum. I'd feel better with someone else in the house. My mother can't wait.' She turns to me. 'You need to know I'm not moving Tyler from school again, he's settling in nicely. If you don't like me here, then move yourself. Anyway,' she bristles, 'why were you so damn sure it was me causing all this grief? I told you it wasn't.'

'It started the same time you moved here. Monique told me you were asking lots of questions about me and then Danny turned up and said you were crazy and out to get me. Things kept happening and it all just seemed to point at you.'

'Well as for the eBay stuff, you should know that I don't even have an account. I've never been on eBay in my life. I wouldn't have a clue how to order anything, never mind do it under several aliases.'

I start to cough, despite the sherry, my throat is really dry.

'Do you want a coffee?' Niall asks. I nod. 'Bettina?'

'Yes, alright.'

'I'll check on the kids and fix them a quick sandwich, if that's okay with you, Bettina?'

She nods. 'Thank you.'

Niall leaves and I feel the draft from the door sweep over me. From down here I can see dust gathered under Bettina's chair and decide I need to do some housework. My carefully ordered life has broken like a smashed meringue over the last few weeks.

'Seb called me on Saturday,' she says.

I try a naive look but it obviously fails.

'Please. Save it. I know full well that you've been in touch with him. I could tell by the way he suddenly ran a mile. Why I thought he was genuinely interested in me, I don't know, really, bearing in mind he practically tripped over his own tongue every time you walked past him.'

Something else dawns on me. 'So you didn't report us to the school saying we were having an affair?'

'Of course not. Look Lauren, I'd normally hate to sound this rude, but right now I really don't give a fuck. You can do what the hell you want with your life, screw Seb, stay with Niall, switch to battery powered. I couldn't give a toss. Your life is of no interest to me beyond Tyler's friendship with Joe. Other than things that connect the kids, I don't want to speak to you, or be involved with you in any way. I just need to keep Tyler's life in order. I don't need any more of your grief or your temper tantrums, or for that matter your selfishness. I'm sorry someone seems to be targeting you at the moment, Lauren, I really am. It must be very scary, not least for where Joe is concerned. I know, because I've been there with Tyler and I'm not trying to top you here, but have you no idea how good you've had it? Moaning about Niall. He's one of the best blokes I've ever met, no-one's perfect. You don't have to work, you can just swan round shops all day going for coffees with your best mate? Then you have an extremely well behaved son, a gorgeous home with two cars and yet you feel the need to practically dry hump the schoolteacher? Grow up and don't get a life, enjoy the one you have.'

She stands up, as Niall heads back through the doorway. 'Sorry Niall, forget the coffee. I'll be off in a minute,' he looks between us, at Bettina's now angry face and my downcast one. If I slide any further down the wall I'll become some of that trapped dirt and dust.

'There's just one last thing I wanted to bring up before I go, and it's the last time I intend to speak of it,' she says. 'The damage that was done to my own house over the weekend... I know it wasn't Danny because he was in the cells, so that really only leaves me with one suspect,' she glares at me. 'What you did makes me sick to my stomach. I hadn't realised you hated me that much Lauren. I realise some of why you felt you needed to do it, but I thought you were better than that.'

'Lauren?' Niall looks at me and then at Bettina. 'What exactly was the damage at your house Bettina?' I listen as she tells him and I watch his face drop. I feel like I'm watching a car with a puncture, where the tyre was filled with love and trust and then it deflates and bleeds until there's nothing much left. How is he going to trust me now?

'Is this true Lauren?' he turns back to me, searching my face for the one glimmer that'll reassure him that it's not me, that its entirely stupid to suppose I could ever do that. I can't meet his eyes. I look away.

'I've lost my bond money and have to pay to fix the damage to the lawn.'

'I'll make sure you're reimbursed, Bettina, as soon as I can,' says Niall. 'Though God knows where the money's going to come from with everything else we've lost or had to pay for lately.'

She goes to get Tyler from the dining room. 'Thanks for his sandwich,' she says and heads out of the door with him.

Niall turns to me.

'I'm not sure I know who you are right now,' he says. 'I think its best you go to your room.'

And like that I'm dismissed like a child, sent to bed for bad behaviour, though my own has been far worse.

As I walk into our bedroom I realise that I can't sleep here. I can't face Niall again when he comes to bed. This room has always been my refuge, but I feel I'll blight it with darkness if I lay my head here. I grab my pyjamas and head off into the spare room. My spare room has always been my workspace, with a bed under the window and the rest of the room taken over by an enormous corner desk where I keep my laptop, printer and boxes of craft supplies from previous creative endeavours. I have shelves covered in craft, art and cookbooks, a pile of notebooks which I collect just because they are pretty, and two square Perspex boxes on the desk, which are usually full of the vintage trinkets for sale on eBay; they're now are as empty as I feel. I pull down the blind to plunge the room into darkness and switch on the small light. I look at my pyjamas. They are far too cheery looking - blue and red tartan bottoms and a grey top with the appliqué 'I've been good all year' - what a joke. I go back into my room, take out a pair of black pyjamas and slip those on. It feels right. I pick up a glass candle holder, wash it in the bathroom and then pour myself a whisky, emptying the bottle. Oh look the spirits all gone I think, just like mine.

CHAPTER EIGHTEEN

Trying to sleep is a waste of time. I stare around the room in the dark trying to make out shapes as my eyes become more accustomed to the lack of light. Thoughts whirl around my mind. Bettina maintains her innocence and it seems to point that way, but is it coincidence that she delivered another blow by telling Niall about the damage to her property? If it's not her than who the hell have I offended? Or is it Niall who has an enemy? Maybe some patient of his has a grudge; he did get crashed into in the car park? I warm to the idea that it has something to do with Niall. But then how would they know so much about me? Has someone been spying on us? I think back to Bettina. If she is innocent, then all along she's just been an anxious mother trying to get settled near her mum and start over. If so, look what I have done, screaming at her in the schoolyard and destroying her property.

I put the light back on wincing at the brightness. I need something to do. I grab my nail polish tub from my shelf. I get out the black and paint my nails to match my mood and pyjamas. If I could make myself disappear I would. My thoughts won't leave me alone. I feel like I'm going crazy. I want to take a holiday from my own head.

In the morning Niall remains in bed. He should have been on an early shift so I assume he's taking a further day off. I get Joe ready for school, just having to call into the bedroom once to grab some clothes. I choose black again, easily identifiable by its darkness in my still colour co-ordinated wardrobe, though there's not a lot to choose from anyway. I sweep my unwashed hair back into a ponytail. A glance in the bathroom mirror shows the truth of the last few days in my face, every agony is mapped out in frown lines and misery.

I walk Joe right up to the school gates this dark and drizzly morning. I'm scared in case someone is following us. I need to make sure he is safely delivered inside. I tell him I just wanted the fresh air by way of an excuse, and he takes this on board in the innocent way children do. It worries me. I feel reassured by the new password system which ensures no stranger can take my child out of school. When Joe's inside I walk back down the driveway, folding my Mac around myself so no-one recognises me. I'm behind three of the other mothers and hear them talking.

'Thought there must have been something going on when they had that fight outside.'

'Fighting over a teacher they reckon. I've never taken to her, seems like she thinks she's better than everyone, swanning about in that vintage shit. Her poor husband and little Joe, he's so sweet.'

'Well just shows you don't know what's happening behind closed doors. Who'd have thought it of Lauren, I thought she was a good one....'

I recognise Tanya's voice coming out from under an umbrella. I turn left and shortcut through the nursery school. We're not supposed to go this way unless we have nursery kids, but I need to escape the narrow minds and prying eyes.

The window is open when I get home, which indicates that Niall is up and about. Honestly it's like living in a fridge when he's around. It's quite cold, yet he has all the windows and the back door open. I usually hate it because once I'm cold it takes hours for me to warm up. Today it will make no difference; I'm numb on the inside anyway. I walk into the room and see Niall fixing his breakfast.

'Joe went off fine.'

'Why wouldn't he?' Niall says, his expression pinched.

'I'm just telling you. How long are you going to be like this? Can't I try and explain?'

'When I'm ready, Lauren. I've enough on my mind sorting out all the insurance and other finances, so don't pressure me right now.'

At no time during this conversation does he ever look up at me.

He points back into the living room. 'Your phone's on the side. The police just dropped it off, said there's nothing further they can do. No evidence of anything. The phone used was a pre-paid, they obviously knew what they were doing.' He goes back to buttering toast and I go into the room and pick up my phone.

I can't face putting it on. I'll sort out a new one today with a new number. I get Niall's laptop and look at my emails. I see one from eBay customer services and click on it.

"Thank you for your email regarding the negative feedback on your account. Whilst we investigate the matter we have set up a temporary limit on your account of three items per week. This will be in place for the next three months whilst we monitor your account for suspicious activity. Please be aware that this limit is provided for your safety and security online."

Three items a week for three months? My business is over. Not that I think I'd have the confidence to sell much again after this. I've lost almost everything. The person texting was right, my dignity is shredded, my personal life is a shambles, my business is over and the cars need insurance work. The only things I have left are Joe and Monique, and hopefully in time Niall will come around. The doorbell rings and I rise to answer it.

'Delivery for Mrs Lauren Lawler.'

I look at the black chrysanthemum wreath being delivered to my door by the local florist.

'There must be some mistake.'

'Are you Lauren Lawler?'

'Yes, but ...'

'Then it's for you.' He taps his pen on his clipboard. 'Are you going to sign for it, or shall I take it back?'

I sign for it and take it back in the house to look at the card. I remove it slowly from the envelope, nervous that it's going to contain poison or something. There's just a plain card and on it is written 'deepest sympathies on the loss of your best friend'. My heart lurches and I feel I need to rush to Monique to warn her, but I remember she's at work. I rush to Niall and show him instead.

'Leave it on the window ledge, I'll show it to the police later. Maybe they can trace who made the order.' He heads through the house towards the hallway. 'I'm going for a drive, Lauren. I need to clear my head.'

He leaves me standing there.

I hear him removing just delivered post from the letterbox and opening an envelope. I go through to see if there's anything for me. Niall has gone deathly white, as if he's in great pain. I'm worried for his health.

'Niall, are you okay? Does your chest hurt?'

He thrusts a photograph at me. It shows myself and Seb on Friday evening. Though our kiss was captured through the living room window, it's perfectly clear what we were doing. I open my mouth to explain but before I can utter a word, Niall beats me to it.

'I will collect Joe from school tonight. Right now, I don't want to see your face or hear any more of your lies. Get the fuck out of this house,' he spits. 'Be gone before I get back or I swear to God I will throw you out myself.' He slams the door and is gone.

I collapse to the floor, all my strength is gone. I am no longer real, just a speck where there once was life.

I don't know how long I lay there for – catatonic – before I feel like I'm looking down on myself and seeing the pathetic wreck that is laid there. I'm transported back to my childhood, when my father could make me feel this way by the sound of his shouting voice, or the crack of his hand; or by my mother's endless words about my uselessness. I sit up in shock. I will *not* go there again. I am Lauren *Lawler* now. I have left my previous persona behind.

I get up and pace around the living room. What shall I do? I realise I want my friend. I want to tell Monique everything; she'll know what to do. I know she'll let me stay over, that will give Niall time to calm down. I go and pack a bag of things I need and then drag out an empty suitcase from the garage. Monique won't be back until around half five. I decide not to ring but to surprise her instead. We can have a fun girly evening and right now I decide I'll go around the charity shops again to try and replace more of my wardrobe. I can also get a new phone. It's a positive thing to do and the thought of it propels me into action. I drag myself into the shower and put on some clean clothes. Before I head out of the door, I write Niall a note telling him where I'll be and that I'll text him my new number. I check that my address book with everyone's telephone numbers is in my bag, and catch sight of my black nails, now the only reminder of my previous mood.

After getting a new phone, I go around the charity shops. It's a perfect shopping day and there seems to be lots of lovely items in my size. I get some Per Una jeans, a Diesel shirt, and several pairs of casual trousers. I buy so much I have to go back to the car mid-trip to drop it off so I can start again. I open the suitcase and place the new items inside, then zip it up.

Before round two I decide to hit my favourite cafe for a cup of life juice aka coffee. My favourite sofa is available and I feel buoyed that the shopping has gone so well. I feel it a sign that my brown couch is free to comfort me. I look at my new phone. It needs charging before I can put the numbers in, so I'll have to do that at Monique's. I sit back and look around. There's a new piece of art on the wall, a kind of tribal mask, carved out of wood. It has a sign under it 'protector of the innocent' and a price tag of a hundred and twenty pounds. It's by a local artist. Is it total coincidence that not only do I love it, but that it appears meant for me? We can't really afford it, but I reason the insurance will come through at some point, my jewellery was worth a decent amount of money. I flag down the waitress and buy it. I head back to the car a second time and place it in the boot.

I spend the rest of the afternoon in the shops buying more items, getting a thrill out of each purchase. I add shoes and bags to the pile. I don't need them but each one gives me happiness. At five I decide to head to the local pizza restaurant to pick up a takeaway for myself and Monique. While I am waiting I watch a family of four eating their meals. They are all so happy, and this is communicated without words. A wipe of one son's mouth; a mother pouring some of her coke into the other son's glass. She and her husband looking at the kids subconsciously and smiling at each other. Their happiness shines out of them like the winter sun, and just like that, it hurts my eyes. I look down at my bags and realise that apart from the things I need, the rest of it won't make me happy. Once again I'm protecting myself with materialistic things that will only provide happiness for brief moments. It can't compare to the love I have for my family. I feel I've made the right decision to stay at Monique's tonight, and then tomorrow I'll go home and stand in Niall's way and protest until he listens. I will fight for my family, they are my life. I take the pizza and go and get the car, putting the purchases in the boot and the pizza on the seat at the side of me.

I pull up to Monique's and press the buzzer. She comes through on the intercom. 'Yeah?'

'It's me. I need a place to stay tonight. I brought pizza.'

There's a moment of silence and she buzzes me through. I walk to her door and I'm surprised to see a guy there. He's tall and good looking, with dark, mussed hair and a flush to his cheeks.

'Oh my God, I'm so sorry, I never thought you might have company.' I cover my mouth with my hands. Once again I've assumed that everyone is there to look after me. 'Sorry, I'll leave and call you later.'

'Matty's just going. Don't worry about it.'

I hold up the box. 'Sure you don't want to share pizza?'

'No I'm okay,' he says, and winks at Monique. 'I've had my fill.'

She rolls her eyes at him and I feel my own face flush. I'm guessing this is Dr Love and look at his ID card hanging from his waistband. He sees me and quickly whips it off. 'Gosh, I'll be losing that if I'm not careful. She didn't give me chance to organise myself, that insatiable friend of yours.' He bounds off saying he'll catch us later and I step into the apartment.

'Well, you were right. He is damn hot,' I say, and place the pizza box on the side in the kitchen. I decide I'll not share my woes with Mon and will enjoy a girly night instead. For once I'm not going to be selfish. I've already maybe spoilt her planned evening.

'He is all that, which is why even though I'd ditched him, he's found his way back into my bed.' She grins. 'Anyway, to what do I owe this honour?'

'You've been a great friend and I want to spoil you. I've bought a couple of DVDs this afternoon,' I get them out of my bag. 'Pick one and we'll have a cinema night.'

She looks at me like she wants to ask me something, but chews on her lip and walks into the kitchen instead to get plates. No eating straight from the box for Monique.

We have a great evening and I feel able to distance myself from what is happening at home. In my mind I'm on a mini-break, with no focus other than Monique, fashion and fun.

After the film ends Monique stands up. 'I'll go and fix up the spare room quickly. I wasn't expecting you.'

'Sorry, I really should have called.'

'Well I would appreciate a call in future, but I forgive you this time. It's been a great night.'

I watch some trash on the TV. I hear Monique banging around putting stuff away and dragging out the sofa bed. She returns. 'It's ready when you are, but leave your clothes and stuff you don't need out here as all the drawers are full. You'll be fine if you stick to the area around the bed, but I don't want you tripping up.'

'No problems, I'll be careful.'

We settle down to watch Big Brother as I haven't seen it for a few days. At eleven I decide to turn in, I don't want to keep Monique up as she's back at work in the morning. I want to get back to see Niall as soon as I can.

I go into her spare room. It's covered in clothes; they are draped all over the surfaces. She's much worse than I am at buying clothes, shoes and bags. I remember I need to charge my new phone, creep back into the living room and get it. I can hear Monique brushing her teeth. I return to my room and look for a suitable socket. As I place the phone on the dressing table I see one of her jewellery holders, one of those that are shaped like a lady's body and a teacup necklace catches my eye. It's just like mine. I feel another pang at its loss. I sit back on the bed thinking about the coincidence. We share the same tastes and have often bought the same thing. I wonder if Monique would let me buy it off her.

I settle under the duvet and think about how embarrassed I felt when I first turned up. A few minutes earlier and I would have interrupted her and Matty 'at it'. I really must learn to think of others more. Another resolution going forward. I know it's early days and he's a lot younger than Mon, but there was a great spark between them, and I hope he'll be able to break through her barriers. Finally, Dr Love has a name, Dr Matty Bailey. I frown, the name sounds familiar, but I can't place where from. Then it comes to me. My eyes open wide and I shoot up in bed. The bloke who crashed into Niall's car – he was called Dr Matthias Bailey. A wave of unease comes over me as I think of this next coincidence. I sit in the dark with my heart beating fast for a long time, until I'm sure that Monique must be asleep. I tiptoe to the bathroom and on my return listen at her door. I can hear the sounds of her snoring, something we've laughed at in the past and now I'm glad of the clear sign of sleep. Back in my room I switch the small lamp on and systematically go through all her drawers and cupboards. I find nothing. I'm about to dismiss my suspicions as stupid when I remember something she said to me when I told her about the break in, that she hoped they didn't come after my shoes and bags. I never mentioned they had been left, so how would she know? A feeling of nausea begins to accompany my rapid heartbeat. I resolve to carry on looking. After about ten minutes I'm about to give up when I spy a vintage style vanity case at the back of a wardrobe. I bought it for her the first Christmas after we met. I open it up and inside find more of my missing jewellery and some photos. One of the photos is the one of Seb leaving my house. My hand shakes as I look through the pile of photos I am clutching. There are a couple of Bettina from what must be a few years ago as she looks younger. As I get to the bottom I find a well-thumbed photo of Monique gazing lovingly up at a man. The man is Danny Southwell.

CHAPTER NINETEEN

I carefully replace the items in the case, remembering the order of them, and get back into bed. Part of me wants to take the case and run, but instead I lie there, thinking there has to be some other explanation. Monique is my best friend. She's shown no sign of knowing Bettina, yet there are old pictures of her. The picture with Danny indicates Monique was either a fan, or worse, a lover. It makes no sense. Why do things to me? What have I done to Monique other than be a good friend? Is this part of Bettina's plan? Are they in it together?

I stare at the ceiling, my heart thumping. What should I do next?

I need to get out of here.

Or do I confront her?

There must be some logical explanation.

I decide I'll stay here tonight. It's not like I have anywhere else to go. Tomorrow at breakfast, I'll tell her the news about Danny if it hasn't broken already and watch her reaction. Maybe she'll give some clue in her behaviour that'll point me in the right direction?

Or maybe I just should get out now, while I have the chance?

But then I'll get no answers. No, I'll stay.
My thoughts circle like a car on a roundabout.

At six I get up as I've barely slept anyway. I fix
some coffee and toast for myself and Monique.
Around half an hour later she enters the kitchen and
stretches, reminding me of a slinky cat. She smiles
at me and I smile back, hoping my face gives
nothing away, whilst feeling like tormented prey.
'Did you sleep okay?' she asks.
'Yes, thank you. That spare bed is surprisingly
comfy. Other than a quick wee I was out like a
light.'
'That's good. I really enjoyed you coming over.'
'Er, yeah, it was great. I'm going to have breakfast
and then head back home, I fancy doing some
baking.' Another lie, in truth I have nowhere to go,
and I'm not sure what to do.
'Are you baking your cupcakes? I can't remember
the last time I had one, you should have made some
yesterday before you came over.'
'Never thought. I'll bring you some soon, promise.'
'Right, well I'll head to the shower. Do you need
one?'
'No I'll just freshen up and get showered at mine.
I'll see you in a bit.'
I stick on a bit of TV whilst I eat my breakfast and
then get dressed. When Monique leaves the shower
I head in and have a quick wash, brush my teeth and
stick my hair back in a ponytail. Looking in the
mirror I think if the circles under my eyes get any
darker, I'll look like I've been run over by dirty

tyres. I gather all my things together, ready to leave and then head back into the lounge to say goodbye to Monique and mention Danny to her. I see she's reading the newspaper, her face is deathly white and her head is in her hands. I reverse my steps back into the bathroom quietly and make more noise on my way out. When I re-enter her face is perky. She looks up at me like a gossip columnist who's been in the toilet next to a drug smoking supermodel, scoring an exclusive. 'You'll never guess what? Bettina's husband's been arrested,' she says.

'Yeah, she told me yesterday.'

'You spoke to Bettina yesterday? Why would you see her? Why didn't you tell me last night?' she shouts with uncharacteristic force.

'I didn't think you'd be interested. It's not like you know them.'

If I hadn't known to look for it, I would have missed the split second hesitation before her reply.

'Course not, but it's major gossip. Sorry, I got a little overexcited, we kind of know her.'

'No worries. Anyway, I need to get off so thanks for a—'

'No, no, no. You can't leave me without info. How come you saw her? Tell me what she said. It says he pushed someone. Does she think he'll get off? Seems unfair if it was an accident.'

'She was there when I got home yesterday, saying she wanted us to know, and that whatever has gone on between us, she still wanted the boys to be able to play as Tyler needs some stability, especially with what's happening with his dad. Other than that she didn't have much to say, other than he's being charged with manslaughter cos he punched the guy and he banged his head.'

'Is she going to see him?'

She's not interested. She's his ex-wife now, so it doesn't really concern her.'

'She's got Danny's son.'

'Her priority is to keep Tyler away from it all, and from the press.'

'So do you think he'll get out?'

'I've no idea, but he's not known for his mild manners is he?'

'Yes, but can you believe Bettina? Look what she's been doing to you. You only have what his poisonous ex-wife says. I'm sure he's an alright bloke really. Maybe she set him up too?'

"She can rot in hell for all I care. She came and told Niall yesterday about Danny. I asked her to leave as soon as I arrived home. I doubt I'll have anything to do with her again, and I'll phone the police again if she starts anything.'

'That's good. Hopefully you'll get back on your feet if she's out from under your hair.'

'Well I live in hope. Anyway you're going to be late for work if you keep on yakking. Who'd have thought – Monique Henry – gossip queen.'

She folds up her fist like a microphone and talks in a reporter style voice. 'Keep in touch, and let me know if there are any new developments.'

'I will.'

'She was alone with Niall when you came home? You need to watch her.'

I nod, grab my overnight bag and head out of the door. I walk calmly down the path towards the stairs, thankful that the driveway isn't visible from Monique's apartment and then I run, feet crunching in gravel, across the car park. I throw my things in the car, jump in the driver's seat and reverse out of my space. I need to tell Niall what I've discovered and fast.

I race through the door when I get home, seeing the car outside and noting that Niall has not gone to work for a third day. I find him in the garden digging the hole required for the garden pond he wants. He looks at me and wipes the sweat from his brow and walks towards me.

'Lauren.'

I can barely get out my words due to being out of breath. 'It's Monique... Niall, I was in her room last night and ..'

He throws down the spade and clutches his temples. 'Good God. You nearly drove Bettina to a nervous breakdown, and now you're starting on Monique?'

'But I–'

'No, I'm not listening to this right now. Look, is there somewhere you can stay another night or two? I'll tell Joe you're on a mini-break. He's used to you abandoning him to babysitters whilst you float off anyway.'

Tears fill my eyes. 'My son is everything to me, don't you dare. Sulk away today, Niall, I'll be back tomorrow. Hopefully by then you'll have grown up.'

'I need some time to think.'

'You can have today.' I stride away from him, picking up my overnight bag from the doorway. I run upstairs and add some clean undies and then go back out the door. I now have another day to find something to do. I need to make a plan of what to do next. However glancing at my watch I see that at the moment it's only just turned half nine. I decide to drive down to the local cinema which is about ten minutes away; there are always some early showings so I decide to kill a couple of hours in there.

After the film I look over the entertainment complex and decide to lunch in the local pizza place. Honestly I have never eaten so much rubbish in my life as I have the last few weeks. I order a coke, and whilst I wait for my pizza, I take my cupcake design notebook and pink biro out of my bag and turn it onto a fresh page. I need to think and make a plan, and when I make plans I make lists. I consider who can help me to get through to Niall and come up with either the most logical or most stupid plan ever. Seb. Seb could help me to make Niall see sense. He'll be gone in less than two weeks. Anyway, what do I have to lose? I write on the list:

1. Ring Seb.

I also need to see Bettina. I need her to wrack her brains and see if she remembers Monique from anywhere.

2. Try to find a way to get Bettina to meet me. That's a start.

3. Maybe speak to Dr Love?

I'm unsure of this as a plan. If Monique has set Niall up then this could tip her off that I'm onto her. Now I'm annoyed that I didn't bring the photos and jewellery with me, but I didn't want her to get suspicious. I just don't understand why she would do this to me. My pizza arrives and I pick at it, struggling to find an appetite. Then I start thinking again, and regret not taking any evidence, maybe then Niall would believe me.

There's only one thing for it.

3. ~~Maybe speak with Dr Love?~~ Go back to Monique's.

I stare at my piece of paper for a while whilst eating a little more pizza. I doodle in the corner, drawing a sun and turning it into a happy face. Then before I know it, I've drawn lightning striking it and rain pouring. I get out my phone and send Seb a text.

I'm sorry to bother you yet again, but I need to ask you a favour. Can we meet at usual pub?

Luckily for me it's the school lunchtime and I get a text back quickly.

I can be there by four. PS You never bother me Lauren.

A minute passes. I get another,

Actually that's not true. You make me extremely hot and bothered.

I smile and wonder if he will ever actually change. I wipe my mouth with a napkin and ask for the bill. It's just gone one and I have until four to do something. I go back to the cinema to pick something else. This morning I chose a comedy in a feeble attempt to cheer myself up. This afternoon

I'm plumping for an ass kicking spectacular. On my way out, sitting in the car, I send Monique a text. Trying to sort stuff out at home. Be in touch soon xxx.

I need to keep things as normal as possible. I drive to the pub with my mind so full of current happenings, that when I arrive I'm not entirely sure how I got there. I don't remember even being conscious of the traffic lights.

Seb is already at the pub. He looks as gorgeous as ever. Dressed in his nerd gear, I want to take off his glasses and rough up his hair. Still furious with Niall, I order a glass of wine. However I'm mindful of the fact I can't drink much more as I need to drive to a local hotel for the evening.

'So, much as it's nice to see you, Lauren, what's this all about?'

I take a large mouthful of wine. 'Niall was sent a picture of us kissing at my house. Now he's convinced we had an affair. I want you to come and tell him it's not true.'

He splutters. 'I don't bloody think so. Not sure I fancy a cosy meet up with your hubby.'

I bite my lip and try to stop my tears. 'Please....I'm desperate. He's kicked me out and won't let me see Joe.'

His brown eyes seem to darken to black. 'He's a total fucking dick, then. Can't he see what he has?' He taps his foot on the floor. 'I'll think about it okay?'

I wipe my eyes. 'Thank you.'

'Is that all you want me for? I have marking to do.'
I grab hold of the top of his hand across the table.
'Please, don't go.'
'Christ, Lauren, what do you want from me? I feel
like a bloody yo-yo.'
'I'm on my own.' I neck my glass of red. 'Please
stay and have a meal with me. I hate being alone.'
He sighs. 'I need to get away from this – from you.'
'Yes,' I spit. 'That's what everyone seems to want,
to get away from me. At most points in my life I
appear to have been some diabolical person that
everyone needs to be rid of.'
I go to the bar to order another glass of red wine.
Sod it. I'll have a bottle. I'll order a taxi to the hotel
and leave the car here. I smirk. I might just leave it
with the door open and the engine running so Niall
gets a call from the police and goes frantic, it would
serve him right. I sit back down and drink another
large mouthful. The blackcurrant and cinnamon
flavours warm my mouth.
'Don't you think you should slow down? You'll be
flat on your back before long,' Seb warns.
I look defiantly at him. 'Isn't that where you want
me anyway?'
I hear his breath hitch. 'I'm going to order some
food, and get you some so you don't fall over.' He
rises from his seat and goes to the bar.
Whilst he's gone I finish off the current glass of
wine and pour myself another. I can already feel it's
going to my head. I feel this slight sensation of
being in a greenhouse, as if I can see everyone but
there's a distance between me and them. I like it.

I'll stop after a third glass as I know I'll be prone to vomiting if I drink any more, lightweight that I am. But one more glass with some food, I should be able to manage and if not, who cares? Seb can call me a cab.

When he returns I follow on from my train of thought.

'I'm going to stop at the Novotel. If I'm a bit squiffy, dial me a cab.'

He picks up the remainder of the wine and moves it out of reach. 'That's you done for the night. Don't do anything you'll regret tomorrow, Lauren.'

I smile up at him and give him the benefit of a full toothed grin. 'I'm a bit pissed, and I'll tell you something,' I lean over the table and mock whisper, 'I've done nothing but be a good person and look where it's got me. My life is ruined. Well stuff it. I'm not behaving right now. I'm getting drunk and having some fun.'

I wander over to the game machine and feel in my pocket for the change I got from the bottle of wine. I stick a few quid in, pressing random buttons as I've never gambled apart from a few goes on the Grand National over the years. There's a series of flashes and noise and then coins come tumbling out into the tray. I've won twenty quid.

'Whoo hoo,' eyes turn towards me and I get a few "well dones" and grins. Seb comes over and takes my arm. 'Our food's here.'

I heartily tuck into my scampi and chips. I smear it in tartare sauce, using up three sachets.

'I had no idea you were such a pig with your food.'

I stick out my tongue and then get a chip and suck all the tartare sauce off. 'Mmmmmmm'.

Seb shuffles in his seat, adjusting himself. 'Jesus, Lauren, what're you trying to do to me?'

I look down at the chip in my mouth and begin to giggle hysterically. I can't stop. I take another chip, dip it in the sauce and lick up and down its length. A woman at the next table gives me a dirty look. I give her a wink back.

'Eat your food. It's time to go before you're kicked out. It's only tea-time for Christ's sake.'

'Why is everyone so boring?' I roll my eyes. 'Do you know, today I made plans and lists? Well to hell with them.' I take out my little notebook and upend it in Seb's pint of beer. He looks skyward. 'I'm going with the flow, by the seat of my pants, throwing caution to the wind.'

'I think you've swallowed a book of clichés along with that wine missus. Come on, let's get you home before you fall over.'

'I have no home. Take me to your home.'

Seb raises his eyebrows. 'You want to come home with me?'

'Yes.' I puff out my chest sexily. 'I want to see your bachelor pad.'

'Jesus, how drunk are you?'

'I'm just merry – merry and bright; bright like the wine was sunshine, and its brought light into my life.'

'I'm going to take you to my flat, but just to make you some coffee and help you sober up. Then I'll drop you off at your hotel.'

'Oh, yes, take me to your home,' I say. 'Now.' I start giggling.

Seb holds my arm to help me out of the pub. I see him roll his eyes at the landlord as he wishes him a good evening.

'Rude.' I mutter.

Seb's place is nothing like I would have guessed. It's a ground floor apartment which we enter through a hallway, like Monique's. It's a lot shabbier though with cracked paintwork and graffiti. Yet when he opens his apartment door, I'm pleasantly surprised. The door opens straight onto a decently sized lounge with a dark brown carpet and neutral walls. He has a large screen television and a green canvas couch. I look at him questioningly.

'Came with the flat. Beggars can't be choosers.'

He goes to switch the kettle on, telling me I'm to have a couple of cups of coffee. I made him take my overnight case out of my car and bring it here, so I wander off to take it into his bedroom. His room is decorated in purples, again no doubt the work of whoever owns the flat. It puts me in mind of an Arabian nights scene, and I giggle thinking of Seb as Shahryah surrounded by nubile young virgins. I don't consider what I'm doing. I put my case in the corner of the room and lay on the bed. I'm not thinking of Niall or anyone else this time, not even Joe, I'm doing what I want; to hell with everyone else.

That's the last I remember until the early hours when Seb accidentally wakes me up as he comes into the room. I see his alarm clock reads two sixteen.

I am thankfully hangover free. I turn to face Seb, who is picking up pillows. I am laid on the top of the bed.

'Sorry,' he says. 'I was trying not to disturb you.'

'That's okay,' my mouth is dry. 'I guess I missed out on the coffee then?'

'Yes, and you'd have loved it, a rich Ethiopian blend. It serves you right for falling asleep.'

I sit up.

'Where are you going?'

'Bathroom. I need some water. Then I'll head to the couch. It's your bed.'

'No, you can have the bed. I'm okay with the couch. I think you need a good night's sleep.'

I head to the bathroom, which has a smart white suite. Although basic, it looks really effective with a black and white checked shower curtain and a black venetian blind. I splash water on my face and have a few sips from the tap. Then I use the loo. I sit for a few minutes, thinking about where I am and that a man who is not my husband is only a few feet away. I strip myself down to my bra and pants, wrap a towel around myself and walk back into the bedroom. Light peeks through the curtains, casting a glow on the room so I can see my way around. I hesitate as to whether to get my pyjamas out of my case, and stand in the room, completely unsure of which way to turn.

'Everything okay?'

One look at his open caring gaze and mussed up hair and the temptation is too much. I'm done resisting. The towel drops to the floor and I climb onto the bed beside him.

I run my hand up his tee shirt and stroke his chest. He has a slight covering of dark hair across his chest and down his navel. He shivers and grabs my hand.

'Are you sure about this, Lauren?'

'Sssshhh.' I place my index finger across his mouth. 'You'll be gone in a few days, remember. I need this to remember you by.'

He bites my finger and turns and backs me into the bed, crushing his chest across mine. His mouth smashes into mine and I thrust my tongue between his teeth. He tastes of his Ethiopian blend. I can't get enough. We kiss on and on, trying to drink each other in. I want as much of him as I can get, knowing this is a one-time only deal. He moves his mouth onto my neck and I twist with delight as he kisses and licks it. It makes me squirm where I'm laid as the ticklishness of it fights with desire. I raise myself up so he can remove my bra. He pauses and looks me in the eyes and says. 'Oh, God, Lauren. I can't believe you're here.'

I silence him with another deep kiss and stroke my hands down his back. I help him remove his shirt and move to sit astride him. I trace the dragon tattoo with the tip of my tongue. He flips me back over and moves himself further down the bed. I can feel his desire pressing against my leg. He takes turns to suck, lick and tease my nipples. I can feel my excitement between my legs, I am so turned on. I pull him back up the bed to kiss me again, and then I slip my hand under the waistband of his pants and stroke him there.

He jerks away from me. 'No.'

I try and put my hand back.

'I said no.'

I look up at him. 'You want this.'

'Yes, but I don't think you do, Lauren.'

He moves himself away from me and runs his hand through his hair. 'Shit, that was so nearly a huge mistake.'

My voice trembles. 'But…why?'

'Because you're hitting out, Lauren. Tell me, how will you feel if Niall apologises and we've slept together?'

I look at the floor.

'If it's over Lauren, and you want us to be together, that's different. But I won't do it this way, do you understand?'

I begin to cry. 'I don't know what I'm doing any more, Seb. I just keep making everything worse.'

'Well I can't decide for you,' he says. 'Next time I won't stop, Lauren, I'll fuck your brains out. I'm not a good guy, don't you get it?' He turns over, his back to me.

Finally, all cried out, I fall back asleep.

When I awake, I move out of Seb's warm arms. My eyes feel swollen and gritty. I pick up my wash bag and go to the bathroom. I check my reflection in the mirror. I look tired and drawn. My eyes are bloodshot. I stare at myself, wondering what on earth is happening to me. What am I doing? I feel I need to wash last night away. Thank goodness Seb stopped me. I feel the tears welling again. I'm such a fool.

As the water washes over me, I rub my wash mitt down myself and scrub away at my skin, relishing the pain. I need to feel something. I massage shampoo into my hair, kneading my skull. I'm pulling Lauren Lawler back together. I'm letting my enemy win and that's not going to happen if I can do anything to prevent it. I dress, dry my hair, and head back into the lounge as Seb's kitchen is very small and has no table. Seb pulls up a coffee table, one of those sets of three that fit neatly under each other, and sets down some coffee and a plate of toast. My stomach growls as I smell the coffee.

'Wow, that smells good,' I say. 'And strong.'

'I think it should be named after me,' he says.

I smile, pleased that he's being normal.

'I'll leave you a key if you like. You're more than welcome to stay here.'

'Thank you. I need to regroup, and think.'

'Well, I'll be gone a week on Saturday. You need to decide if you want to fight for your marriage and get your life back together, or,' he pauses, 'you can come with me.'

I fall silent for a while, because whilst I know I do want my marriage to work, there's a small part of me that wants to be with Seb; a tiny chink of obsidian fighting to be seen amongst diamond. I know Seb has been a little deviation from the route of my life, a wrong turning on the journey, that to me, has begun and will end with Niall.

'Well things are slightly more complicated than that,' I say and fill him in about Monique.

'She must be mentally ill if she's been doing things like that.'

'I feel like the Monique I've known for the past five years was a mirage, and now I'm left with this new person who I don't know at all. What I do know though, is that I need to get Bettina to speak to me, and then I need to see Niall.

'It sounds like you have some things to occupy you today. As I said, stay here as long as you need to.'

'Will you come with me to see Niall later?'

'That's a bit of an ask, Lauren. Look, I'll think about it whilst I'm at work. Go see Bettina and take it from there. Maybe it's time to step out from all the protection you place around yourself and take some chances.' He kisses me swiftly on the cheek and leaves for work.

I get out my mobile phone and call Niall.

'I'll be picking Joe up from school and coming home.'

'I've got school covered Lauren. I've taken the rest of the week off.'

'You don't seem to be listening. I will be picking my son up at three fifteen. I don't know why on earth I've let you boss me around this week. Sure I've not told the whole truth, but I've done nothing to deserve being shut out of my own home. So tonight, I *will* be home and you'll listen to what I have to say if you have any ounce of compassion in your bones. If not, then you can pack your own Niall, because I'm staying with my son.'

There's silence at the other end of the phone. I feel sick whilst I wait to hear what his reply will be.

'I'll see you later.'

My outtake of breath makes me go dizzy.

I drive to Bettina's and pray that she's in. As I walk up her driveway I see evidence of the damage I've caused to the garden, as yet not repaired. There are yellow dry patches on the garden where the weed killer is taking effect and turned over earth where I pulled out the plants. It looks like a mole's had an acid trip on the lawn. I knock on the door and step back.

Within a minute she opens the door. 'Get away from my house or I'll phone the police.'

'Bettina. I know we aren't friends, but I desperately need to talk to you.'

'I'm not a sounding board for the woes of Lauren Lawler, you have Monique for that.'

'That's why I'm here,' I pause. 'I think Monique's the one who's been doing all this.'

She stares at me, eyes narrowing. 'Why on earth would she do that?'

'Because of Danny. She may have been his lover.'

She sighs, the cheated on wife discovering yet another infidelity of her husband.

She steps away from the door. 'You'd better come in.'

CHAPTER TWENTY

Stepping through the hallway, I realise that this is the first time I've actually been inside Bettina's rented house. We go into the lounge. There are packing boxes piled in the corner and the room is noticeably bare. It's decorated in the old nineties style of burnt orange wallpaper with a floral border around the middle. It has laminate flooring, an orange sofa and a beanbag. There are an array of toys around the beanbag and a folded back copy of Hello! lies on the sofa.

'I've just made a pot of coffee. I suppose asking if you want one's a silly question?'

'A bit.' My mouth attempts a smile.

'Take a seat. I'll be back in a sec.'

She brings in two mugs of coffee and a plate of chocolate biscuits on a tray, setting it on the floor in front of us.

'Sorry. I've packed the table.'

'Oh, yeah, right.'

'I haven't seen you at school the last few days? Niall said you were on a mini-break?'

'Niall threw me out after a photo arrived of Seb leaving our house.'

'Oh.'

'It's not what you think. He came around because I needed some advice, but presented with that picture on the back of everything else…Niall found me guilty as charged.'

'I'm sure he's just angry and bewildered. I've been there. You don't know what to believe.'

'Yes, well aren't we all? Anyway, I'm going back home tonight to talk to him and try and get him to see reason, then the ball's in his court. I'm tired of it. If he wants to pack his bags, he can go.'

'You don't mean that, Lauren. You love Niall.'

'Yeah? Well maybe that's not enough. Right now, I'm just focussed on Joe. I want to be near my son, and if that means it's just him and me, so be it.'

'He'd miss his father like crazy. Tyler does, and look what a moron he is. Forget your bitterness, Lauren. Niall's not your mother and father. He's hurt. This has affected him too and he must be scared of what could happen to Joe, just like you are.'

I wince as she mentions my parents, but perhaps she's right. I'm building up a wall ready to protect myself again.

'I'll see how it goes later. Right now, I need to talk to you about Monique.'

I explain about finding the photos in the vanity case, about several of them being a younger Bettina, and tell her about the one of Monique and Danny.

'Well if she had an affair with him, I never knew about it. All the ones I knew about were stereotypical blondes with big boobs.'

'I don't understand why she would attack me though. I've got no real connection to Danny.'

'Who knows how a weirdo's mind works. All the time you've known her, has she ever displayed any strange behaviour, stalked anyone or anything?'

'No, she's just been my best mate. We've been there for each other for everything over the last five years. As soon as I met her at yoga I felt like we'd known each other forever.' My voice cracks. 'I can't believe she could be behind all this. I mean, she's just been through a miscarriage...'

There's an uncomfortable silence for a minute or so. 'How sure are you that she actually had a miscarriage?'

I think back. I never saw evidence of any blood or a mess, all I had was Monique's tears and her word. 'Making something like that up would be totally sick.'

'You reckon?'

I frown. 'But why? If it wasn't genuine, what did she achieve by faking it?'

'I have no idea. We need to try and get more of a clue.'

'I'm thinking about going back and gathering some evidence, see if I can find out any more, but I don't know. I feel like I need to talk to Niall first. He's always so good at thinking of what to do.' This makes me feel sad. I've always depended on Niall, maybe too much. Will he be there now when I really need him, or should I do things myself?

'We need to get this sorted as soon as possible. You talk to Niall tonight, and I'll call you in the morning. When you've gone I'll ring the prison and try and set up a visit for tomorrow morning. Danny's allowed three visits a week at the moment, so hopefully I'll be able to get to see him. I'll ask him how he knows Monique.'

'That'd be great.' I realise I've not drunk any of my coffee and leave it untouched. 'Maybe I need to speak to Monique's Doctor Love as well, find out if he was asked to crash into Niall's car? It seems too coincidental now.'

'I wouldn't at the moment. He might tip Monique off.'

'You're right. Okay, I'll speak to you in the morning. I'm sorry I had to come and bug you yet again.'

'It seems we're in this together, Lauren, for whatever reason.'

'Yeah, well let's try and find out what that is.'

I get a hero's welcome from Joe at school. 'Mum, you're back. Please don't go away for as long again.'

'I won't, I promise.' My words are the truth. I won't be leaving Joe again for a long while. I need to know he's safe, and I need him to know he can rely on me to look after him. Once again I feel rage at Niall for taking precious time with my son away from me.

Seeing Niall makes me feel like I'm facing the executioner. He ruffles Joe's hair as he goes to hug him. The usual "have you had a nice day, Joe" is answered with "fine," and then Joe's off to his room, regardless of the fact he hasn't seen me for days. It makes me feel warm inside, that the thought of me being here is enough.

'Let's hear it then, your latest version of the truth.'

I don't bite back. I take a seat diagonally across from Niall at the dining table. He sits back in the chair with his arms folded. He looks impenetrable and I need to get through to him. So I begin.

'The other night at Monique's, I found some of my stolen jewellery in a case in her wardrobe.' Niall opens his mouth to speak and I hold up my hand. 'Let me finish. There were some photos of Bettina from a few years ago in there too, and the photo of me and Seb that was delivered through the post to you. And… an old picture of Monique looking very loved up with Danny Southwell. My assumption then, is that for whatever reason, but connected to Danny and Bettina, Monique is behind everything that's happened. Also,' I take a deep breath, 'Monique's boyfriend is the doctor who crashed into your car.'

'I'll kill her.' Niall is out of the chair with his face in a grimace and his fists clenched. 'Get the phone. I'm calling the police.'

'That's the thing though Niall. I don't have the photos or the jewellery. I didn't want to tip her off so I left them there.'

'Well if we ring the police now we can show them where it all is.'

'But then I may never know why she targeted us. What if she's moved everything? I want to go back to the apartment and try and see if I can find anything else.'

'You must be bloody joking. You can't go there now. Who knows what she'll do?'

'If she was going to harm me, Niall, she's had plenty of opportunity to do that already. I don't know what her game is, but I do know it's not to hurt me.'

He folds his arms across his chest. 'Well, I don't know how you expect me to just sit here while you enter the monster's lair.'

'I'll be fine. I need to do this. I promise, any sign of something iffy and I'll be out of there. I thought I'd go tomorrow morning. I'll tell her we've fallen out, so she won't be suspicious of my turning up at her house. I'll find some way of getting the stuff and get out. Hopefully I won't be long.'

I uncross my legs as I'm getting pins and needles in one foot and shake it out. 'There is something I need you to do, though. Is there anyone at the hospital who could look up whether or not Monique attended A&E, or the antenatal ward? Bettina reckons she might have faked the miscarriage.'

He peers at me with his forehead all creasing. 'Faked a miscarriage? I just can't take this all in, Lauren.' He sighs. 'It breaks all the rules of confidentiality, but I'll ring our secretary. Write me her date of birth and the first line of her address.'

He passes me a post-it note and pen. I quickly scribble them down and he goes off into the lounge. He returns a couple of minutes later.

'Monique hasn't been anywhere near a hospital since she's been in Sheffield. She's not even on the system.'

'Are you sure they inputted her details correctly?'

'She did what's called a soundex – it looks for anyone remotely relating to the details. There was nothing.'

And with that, one of the branches of my heart snaps. My best friend is not who she seems.

For the rest of the evening we imitate normal family life, with the usual sit down meal and bath time, then I go to my own room whilst Niall sits in the lounge. My own bed feels wonderful. I dive under the sheets, pulling the covers up around me and spend a long time wondering what the next day will bring.

I ring Monique the following morning and she's delighted that I'm coming over. I never usually see her on a Friday as it's her 'working from home day', but obviously being given a chance to catch up on developments means she'll do her work later. 'Bring some of your baking,' she says. 'I'm in the mood for something delicious.'

Damn. I forgot I was supposed to have been baking. I pick up a tupperware box. I'll call into a bakery on my way over and hope I can wing it.

On arrival, I'm ushered into the lounge where she is dressed in a long burgundy silk chemise with black lace trim and matching gown. She looks like she needs one of those long cigarettes they had in the nineteen twenties. I don't know if I should be afraid of her or act differently, but she just appears to be my same old mate. I just can't get over the fact that she could be anything else. She sits on the settee and indicates I should take a seat on the other one, then passes me a drink. 'I'm being decadent today, I've made Mimosas.'

'Oh, any reason why?' I ask

'A few things I've had in the pipeline seem to be coming to fruition. I feel we should celebrate. Also, it will help cheer you up. What's Niall done this time, anyway?'

I must act normal. 'He's had a big go at me about everything. I assume it's the stress, but I'm not putting up with it anymore.'

'Good girl. Right, what did you bake?'

I get out the cupcakes I've bought; all pink icing and coated in sprinkles. They smell amazing, either recently cooked or warmed through by the bakery. Thankfully made in the shop and not of uniform size, I can get away with having not baked them myself.

'Have you heard anything else about the break in? Are they going to replace your clothes?'

'They will do, but these things take time, don't they?'

She takes a bite of cupcake. 'Umm, these are gorgeous, you should think of selling them in a shop.'

Does she know? I need to act fast and get her out of here. I feel sick.

'Is everything all right Lauren?'

'No.' I hold my guts as if I'm in severe pain. 'Owww, it really hurts.'

'What is it? Shall I get you a hot water bottle?'

'It won't go without medicine. Can you fetch me some if I give you the money? Your local chemist isn't far, is it?' I push the half eaten cupcake and the bubbling Mimosa out of the way. 'I knew I shouldn't have had them. Serves me right for trying to have fun when my life's a pile of steaming dung.'

'Honestly, Lo, there's always a drama when you're around. Have you thought of applying for your equity card?'

I manage a brave smile. 'I feel a bit sick.'

'Go to the bathroom,' she orders pointing. 'I'll get straight dressed and go to the chemist. It shouldn't take me long in the car. By the way, if you puke, you're cleaning it up. I might be your best mate, but even I don't love you that much.'

I wander to the bathroom clutching my stomach as she goes to get ready.

The minute she leaves the flat I run straight into the spare room. The vanity case is still at the back of the wardrobe. I grab it, and with hands shaking so much I can barely open it, I record with the tiny Flip camcorder I have in my pocket and then remove the photos and jewellery and put them down my bra. I have about ten minutes or so before she's back if there's no queue, so I keep an eye on my watch as I move around the room. As I pass her dressing table I bang into the corner bruising my leg and making myself go light headed with the pain. As I do so, I hear something falling down the back of it. Mindful to not move anything visible, lest she get suspicious whilst I'm there, I pull out the dresser to see what fell. Behind is a cheap looking handset. I'd put money on it being the one used to message me. I run and place it at the bottom of my handbag, remove the photos and jewellery from my bra and stuff them inside as well. Once I'm back in the room I shove the dresser into its original position. I look around the room again, but in full on panic mode with the adrenaline kicking my ass I realise that I really am about to be sick. I run back to the bathroom and get there just in time; a half eaten cupcake mixed with Mimosa shoots into the toilet bowl. The look and smell of it is enough that I begin to heave again and that's how Monique finds me, sweating and bent over the toilet seat.

'Oh gosh, you really are ill, aren't you, Lo?'

I nod my head. I feel clammy and sweaty. I feel really rough now. 'I think it's best if I head home and go to bed.'

'Nonsense. You can have a rest here. The spare room--'

She looks towards the spare room and frowns. 'I'm sure I closed that door.'

'I've been in here since you left,' I lie. 'How can you know how you left a door, anyway? I don't know how I leave the house in a morning, never mind what chaos I leave behind.'

'It's just who I am,' says Monique. 'I always close every door. It's just one of my little rituals.'

My mouth feels dry. How have I never noticed this before?

'Anyway,' she says, 'either I forgot for once, or it's blown open. I don't know why I'm thinking of that whilst my best friend is ill. She rinses out a face cloth, folds it over and gives it me to hold to my head. You stay there. I'll get the spare room ready for you to have a sleep. I'll take the laptop into the lounge and work from there.' She gets up and strides purposefully towards the spare room. I realise that my game is probably up, so I do the only thing I can think of under the circumstances, I grab my bag and run, closing the door silently behind me.

I head towards the car, my legs feel so wobbly they threaten to give way on me, but I manage to get in and start it straight up. Once again I find myself blasting off in the car out of the communal driveway. I really must get a job at a racetrack for my next career, I'd be damn good at it. I drive until I am well away from her apartment and park myself in a local supermarket car park, and then I sit and shake.

My phone rings and I nearly die with fright. It's Bettina.

'Hello.'

'Have you been running? You sound out of breath.'

'I've just legged it from Monique's.'

'Crikey, how did that go then?'

'I got everything, but I think she sprang me. I left the spare room door open.'

'What do you think she'll do now?'

'Goodness knows. We need our evidence together for tonight so we can go to the police before she does anything stupid. Anyway, I panicked. She might have genuinely been going in the spare room to get it ready for me staying, and now I've run off and given her a reason to be suspicious.'

'You'd better ring her with some kind of excuse, just in case.'

'Good idea.'

'Well I was calling to let you know that I'm just about to go in and see Danny, so wish me luck.'

'Good luck.'

'I'll give you another call when I get out.'

'Actually…do you want to come over to ours when you've done? Niall will be there and then we can all decide where we go from here.'

'Okay, I'll see you this afternoon sometime. I'll ring when I'm on my way.'

I dial Monique's number. 'Hello,' she sounds agitated.

'Monique, it's me.'

'Where the hell are you? One minute you're puking in my loo, the next you've disappeared.'

'I wanted my own bed.'

'Well, you could have said. I had no idea where you were. I looked around the apartment and the grounds thinking you might have collapsed somewhere.'

'I'm sorry, Mon, I didn't want to worry you. I just panicked and wanted to get back home.'

'Is that where you are now?'

'Yes,' I lie. 'In bed. Not that Niall is taking any notice of me being ill. He's a pig.'

'Well, I've told you that from the beginning. You should've stayed with me.'

'I know.'

'So are you staying at home all day now?'

'Yes.'

'Well, look after yourself, and Lauren -'

'Yes?'

'About the spare room.'

I think my heart actually pauses. 'Hmm?'

'It was me. I left the window open. Sorry for seeming paranoid.'

'I never gave it another thought.'

'Well ring me when you're feeling better. I'm sure we'll see each other soon.'

'We will. Thanks for everything, Mon.'

I put the phone down. I'm deeply worried now, because the window in Monique's spare room was definitely closed.

I drive back home carefully, on alert to anything untoward and jumping if another car moves anywhere near me. I feel parched. The first thing I do when I get home is to run upstairs, swill water around my mouth and then brush my teeth. So I'm more than a little shocked when I eventually walk into the living room and find Niall on the settee with a pack of frozen vegetables on his fist. Seb clutches another bag against what I guess is the beginnings of a black eye.

'Do you want to sit down, Lauren?' Niall asks.

CHAPTER TWENTY-ONE

I'm not sure my poor heart can take much more of this stress today. I swear it'll be grey rinses from now on, not blonde highlights.

'How come you're not at work?' I ask Seb.

'Yes, Lauren, I'm fine, thank you,' he states with snarled sarcasm.'

'I can see you're not fine. I can also make out that you've connected with my husband's fists, being that I am not entirely stupid.'

'The head teacher gave me the afternoon off.'

'Your mother let you finish early?'

'Mother?' Niall sniggers. 'Mrs Sullivan's your mother?' He bursts into laughter. 'Oh my, where's Jeremy Beadle, seriously, cos all of this has to be someone's idea of a sick joke.'

I take note of the fact there are two cans of beer on the coffee table.

'So did you start drinking before or after the fight?'

'He punched me the minute he opened the door,' says Seb, looking at me like a wounded puppy. 'Didn't even give me a chance to speak.'

'Yeah, well mate. Last time I saw you, was on a photo kissing my wife, what'd you expect?'

'I've explained that now. I have no interest in your wife whatsoever.'

I feel a bit insulted but realise it's best to keep my mouth closed on this one. 'So you finally believe me?' I state.

'Yes, well, with all this Monique business, I was already thinking you'd probably been set up, but I was still wondering what he was doing at the house. He's explained it all now, and it's sorted.' He turns to Seb. 'Do you fancy another beer, mate?'

'No thanks, I need to be able to drive home.'

'Good point. I'll just shift these tins or she'll be moaning.'

Whilst he pops into the kitchen I look at Seb and he winks at me with his good eye.

Niall comes back with a cloth and wipes the table down. However, not to make me completely think he's been abducted by aliens, he leaves the cloth on the table and sits back down. 'So, er, you got a lady then, Seb?'

'There was someone, but they didn't feel the same way about me, so I'm planning on going Down Under for a while.'

I have to cough to cover a snort and then I replay back what he's said and I feel sad. I've used this guy and deserted him, so beach life should suit him well.

'We've talked about going to Australia in the past,' says Niall. 'I can go with work over there through being a nurse. I guess that's the same with you, are they crying out for teachers?'

'Yes. Are you considering it then, in light of what's happened?' Seb asks Niall.

They both look towards me and I feel uncomfortable under their gazes, and unsure as to whom I should look at.

I turn towards Seb. 'No, though I am asking Niall to consider a move. I'd like to go to Staffordshire to be nearer his parents. I think it would be nice for Joe.'

'Sounds sensible to me,' says Seb, looking at Niall. 'I do think a fresh start away from this madness is what you need.'

'Well we still need to talk about it, but it's definitely a possibility.' Niall looks at me and gives me a look and a half smile that for the first time in a long time, gives me hope again for us.

'Right, well I'd better be off then,' says Seb. 'I'll leave you to it. Good luck with the police later. I'll be around until a week on Saturday if they need me for statements or anything.'

'Thanks, I'll show you out,' I say.

He stands up and shakes Niall's unbruised hand. 'See you mate, take care of this lady, she's a good one.'

'I know, that's why I married her.' I hear the Neanderthal coming out of Niall, so head Seb towards the door quickly.

As he stands in the doorway he turns towards me and I get the full melting chocolate brown eyes. 'Here,' he says, and hands me a piece of paper, taking time to stroke my hand as he leaves it in my grasp. My hand tingles.

'What is it?' I whisper.

'My address in Australia. I'll be there for a couple of months. If it doesn't work out with Niall, you know where to find me. I'm not saying goodbye Lauren.' With that he walks away and I know that although there's a chance I'll bump into him at school, it's possible that this will be the last time I'll ever see him. I close the door on him and on that part of my life. I tear the paper into tiny pieces which I place into my pocket, knowing that even if I put it all together again, a piece would always be missing.

I walk back into the lounge and into Niall's embrace. He covers me with his arms like my warm duvet. I hope this episode in our lives has passed and we can go on to the next. Anyone who thinks a marriage is always love and flowers is fooling themselves. Marriage is hard work. Sometimes you travel on different paths as you grow, but if you're lucky enough, those paths reunite and the journey is good again. I hope that Niall and I will get through this, as in all these years it's not been our first bump in the road, although it's proving to be the largest to date. I sink into his hug and feel relief overwhelm me.

'So what do we do now?' asks Niall.

'We wait.'

Bettina arrives just after two. The day has turned pleasant, so we sit in the garden on my bench. Niall brings out a fold up chair so he can sit with us. We sit expectantly, there are no pleasantries exchanged, we just want to try and get to the bottom of the situation.

'Well it took me to say Tyler may be in danger, but once he got that, it all came out. I think I'm going to need some more therapy after this.'

'Won't we all,' says Niall.

'Danny says he met Monique when I was pregnant with Tyler.' She sits stony faced. 'So he was probably never faithful to me at all.'

'I'm sorry, Bettina.'

She shrugs. 'I got over Danny Southwell a long time ago. Anyway, they had, by all accounts, a torrid affair, for about a year. She wanted to get serious and asked him to leave me, and of course he said no. He told her she wasn't his only lover and he didn't need another wife because he already had one.

'What a charming man. Why on earth did you stay with him so long?' asks Niall.

'You do what you can for your kids. I thought Tyler needed his dad.'

Niall nods.

'She threatened to tell me everything apparently. Danny told her to go ahead because I knew anyway, and that there was no way he'd leave, he had his son to think about. She gave him a load of hassle, saying that kids always got in the way of things and she was sick of it.'

'Hang on a minute,' I say. 'This is like, nine or ten years ago?'

'So?'

'That's around the time her husband left her because he wanted kids. Looks like it became a pattern for her; rejected for children again.'

Apparently she sent him poison pen letters, turned up at bars he was in. He had to threaten her with the police. She said he'd come around eventually and she could wait.' He just put it down to her being another possessive bimbo. He's met quite a few over the years.'

'So has he any idea why she came to Sheffield? That was five years before you arrived. She couldn't possibly have known you'd move here.'

'No. That he has no idea about. He fails to see the connection with you, other than he believes he probably discussed my 'obsession' with you.'

'I don't get you,' says Niall.

'It was one of his "my wife doesn't understand me" lines. I had issues with Lauren over school. He'd tell his girlfriends I was obsessed with a former school friend, made out I made his life hell. Sound familiar?'

'That's what he told me,' I say.

'Yes, well that's the only connection to you that was made, so we have to assume that she befriended you to get at me.'

'That makes no sense. We weren't in touch.'

'Well, I don't have any other ideas.'

'At least we know what set her off now.' I'm still in total shock that my mate has turned into a crazy lady. 'I think it's time to ring the police.'

The police take the phone, the photos and brief statements from us. They say they'll need to talk to us again later, but for now they just intend to pick her up. They call to say she's not at the apartment, but they'll keep checking in until she appears. We go to collect the kids from school, aware that for now it's just a waiting game.

The kids are full of it as they come out. 'I've had a great day mum,' Joe squeals. 'We had a class treat and watched a video.'

'Remind me to retrain as a teacher,' I tell Joe. 'Cos that sounds like fun.'

We walk down the drive together and say goodbye at the bottom. Bettina and Tyler walk off in the opposite direction. As the weather's nice we walked to school to pick up the kids, so I look forward to a nice stroll home with my son. What I'm not expecting is for my path to cross with that of Dr Love.

'What the hell?'

'I need to speak to you.'

I turn to Joe. 'Mum won't be a minute, Hun. Just wait here whilst I talk to Matt.'

'Who are you?' Joe asks him bluntly.

'Its Auntie Mon's boyfriend, Joe, don't be rude.'

Joe stands at my side looking up the street and fidgeting. It's impossible for him to keep still. I smile and then turn back to Matt.

I speak in hushed tones. 'We've called the police, so they'll be looking for you in connection with the crash into our car.'

His face turns grim. 'It's my word against your husband's. I've got a witness, and anyway, I'm a doctor.'

'Yes, but you're linked with Monique, whose turned fifteen shades of crazy, so maybe your statement won't hold as much clout as you think.'

Joe tugs my arm. 'Mum, mum.'

'Just a minute, Joe.' People are bustling around us in their quest to get home from school as quickly as possible. This is not the best place to hold a conversation but I need to find out as much as I can from this man.

'Why did she ask you to crash into his car?'

'I'm not going into that with *you*.'

'So why are you here? Why bother coming all the way here? You must have had some reason?'

He smirks and gets in the car that has pulled alongside us. It hares off down the street.

I turn around to tell Joe that we need to get home, but he's not there. He's gone from my side whilst I was distracted by Dr Love. I realise the words out of Joe's mouth weren't 'Mum, Mum,' they were 'Mon, Mon.'

My legs give way and a scream leaves my body at a noise level and with a strength I didn't know I had.

Someone calls the police. It's all a blur. My voice screams for Joe, and then as much as I try and fight it, knowing I need to keep on top of things for Joe, it all goes dark.

I come round in Mrs Sullivan's office, laid on the floor with my head on a jacket and my heels perched on the edge of a child's chair. I'm told Niall is on his way. A policewoman is sitting in the corner and I realise there is someone to the right of me, a paramedic. 'Okay Mrs Lawler, stay where you are a moment."

I ignore him and sit up. I go dizzy and feel faint again. What sort of mother am I? My child needs me and I can't help for fainting.

'I'll make her a cup of sweet tea,' says Mrs Sullivan, 'and get her a biscuit.'

My son is missing and they think I have time to drink tea and eat biscuits? Yet I know that if I don't take this time I'll be of no use to anyone. A trickle of water slides down my face. Niall, who has now arrived and been briefed, looks at me with concern.

'The police are looking for them, but can you remember the number plate or make of the car?'

'No,' I sob. 'It wasn't Monique's car.' I curl up in a foetal position. 'I only know it was dark blue. What the hell use am I? I don't even know the make of it.'

'Stop it, Lauren.'

'I let her take my child.'

'Before you fainted, you told the people with you that Dr Bailey deliberately distracted you. Is that true?' The policewoman moves over toward me.

'Yes.' My eyes open wide. 'She hates children, what does she want with Joe? What if she harms him? Oh God I can't bear it.'

She places a hand on my shoulder. 'They won't be far. We've all the local airports and other travel stations covered.'

A fresh wave of horror washes over me. I never thought she might take him away somewhere. 'Joe, Joe, Joe.' I sit up and rock back and forth. 'My baby, my baby.' I stand up and a burst of adrenaline shoots through me. 'I'll fucking kill her.'

The policewoman guides me back to a seat. 'You need to calm down Mrs Lawler.' She hands me my tea. I take a sip and wince as it burns my tongue. It's sweet and disgusting. The policewoman urges me to take another sip. 'It's what you need right now. We need you to calm down so that we can ask you some questions. Now don't worry about the make of the car. There were other witnesses around who recognised it as a Mazda three, so that's one further detail we have to go on. It's not Dr Bailey's car, so we're currently looking into car rental places to see if we can get a positive ID that way.'

Of course, I'm the key witness and so far I've been no use to anybody, least of all Joe. I take a few deep breaths and sip the tea slowly. I ask for a biscuit and force it down. After a few minutes and two biscuits I feel calmer. 'Okay, ask away.'

I recall the conversation with Dr Bailey and how he'd obviously been there to distract me whilst Monique got Joe in the car. I told them how I'd just thought Joe was being his usual annoying 'mum, mum, mum' self, and I have to bite my tongue, deliberately hurting myself until I taste blood, in order to stop from falling apart again. 'He was saying Mon, Niall,' I say, looking up at him and seeing my pain reflected in his face. 'I wasn't listening properly. I'm a hopeless mother.'

Niall comes over and gets down on his knees so he's looking me in the eyes. His eyes flash with anger. 'You are not a hopeless mother. Our son has wanted for nothing. But now is not about your ability as a mother Lauren. It's not about you and it's not about your past. It's about now and Joe and I need you to get yourself out of this funk and into a place where you can help get our son back. Do you understand what I'm saying, Lauren?'

I feel like I've been slapped in the face, but in a good way, if that's possible. As if I was sleepwalking, about to go off a cliff edge and the slap was to wake me up and bring me back from danger.

'You're right. I've got my mobile on me. We need to go looking for Joe ourselves.'

The policewoman starts to shake her head. 'Leave it to us, we've everything covered. Why don't you take her home, Mr Lawler?'

'I'm not sitting around whilst that cow has my son somewhere.' I snap. 'You have my number if there are developments.' I get up from my chair, feeling stronger now that I have a purpose. 'Niall, let's go, we need to find our son.'

He walks with me towards the door.

'I'll call you later, Lauren, and see how you're getting on,' says Mrs Sullivan. 'You know we're here for you if you need anything.'

'Thank you,' I tell her, and leave the school.

We sit in Niall's car thinking about what we should do next. 'What if she goes for Tyler next?'

Bettina turns hysterical when we tell her and then catapults into me, holding me in her arms. 'Oh God, Lauren, I'll help anyway I can. I feel responsible for getting you involved in all this.'

I stiffen.

'There's no reason behind this, she's a nutter,' says Niall. 'Anyway, you may need to think about getting some protection from the police until she's caught.

'I'm going to drop Tyler off with my mum,' she says. With the police there, they'll be safe. I feel partly responsible for her behaviour. So, no arguing, but what's the plan?

'We're going to look anywhere we can think of, where she might take him.' I say.

'Well, I'm coming with you, let's go.'

CHAPTER TWENTY-TWO

I wait at Bettina's while Niall takes her to her mother's to drop Tyler off. I pace around the house wondering why I didn't go with them rather than hanging around here, but it had been agreed they would return to the house so we could think of the best way to approach things. I just want to be out there looking for my kid. I'm surprised the police haven't called with any updates, and then I remember, of course, my mobile. I try and call Monique's home number, but it just goes to the machine. I leave a message.

'Mon, it's me. I don't know why you've taken Joe. Please don't hurt him and please ring me. I thought we were friends.' I don't know what else to say and feel my voice breaking on the words so I hang up. I open the keypad and text the same message to her mobile. I sit on my knees next to the window ledge and pray that she'll make contact and bring me back my son.

Niall and Bettina return within twenty-five minutes. He looks at me hopefully and I watch his face drop as I have nothing to offer him.

'I've called and texted,' I state. 'Nothing yet.'

'We need to come up with a list of places she might have taken him,' says Niall. 'She's obviously not stupid enough to go back home.'

We sit and think and come up with the following:

Coffee shop

Gym

Supermarket

Toy shops.

'It's a start,' says Niall. 'Let's go.'

We spend a few hours trailing around all the places we can think of, but find nothing. It's early evening and though still light, it's beginning to fade. It strikes me that I might have to spend the whole evening without my son. From there I start to think what if I never get him back, never see him again?

'I think for now we need to go back home,' says Niall. 'We'll leave it to the police and try again tomorrow morning.'

'We can't give up Niall. We have to keep looking.'

'We need rest and some food. Remember what you're always saying to Joe? A car can't run without petrol? Well you need to take your own advice. We'll go home, get some food and rest, and then we'll take it from there, okay? If we think of anywhere else to look tonight, I promise, I'll be the first one out of the door.'

My shoulders slump and I sit back in the front seat of the car, my eyes scan the road all the way back to Bettina's mother's house.

'Ring me if there's anything and if you go back out. I want to be there. I have my own issues with that bitch.'

'We'll keep you informed,' says Niall, 'but any issues you have, you need to keep a hold of. Joe's our concern right now. Not the reasons she wanted to hurt us.'

Bettina looks contrite. 'You're right, of course. I'm sorry, I'm just tired. I can't imagine what you're going through. When I think about it I just get so damn angry.

'Get some rest,' says Niall, 'We'll ring you later.'

'Right now I just want to hug my son,' she says. 'Oh my God, I'm sorry, that was really insensitive.'

'No it's not, it's what any mum would do,' I say. 'Go and hug him Bettina, and don't let him go.'

We drive back to our own house in silence, both too busy searching. We wander around inside. The house seems so empty, and quiet. My insides twist, I can feel the impression of Joe in the house, echoes of him running around making noises as his Lego figures begin battles with each other, or his voice shouting 'Muuuuuum, I need you.' I walk upstairs and into his bedroom. It's a complete mess. There are figures all over the floor. His pyjamas are thrown in a heap where he took them off, and the books and magazines he's read are strewn across the bookshelves rather than being placed back in a tidy order. I think of all the times I've nagged him to tidy his bedroom and now I just want to see him in this room, being Joe; a messy, nine year old kid. I don't need to close his bedroom curtains, yet I do. I see his bedtime pal, a soft blue rabbit that he still takes to bed, a reminder to me that he's still my little boy, no matter how fast he seems to be growing up. I curl up on his bed with the rabbit and hold it close, breathing in the smell of Joe on it, and wondering where my son will be spending the night, praying he is safe and warm. I tell Joe goodnight and hope wherever he is he can hear me. I fall asleep on his bed, stress makes me blank everything out.

For a few blissful moments when I wake, I have peace, and then it all floods back. How can I have fallen asleep whilst my son is missing? I don't know what the time is, but it's becoming lighter. I run to our bedroom where Niall is asleep, sitting up in bed, my mobile at the side of his own. I pick it up but there are no messages or missed calls. It does inform me however that it has just passed five am. I ring Monique's number again.

'Mum?'

'Joe? Oh my God, Joe. Are you okay?'

Niall shoots up in bed. 'You've got him?'

I wave a finger to warn him to be quiet.

'Hi mum, you have to be quiet cos Auntie Mon is sleeping. She was awake nearly all night. You've nearly woke her up. It's really early you know?'

'Joe, where are you? Do you know?'

'Have you forgotten silly? Auntie Mon said she'd told you where we were going. She said it was a surprise.'

'Is Matt with you?'

'No. Auntie Mon took him home. It's been awesome mum, she's bought me new clothes and toys and everything.'

'Joe listen to me. I've forgotten where she said she was taking you. Can you tell me?'

'We're in Manchester. We've been to the Science and Industry Museum, and today she's taking me to Legoland Discovery. She's promised me loads of Legos.'

'Joe, something's happened and I need you back home. Nothing to worry about, but the police need to see Monique.'

'Has her mum died?'

'No, but it's something like that. I don't want you to worry her, so I'm going to come and get you both, and I don't want you to tell her anything okay? Not even that you've talked to me. Can you do that?'

'Course I can. I'm not two.'

'Do you know where you are?

'We're in a hotel called Doubletree. It's easy to remember cos you just have to think of two trees. It's near the train station cos we didn't have to walk far. I need to go now mum, Auntie Mon's waking up.'

'Okay, Sweetie, try and stay at the hotel as long as you can.'

'Okay, Mum.'

He hangs up and I shout all the details at Niall. He calls the police and I ring Bettina, whilst throwing things in my handbag.

The police tell us to wait to hear from them. We have no intention of waiting in Sheffield, so they agree that we can travel to Manchester, and we arrange to wait in a cafe upstairs in Piccadilly Train Station.

I've never known such extremes of time, the journey was fraught and passed in the blink of an eye; we were so busy trying to rush there. Now waiting at this station, I feel like I'm in a scene from The Matrix, like time is passing so slowly I can see people moving in extreme slow motion. A policeman comes upstairs and approaches us; he's an older guy, grey and balding. He's overweight and I wonder how he can possibly run after anyone who might have my son. They surely should all be built like Superman. But of course he isn't a superhero, just an ordinary person. I simultaneously feel sorry for the fat copper at the same time as I want to grab every fit young person in the train station and get them to help us.

He sits down alongside us and introduces himself as PC Trevor Irwin. The three of us are sitting with untouched drinks, bought only because we felt we needed to justify taking up the area.

We all wait for him to speak. It's the longest moment of my life to date.

He places his hands on his knees. 'I'm sorry, but they'd checked out before we got there.'

It's too much. I hunch over and clutch my head in my hands. 'They can't be far. How could you let them get away? Niall, oh God, Niall.'

He places his arm around me. 'Sssshhh, it's okay.'

'What if we never find him?'

I place my hands over my eyes. He's gone again. This morning he seemed within reach, and now he could be anywhere.

'We've got people stationed at Lego Discovery,' says PC Irwin.

'She'll not go there now,' I say. 'Joe either told her I'd called, or she figured it out. Either way, she'll be on her way somewhere else by now.'

'Well at least you can feel reassured that she's keeping him safe.'

'Reassured?' I shout and others in the cafe turn and look at us. 'She could be doing anything to him.'

He turns and places a hand on my arm. I want to smack it off.

'Does she have a good relationship with your son? You said he seemed happy when he called? Maybe she's genuinely taken him on a break.'

'Niall, get this man away from me, I swear to God…'

'With all respect PC Irwin, our son has been abducted by someone with a Personality Disorder. Hence the great police intervention.'

'Okay, Mr Lawler, fair enough. I just hoped it could be a mistake. We're doing all we can.'

'She could hurt him,' I say. 'When she's caught she's going to end up in prison, so what does she have to lose?'

'There's a big difference between kidnapping and murder, Mrs Lawler, and to be honest, if she's really lost it upstairs,' PC Irwin points to his forehead as if I don't understand what he means, 'it's a psychiatric ward that'll end up with her.'

'You mean she can kidnap my son and not even go to jail?'

'If she's mad, they usually end up in a secure ward like Rampton, near Nottingham. That'd be my bet with someone like her.'

'Do they let them out?'

'Depends what they've done, and if they're able to function in society again.'

'So potentially she could walk free?'

'Yeah, if they feel she's recovered.'

'That's ridiculous.'

'Yeah, well that's the system. Between you and me I can't say I agree with it. I'll be glad when I retire in a few years. All I do is arrest folks and watch half of them walk free and the others aren't inside for two minutes before they're back out robbing innocent folks, but anyway, you don't need to hear my moaning. We'll keep in touch, but for now, you need to decide whether to stay in Manchester or head back home.'

I look at Niall.

'We'll head back home,' he says. 'I doubt she's still in Manchester.'

Its then that PC Irwin's radio crackles into action.

'Excuse me a moment.'

He walks over to the edge of the coffee section. I wait a moment and then jump up and follow him, if there's news I want to listen. From this point you can look out over the crowds of people arriving in Manchester or rushing to catch trains out of here. They resemble little busy worker ants, everyone doing a job they think is important but really in the scheme of life, it's a small part of everything. I consider all these people with their own stories. I wonder if anyone else's is as hellish as ours is right now? Are Joe and Monique maybe down there somewhere?

PC Irwin turns to me. 'Well there's nothing with regards to Miss Henry and little Joe, but they've arrested a Dr Matt Bailey. Apparently he had the brass neck to turn up for work today.'

'That's it then.' Niall stands up and looks from the copper to myself and Bettina. 'He's our best lead, so let's head back to Sheffield.'

We actually start to feel a little hungry so we stop off at a McDonald's drive thru for a small meal. I order a happy meal and put the toy that comes with it safely away in the glove box to give to Joe when he's finally home. I have to believe he will be back soon. Whilst we're parked, I decide to send another text to Monique, not that she's answered the several I've sent so far.

'We can get past this, whatever the problem is. Don't make it worse, send Joe home. Put him on a train, he'll be fine. I'll wait at the station for him. Run away. Just please let him come home.'

'The police told you not to contact her, they have strict procedures,' Niall huffs and looks at me, 'but then again, when have you ever done as you're told? You're wasting your time you know?'

I turn my head away from him in disgust and look out of the window.

Bettina rings home to check that Tyler is okay. 'He's not missing me at all, being spoilt rotten by his grandmother. Apparently she's let him have chocolate for dinner. *Chocolate.*'

It brings a rare smile to my face. In the school holidays, Joe and myself quite often eat a chocolate breakfast from the secret stash I keep hidden upstairs away from the two male chocoholics in my home. It means we can laze around in bed until lunchtime, watching TV. Then when Niall gets home from work, we tease him by saying we had a pyjama morning and he pretends to be disgusted that we had chocolate for breakfast. Good times and I have to believe, to have faith that those times will be back. I vow to let Joe have a chocolate breakfast once he's back with us.

'Sounds yummy to me.' I say.

'What is?'

'A chocolate lunch.'

'Lauren, I said that over five minutes ago.'

'Oh, sorry.'

'Why don't you rest your head and try and catch a bit of sleep,' says Niall. 'We've got about another thirty minutes before we're home, you look all in.'

I do as he says and shut my eyes. The food in my belly and the lull of the car take over and give me half an hour of peace from the current hell of existence.

We drop Bettina off at her mother's once again. It begins to feel like Groundhog Day. Niall promises to let her know as soon as we hear anything. We've been home less than half an hour when there's a knock at the door. Why does no-one ever ring the doorbell? It's PC Sheldon, the local bobby who we first met when the burglary had happened.

'Hello, Mr & Mrs Lawler. I've just come to update you on our interview with Dr Bailey. Can I come in?'

We show him through to the lounge. We are so calm and well mannered, when I know that all we really want to do is yell at him to tell us what's going on. Niall goes through the motions of asking if he wants a drink and he says yes. I am in turmoil inside, and this guy wants us to wait while we get him a drink? This is another Matrix scene that extends on for what seems like twenty minutes, but can only really be about three.

PC Sheldon wriggles his bottom on the settee to get in a comfy position and thanks Niall for the tea placed in his hands.

'You'd be amazed how many people don't offer you a drink. I'm parched. I've not had a chance to call anywhere for one, been really busy today.'

'No problem,' says Niall. 'What do you have to tell us?'

'Right,' says PC Sheldon sitting forwards. 'We've had Matt Bailey in custody since nine thirty this morning when, as I believe you've been told, he turned up to work. He was accompanied to the station where he requested legal representation and was then interviewed.'

'Does he know what she wants with Joe, and did he say why he'd been helping Monique?' Niall asks.

'It appears he's been rather duped by Miss Henry. She told him that you, Mrs Lawler, had stolen Mr Lawler,' he nods towards Niall, 'away from her, and that you'd taken away their adopted son Joe.'

'What?'

'Indeed. He says he had no reason to disbelieve her, she showed him photos of herself with Joe–'

'Photos *we've* taken of her with our son?' I say.

'Well, anyway, he was convinced. In relation to the crash into your husband's car, she got him to ask a colleague to be a witness against Mr Lawler, so that you,' he again nods at Niall, 'would be blamed.' She told him she was trying to discredit Mr Lawler as a father figure in order to get her son back. Mr Bailey, for all his brains as a Doctor, obviously must have left his decisions to another part of his anatomy.'

Niall looks at him, unamused, and the policeman flushes slightly and coughs.

'Anyway, she then told him that Mrs Lawler had been violent with Joe, and he agreed to help get him back after school, thinking that she was going to take him home and call social services. She dropped him off home saying she'd be in touch when she had things sorted and that was the last he'd heard. He's rather shocked at the reality of the situation.'

'I'd like five minutes with that man alone,' says Niall. 'Can you arrange it?'

'I'm afraid not, although I do understand how you must be feeling.'

Niall looks at him with such menace and fire, I imagine PC Sheldon's eyebrows singeing off.

'I haven't had personal experience of kidnap, but I do have to handle delivering and hearing bad news day in and day out; some of the things that happen to people,' he pauses, 'well, let's just say that I've felt similar to how you must feel now.'

I look at PC Sheldon, his youth belies the fact that during his career he's no doubt been the bearer of bad news, over and over again.

'I know what you're trying to say,' I tell him, 'and of course you can't beat him up, Niall, however you feel. He's just another misguided fool who took in what she said – like me, in fact. Do you want five minutes in a room with me about what I've let happen to Joe?'

'Don't be ridiculous.' He stands up and smacks his fist into the door, the same fist that had punched Seb in the eye.

'Dear God,' I state. 'Give me strength.' I go and fetch a bag of frozen vegetables and a tea-towel from the kitchen. I hand them to him. Both he and PC Sheldon have sat in perfect silence whilst I've done this.

'I still don't understand why she's doing this to us. I haven't done anything to her. Do you think she's one of those people who have gone mad because they haven't got kids? She faked a miscarriage, you know?'

'I don't know,' he answers honestly. 'It's usually a baby that's taken in that sort of case." 'Well, if that's all,' I say, 'we'd like to be alone for a while.'

'Oh, of course. They're charging Dr Bailey with -'

I hold my hand up. 'I don't really care what happens to him. He's nothing to me. I just want my son back.'

He nods.

I let him out and return to the lounge. My phone beeps. I run to it and look at the screen.

17 Ruskley Park Road. Bring Bettina and no police. If I see a policeman I'm out of here with your son. You want him, I want Bettina. I'll swap you. Seven pm.'

'Niall,' I gasp. 'It's her.'

CHAPTER TWENTY-THREE

We spend the next couple of hours debating whether or not to call the police. We agree we won't at this time, but make sure we have our mobiles close to hand. I put my 'attack alarm' just inside the top of my pants. We agree to travel in separate cars. Niall still has his courtesy car that hopefully Monique won't have seen. He works out a route that means he'll be parked further down the street, while I will be there with Bettina. We call her and not surprisingly, faced with such a situation, she says she needs time to think about it and will call us back.

'No, I'm on my way to yours now,' I say. 'Do not phone the police and put my son's life at risk, but have a decision of whether or not you're coming when I get there.'

I pull up outside her mum's house at six fifteen. There's no way I'm being late. I run up to the doorway and ring the bell. Bettina comes to the door; she's still in her slippers.

I fold my arms. 'So you're not coming then? Do you not care about my son?'

'I don't know what to do, Lauren. If she does something to me, she would potentially leave Tyler without a mother. He's already got a waste of space for a dad.'

I grip my head in my hands, messing up my hair. 'But if you don't go, she might harm Joe and I'd never see him again. Can you live with yourself if something happens to him? Well, can you?'

'No.' She sighs and grabs her coat and stuffs her feet in her shoes. 'I'm just going to tell them I'm going out.'

Five minutes pass. I can't keep my legs and arms still and keep looking at my watch.

She appears in the doorway with her bag.

'Come on, or we'll be late,' I yell.

'I've just been saying goodbye to my son and mother, Lauren. How do I know I'll even be back?'

'Because we aren't going to let anything happen to each other,' I look her directly in the eyes.' We're in this together, whatever the reason, remember?'

We arrive at the given address and knock. Monique looks out of the door and quickly up and down the street, as if expecting armed policemen to be surrounding her house.

'We didn't ring the police, Monique. Where's Joe?'

She looks completely unruffled and unfazed. 'He's inside, all packed and ready to go. He's fine, Lauren, I wouldn't have hurt him.'

My eyes narrow. 'No, kidnapping won't have done him any harm at all.'

'He's got no idea I took him, he thinks it was a special trip with Auntie Mon, and if you've any sense you'll keep it that way.' She smiles. 'We've had a good time.'

I have to hold my own hands tightly as I want to punch her, but I want Joe more.

'Okay,' she says, 'so here's what we do. You come inside and you can take Joe, and then you leave. 'She', she points at Bettina, 'stays. I need to speak to her.'

'I have another idea,' I say. 'I want to know why you've done this and why I was involved, so let Joe come out and walk down the road to Niall's car.'

Monique's eyes shoot down the street and she attempts to slam the door, but I'm too fast and hold it open. 'There are no police, it's just Niall. Let him take Joe home and let me and Bettina in.'

She considers this for a minute. 'Suit yourself. Just don't try anything funny.' She flashes a kitchen knife from within her pocket at me, and opens the door.

'Muuuuuuum,' Joe runs up to me with the biggest hug. I will never moan about hearing him repeat this familiar word over and over ever again. It's the most beautiful sound I've ever heard next to his first cry as he entered the world and my life. 'I have had the best time. Auntie Mon has spoilt me to death.'

The word death makes me gasp; it could so easily have been that tragic.

'Well, your dad's waiting for you down the road,' I say, 'so get your stuff together cos he can't wait to see you.'

'Oki-doki. Look at this Lego mum, its Loki and Iron Man and -'

'Joe, I promise I'll spend as long as you want going through your toys later, but right now you need a cuddle with your dad and to have a bath.'

He runs off to get his stuff and we stand and wait for him in perfect silence. He's back within a couple of minutes with a heaving duffle bag and a carrier bag full of stuff. He throws himself at Monique, arms outstretched. 'Thanks Auntie Mon, that was brilliant. Can we do it again sometime?'

She reaches down to him and looks at me with a smirk whilst she strokes her hand down my son's hair. 'Well that'll be up to your mum now, won't it? But I'd absolutely love to.'

He comes and gets hold of my hand, something he doesn't do very often now he's nine, and definitely not in public. 'Right, I'm ready mum.'

'Okay darling, well I'll be home really soon, but me and Bettina just need to stay with Monique a little while.'

'Oh, is that cos of Auntie Mon's mummy? You were wrong. She said she's fine now, so you don't need to worry.'

'No it's something else. Your dad's brought his car. I'll show you where he's parked.' I walk to the door. 'I won't be long and then I'm going to read you so many bedtime stories when I get back you'll be begging me to stop and let you sleep.'

'That won't ever happen, Mum. I can stay up til midnight. Are you having a bit of girly time? Dad says you talk about shoes non-stop, I thought it was boring, but I guess it's just like me liking Lego.'

'It is, and yes that's what we're going to do, just for a little while, cos we've missed Monique.'

I open the door and I needn't have worried about him getting to Niall, he's outside the door. He grabs Joe in a hug. I give him a warning look and Niall bets him to a race to see who can reach the car first. I reach into my pocket and press the send button on the text I typed in earlier.

Give me one hour after you get home and then call the police.

'Well, this is very civilised, but I don't like being left two against one, so for now, Bettina, I'd be very grateful if you'd go in there.' Monique opens a door to our right. It opens into a large closet. 'There's no window, so you won't be able to contact anyone, but there's a light and a single bed in there to sit on.'

I nod at Bettina and she goes in.

Monique slides a hook and eye across the door closing.

'This way Lo,' she says indicating a lounge, which is small and basically furnished. There's a feature wall painted light blue, and navy cord carpet with pink floral curtains. 'Oh Lauren, you're dying to know what's happening, aren't you? This,' she sweeps her hand around to indicate the room, 'is one of my rentals. My dad left me some money when he died and I invested it in property. It's recently become vacant, though it's rented again from next month.' She smiles. 'Where did you think my money comes from? I only work three days a week.'

I had honestly never given it a thought.

'I wish you could see your face,' she laughs. 'You've been provided for, and for so long, that you've no idea what the cost of living is. Well I'll give you a little tip, Lo, when you leave here, try and stand on your own two feet, because the pathetic, hard done by, bored housewife thing is so last year.'

'So you were never genuinely my friend?' I ask.

'Oh no, that's where you're wrong,' she says. 'Take a seat. Let's have our usual coffee shall we? I always enjoy them.' She gets up to head into the kitchen and turns back seeing me eyeing the door keeping Bettina in. 'Make any moves towards that door and I'll walk in there and stab her. Or maybe,' she gets the knife from her pocket and looks at it, 'I'll do you, and then there'll be no bedtime stories for Joe after all.'

I sink into the chair and wait for her to return.

She places the coffee in front of me. I have no intention of drinking it, but take pretend sips. I don't trust her; it could have anything in it. She looks at me, smiling.

'If I was going to do something to you, I could think of better things than spiking your coffee, maybe cutting your car brakes or something. That would have been interesting.'

I look at her in horror and she cackles with laughter. 'I'm joking, Lauren. Oh dear, I fear our friendship is forever ruined. Oh well.'

The woman is sick in the head. I don't know why I came for an explanation. We should have tried to overpower her while we had the chance.

'Why do you want to talk to Bettina?'

'I want Tyler.'

I shake my head. 'You are joking?'

She crosses her legs. 'That child is the one thing that's kept myself and Danny apart all these years. I get Tyler. I get Danny.'

'I can see you now, "Mum of the Year".'

'I don't need to be a fantastic mother. He can afford nannies. I just need the child to be ours.'

'You're insane.'

I'm not prepared as she punches me in the nose. I feel a burning sensation and feel a trickle run from my nostril.

'Let's not forget where we are, and who is calling the shots Lauren. Now, I suggest you sit there and be quiet, or I'll kick you out and start on your friend.'

I nod. My nose is throbbing.

She looks at her hand as if I might have ruined her manicure with my nose. 'I've followed Leeds United since I was young, you know. My dad got me into it. After Toby left I didn't know what to do with myself, so I started going to games again. I met Danny in the local bar the team went to after matches. He was an amazing player, and so sexy. He told me what a bitch his wife was and that he was only staying with her because of their kid. He said she'd got pregnant to trap him, and that they'd been together since school. He tried to dump her, but he was stuck with her because of the kid. I told him I never wanted children and he thought that was fantastic. We fell in love.'

I want to laugh, to ask her if she's heard herself. She sounds like a fourteen year old with a crush, not a grown woman, but I keep my mouth shut and continue to listen.

'We saw each other for months. I asked him to leave her and move in with me. He'd still see the kid on the weekends but he'd be child free the rest of the time. He told me I must be joking. He didn't want to be a part-time dad, the football took him away often enough. So I suggested he try to get custody of Tyler and I'd help him. He told me all about her fixation with you, he was going to exploit that and make her seem crazy. I thought then we'd be together.' She puts her drink down on the mat hard. 'But he told me he didn't need another wife, he could have his needs met by any number of bimbos hanging around the club, so he finished with me.' She smiles to herself. 'I decided I would play the long game. I knew the marriage wouldn't last, and in the meantime, I wanted to be friends with the girl who had never fallen for Bettina's charm. The one person who'd got into his wife's mind and messed with her head.'

'Me?' I state.

'It didn't take long to track you down. A bit of Googling and Facebook and I soon had your details. You really should tighten up your security settings, Lo.'

I did – after friending Seb.

'So that was that. I met you at yoga and surprisingly, I genuinely clicked with you. I really was your best friend.'

She looks at me. Does she expect me to thank her?

'But then of course Bettina came back and you made friends with her. The *one* person I expected to tell her to take a running jump, and you fucking befriended her. ' Then the stupid bitch asks to come to the cinema with me. *You* were *my* friend, not hers.' She wrings her hands. 'YOU RUINED EVERYTHING,' she roars.

'W-why the fake pregnancy and miscarriage?'

'To get you to spend some time *with me*; away from Niall and Joe, and Bettina, and from whatever the fuck was going on with Seb. I was losing you, Lauren. You hurt me.'

'Why did you take Joe? You know what he means to me. How could you do that?'

'I panicked. I knew you'd seen the photos and jewellery, so I got Matt to help me to get Joe. God that man's gullible – great lay though. I figured if I had Joe you'd hold off the police, but you didn't, did you? So now I'm left in this situation. Anyway, I figured we could come to some arrangement, so here you are. You can say I was innocent and we'll get Bettina to confess to the crimes.'

Monique's eyes glitter. 'If she wants to keep Tyler safe, she'll do it. I'll take Tyler to visit his dad in prison. Once he's released, which of course, he will be, we can live together somewhere.'

Her speech becomes rapid. 'He could get a transfer to Real Madrid, maybe even Barcelona.' She looks at me, a pitying smile on her face. 'Me and Danny have a connection. That's how I always knew Niall wasn't the one for you. You don't get each other like we do. He's the only man I've ever really loved, and once I have Tyler we can all be together.'

She gets up and reaches for my coffee cup. 'What a waste of good coffee,' she says. I snatch my alarm out from my waistband and blast it into her ear. She wobbles backward, dropping the coffee and I upend the coffee table, knocking her to the floor. I fly out of the room, past the spare room door and flip the latch. Bettina hurtles through the door and we race outside to my car. I'm fumbling with the key fob to get the car open and just manage it as Monique races out of the house shouting, 'I should never have let Joe go, you traitorous bitch.'

'Get in the car,' I yell at Bettina. She hesitates. 'Do it,' I shout.

I judge that I might not make it round to the driver's side so I run to the back of the car and flip the boot open. Inside is the carved mask I bought in the coffee shop. As Monique rushes towards me, waving the kitchen knife, I swing the mask with all my strength. It hits her head and I watch her drop to the floor. Then aware that she might yet get up again, I run and dive into the driver's seat. 'Hold on,' I yell at Bettina. I check my mirrors. There is no-one around. One more look behind me and I see Monique beginning to get up, clutching her head. I put the gear stick in reverse and start to accelerate. I take off the handbrake, let up the clutch and shoot backwards.

There's a large thump. We're lucky not to have hurt ourselves with the whiplash as the car jerks. I sit behind the wheel, my heartbeat thudding in my chest. I turn to Bettina. 'That was an accident.'

Her face has drained of colour and she looks like she's going to be sick, but she nods her head. 'Absolutely.'

She reaches for my hand. I squeeze hers tightly.

I hear sirens in the distance and in a few minutes police cars and an ambulance begin to appear. Niall came through and called them. We get out of the car and they take us to the ambulance, where our shoulders are covered with blankets. A number of policemen gather around the back of the car. Monique is covered in a blanket as well, only hers stretches the whole way over her body.

EPILOGUE

Things moved quickly after that. The police concluded that Monique's death was an accident, caused by us trying to get away from the house with her in pursuit holding a weapon. I sold the car soon after. I couldn't bear to see it again.

Joe and Tyler had the last two weeks off school due to the publicity surrounding the case. I sat with Joe and told him about Monique. I skirted around the main issues and just said that she had mental health problems and her death was a tragic accident. I've kept newspapers out of his way, but I know he'll find out the truth one day. Being nine years old, Joe accepted what I told him. He and Tyler seemed more bothered that they got eight weeks off school instead of six. They spent the last two weeks of term at each other's house, playing Lego. It must be good to be nine and able to deal with things so easily.

We put our house up for sale, and while we await a buyer we are living with Niall's mum and dad. Niall got a transfer to a post in Stafford Hospital. His employers were really helpful with his transfer, possibly because his infamy was stopping a lot of people from getting on with their work. I am enjoying having the security of family around me. We are being spoilt rotten as Rebecca cooks most of the meals, and insists that we have at least one 'date night' a week. This means that Niall and myself are enjoying some alone time, though we desperately miss Joe, even if it's just for one evening. We can't help it. I think we'll always be a bit overprotective now.

I spend loads of time with Joe though. He started his new school a few weeks ago and has made a few friends already, though he says he misses Tyler. I make sure I'm there to take him and collect him every day. I realise it's not practical and hopefully sometime soon I'll be able to trust Glen or Rebecca to pick him up occasionally, but for now it has to be me. That's just the way it is and they understand.

Niall and I are getting there slowly. Like I've said, relationships take work and they're not always on an up, but the time we're getting together is helping us heal. We're seeing a marriage counsellor and he knows how close I came to cheating on him with Seb. We're both accepting some responsibility. I'm positive about our future.

Mrs Sullivan told me that Seb moved to Australia as planned and was settling in well. She wrote me a lovely reference to take with me to Stafford and I'm volunteering as a Teaching Assistant at the local school (the one Joe goes to, but I don't look after his class, that would be sooo embarrassing). I'm hoping that eventually it will lead to paid work, but for now I'm just enjoying the interaction with the children. I look out for the quiet ones who are singled out by others; I try and help raise their confidence. I realise that being in touch with Mrs

Sullivan means that I have a link to Seb. I hope one day I'll hear that he's met someone and settled down. She'll be a lucky woman, and I'll always be slightly jealous.

I left the eBay account closed. I no longer find the need to search and scour for bargains, but look closer to home for any comfort I need. I gave my jewellery away to charity as I felt it was tainted after being in Monique's hands.

Niall was cleared of being responsible for the car accident and Matt Bailey's insurers paid out. His job as a doctor is under review, but we know how hard it is to lose your license to practice in a medical establishment; maybe his forthcoming court case will be more productive.

The insurance paid out on the damage to my belongings. I've put most of it in the bank. Maybe we'll have a holiday, though being in Staffordshire so far, with the countryside, fresh air and animals feels like a permanent one anyway.

Once we left for Stafford, Bettina and I agreed to no longer stay in touch. It was felt that we knew far too much about each other's lives; it was an unhealthy relationship and would be difficult to maintain over a distance anyway. She can now have the fresh start she needs, now the fuss is dying down. We looked at each other in mutual understanding as we said goodbye for the last time; some things were never to be spoken about.

Danny remains on remand for manslaughter. He's expected to be sentenced and remain behind bars for a number of years.

I told Niall I deliberately reversed over Monique, for we have no secrets now. He was shocked, but said if the circumstances had arisen and he was behind the wheel he's sure he would have done the same. Niall, Bettina and I therefore hold this secret between us. I'm sorry but I can't even regret it.

Monique's family were notified of her death. We didn't attend the funeral and I don't know which family turned out to say goodbye. I wonder what her own family history was, whether it had an effect on who she was as a person? I no longer feel defined by my own. I'm a strong individual now, as well as whole within my family unit.

I make my last visit to Sheffield. I walk through the churchyard. My red stilettos kicking up gravel as I walk. I search for the mound of newly dug earth. Locating it, I place a wreath of black flowers on the grave. They're identical to the ones she sent to my house for my best friend. It's only right she received them.

'Goodbye Monique. Rest in Peace.' I say. I know that I can rest in peace myself, now that Monique is underneath.

I turn on my heel and walk away.

THE END

ABOUT THE AUTHOR

Andie M. Long is a bonkers mother of one, who spends most of her time when not working as a Research Administrator/Medical Secretary; reading, writing, on Facebook, drinking coffee, baking cakes and letting her son wind her around his twelve year old finger. She has a long suffering partner. Underneath is her second novel, following *The Alphabet Game*, though she wrote it first. She lives in Sheffield, UK.

Enjoyed this book? Please leave a review on Amazon and Goodreads.

Contact the author at:
www.facebook.com/andiemlongwriter
Twitter: @andiemichelle
Goodreads:
https://www.goodreads.com/andiemichelle

ALSO BY ANDIE M. LONG

THE ALPHABET GAME - THE COMPLETE SERIES: A TO X, Y, Z.

Read all four parts of The Alphabet Game in one complete volume.

Stella Mulroney is playing a game. It's taken her two years but she finally has an interview at Gregory & Sons, the top London law firm that looks after her stepfather's interests. She plans to discover what her Multi-millionaire Stepdaddy really invests in and bring him down. Unwittingly, she's caught the attention of Hot Alpha Gabriel 'Gabe' Gregory, son of her Stepfather's top Lawyer. He wants to know why Stella has such a need for revenge and would prefer her to channel that fury into a game of his own, 'The Alphabet Game'. After all, his is much more fun to play. With a thoroughly evil bad guy, secrets, lies, murder, twists, turns, hot sex and love, this is a game not to be missed ...

Genre: Erotic Romance/Suspense 18+

37426532R00184

Made in the USA
Charleston, SC
09 January 2015